I0817899

TWILIGHT SEEKER

DAYBREAKER BOOK ONE

PIPPA DACOSTA

www.pippadacosta.com

Exclusive character artwork designed by Azur © 2019
Hardback Interior Design and Typeset by The Illustrated Author Design Services
Edited using US English

On the border between the old world and the new, the Night Station welcomes you. Is it blood diamonds you seek, fair traveler? Or something more intimate, perhaps? Come, take my hand and walk among us. I'll show you where the vampires laugh, their teeth sharp in the light. Best you guard your delicate throat, for worse monsters prowl these shadows.

Our fair hostess, you see her there? Miss Lynher Aris. A dream in satin and silk. Beware the beautiful, dear traveler. Didn't you know? They say, by night, she entertains the Dark Ones, but by day, she leads the resistance. By day, she goes by another name: Daybreaker.

Hush, let's not speak of such things. This night is made for revelry. Stay until the dawn train's whistle breaks the spell. Drink and gamble and partake in all the sins you wish, for there are no laws at the edge of the worlds.

Wait. Heed this, dear traveler. Do not linger among the shadows. Do not question those with magic in their eyes. Some foolish souls arrive at the Night Station demanding answers. Those travelers do not see the break of dawn. This glorious station, poised on the border between two worlds, caught between day and night, swallows those it deems unworthy. Myth and rumor, of course, but stay in the light, do not succumb to silver whispers, and turn away from locked doors.

There is a hunger in you, traveler. You feel its spell? The Night Station has you now. Welcome to the end of the world.

1
NIGHT

"Charmaine of House Nether is complaining about the view from her room. The east wing watch reports there are brownies in the cellars, and there's a succubus arriving on the midnight train. We're short on space, so I'll house her with the—"

"Don't say vampires." I pulled on my corset laces, cinching the dress tight, and slotted two throwing knives into a hidden sheath against the small of my back. I rarely resorted to knives to defend myself, but it never hurt to be prepared.

My assistant, Etienne, blinked. "Do they not get along?"

He carried himself well, upright and proud, with a stern face few would argue with. His staff uniform, a black cotton waistcoat and purple silk shirt, suited his dark skin and short ebony hair. The purple shirt highlighted an odd shade of mauve in his otherwise dark eyes. He had the same battle-weary old eyes most of us did, at least those of us who survived on the border between the old and new worlds, but he wasn't as old as those eyes suggested. As all the station staff were orphans, ages were guesses anyway.

"I once housed a succubus near a vampire," I explained, tying off the lace-lined silk dress—the colors black and purple to match all the Night Station staff—and scooped up my overcoat, buttoning it up under my chin. "The repair bill left us on rations for three weeks. Vampires and succubae get along *too well.*"

"Ah, I see." Etienne's voice trembled with nerves. "Then the demons drive the vampires—what is the word, *loopy*?"

"No, the other way around…" I circled a hand in the air, heading for the dressing room door. Vampires could charm the heart out of anyone and anything, and they loved nothing better than screwing with their demonic cousins, but they rarely killed succubae. What they did to them was far worse. Etienne would soon learn the needs of all the Dark Ones. "I'll tell you more later." If he had a later. "And don't say *loopy*. It offends lycanthropes. Just keep the succubus housed far away from the vampireguard."

"Goodness, there is much to remember," he uttered, a touch of his native European accent slipping through. It reminded me of the way Gerome's voice had sounded, before the vampireguard killed him.

"Yes. Yes, there is." Something like sympathy tugged on my heart, giving me pause. "Check in with me regularly. If you can't find me, report to Staff Manager Bee. You will have questions. You will face impossible situations. You'll be challenged and possibly attacked. Respond with courtesy. Stay aloof, stay calm, stay above it all. The Dark Ones will posture and threaten, but they cannot hurt you here." That last sentence almost lodged in my throat. I'd been lying a lot lately. "Are you ready?"

He blinked. "I er… I think so, yes."

He wasn't. Nobody was. I'd been the Night Station's hostess for almost two years, and every night I learned I'd never be ready. All anyone could do was hope dawn came quickly.

My predecessor, Gerome, had excelled as a host. I'd known him all my life. He'd jiggled me on his knee as a child, in a memory almost too sweet to be mine. He'd retired two years ago and handed me my own key. Last month, he'd started a night shift and never returned. The vampireguard had driven an iron railway spike through his heart.

Unlike the Dark Ones, humans didn't get up from that. Under this roof, safety was relative.

If Etienne survived the week, it'd be a miracle, and I'd used my monthly quota of those.

"You'll do just fine."

A shadow fell over his expression. He'd heard the lie, but I wasn't here to hold his hand. We all made our own way into the night. I had my own problems to contend with.

At the door, I closed my hand around the brass handle, lifted my chin, and breathed in, filling my lungs, expanding my chest, and spilling cool, calm control through my veins. Nerves and adrenaline tried to rattle through me. This usually happened. I was human, after all. It took a conscious effort to quell the heady mix of fear and excitement. Lately, the fear had gotten worse.

The shakes stopped. My heart slowed. My thoughts fell quiet.

Exhaling, I opened the door.

The night shift had begun.

Laughter tickled the air. Gaslit chandeliers scattered light; it danced and sparkled among the jeweled sea of people filling the grand hall. Glances were sharp. The teeth behind that laughter even sharper. As I descended the sweeping staircase, I wore my role as hostess like armor. I knew most of the creatures here by their real names and took their offered hands, greeting them into my domain. I cruised through their numbers, a minnow trapped inside a tank of hungry sharks.

Tails licked across the polished marble floor. Magic throbbed around beings best avoided. When they laughed, I laughed with them. When they smiled and charmed, I fluttered my lashes and played their game. It was a dangerous dance I'd spent my life perfecting. These sharks needed their little fish. Without me, this sanctuary wouldn't exist. Without me, the vampireguard would find it difficult to transport their bloodslaves from the old world to their farms. Without me, the demons would be trapped in their hell, feasting on one another instead of humans. Without me, the fae would still be hiding in the earth, bored out of their trickster minds. This station was my castle. I had the power here.

They need me—they need me—they need me, I silently repeated over and over. The mantra beat through my thoughts like a second heart pumping a reason to keep on moving, to keep smiling, to keep seducing and distracting and entertaining, and to keep the great cogs of the Night Station turning. Gerome had told me the prettiest things had the sharpest bites, and that was true of 90% of the guests. The other 10% you never saw coming.

After an hour of silver compliments spilling from my lips, instincts ran a cool finger down my spine. I lifted my gaze to the huge clock over the Grand Hall. Its hands were as tall as me, a reminder that every creature here was constrained by time. The hour hand clunked over to join the minute hand at midnight. Right on cue, a train's piercing whistle announced the newest arrivals.

"Do excuse me." I dipped my chin respectfully at my small crowd and carved through the fray to the wall of arched doorways and out onto Platform One. The thousand-foot-long platform ran the length of the entire station, the white line a barrier that kept all the bad things out there, in the dark.

The night air tasted sweet, like fresh rain. Laughter and chatter filled the air outside too, but the thunderous sound of the arriving train devoured all sound but my rapid heartbeat. Guests looked up, intrigued and bespelled by the single beam of light tunneling through the dark toward them.

Steam rolled and boiled alongside the iron beast. The midnight train hissed. Her wheels screamed, and she ground to a halt. Inside her engine, her furnace heart throbbed and growled. The train had terrified me as a child. I'd learned to live with her, but the fear had never really vanished. Most thought of her as just iron and coal and fire, but my gut told me she was alive in the same way the station was.

I dipped my head and whispered, "Hello."

More steam huffed from her stack.

Etienne's fast approach through the gathering crowd caught my eye. Strands of his slicked-back hair had fallen loose and licked at his cheeks, but the rest of him had held up well through his first hour. His unblinking glare told another story. "We have a problem."

The train's hissing hid his words from most of the gathered guests, but they'd notice his agitated state.

"That's your job, Etienne." I smiled at him, too aware of the many eyes riding us.

The train pulled eight black carriages, each one encrusted with elaborate carvings like icing on a cake. Their window shutters lay open, revealing the arrivals readying to depart. Not all trains that came through this station were as luxurious. Most clattered through, brakes screaming, windows black. Death rode those unstoppable trains.

"Ma'am?"

I blinked, refocusing my thoughts. "Go on, Etienne."

"The vampireguard is preparing for an arrival." He tilted his head, gesturing farther down the platform.

The black- and red-clad vampireguard had spilled onto the platform in larger numbers than usual. Most of the time, the VG strategically spread themselves among the crowds, but clustered together like that, they reminded me of ants. Black and red ants. They pushed the crowd back to open a line from a carriage to the station doors, expecting an important member of their own. I hadn't realized so many of the VG had checked in during the past few nights. Vampires in such large numbers always meant trouble.

"Why was I not informed?"

Etienne cleared his throat. "It appears they didn't know until a few moments ago."

A surprise arrival? I hated surprises. Throwing so many Dark Ones under one roof required planning and forethought. Guests attended the Night Station for its perceived safety. Without knowing who was arriving, I couldn't keep them safe. *Anything* might disembark the train. This was reckless. The VG should have informed me. Typical vampires.

I picked up my skirts. "Well then, I'd best go see—"

Etienne blocked my path. "Wait."

I looked into his eyes. I didn't know Etienne as well as I wanted to, but he had always seemed passive, until this moment. I could appreciate someone who wasn't afraid to block my path, although I'd have preferred to appreciate it away from my guests.

"They say… I heard…" he stammered, fast losing the bravado that had impressed me.

"Spit it out. There's nothing you can say that I haven't heard before."

"Ghost."

"What?"

Taking a deep breath, he dipped his chin and stepped closer. He was taller than me and had to lean down a little to whisper, "They say the arrival is the Ghost, ma'am."

The Ghost, not *a* ghost. We had plenty of those. I blinked again, fighting to keep my composure. Nearby ears pricked at the name. I couldn't let my surprise show, even as my heart stuttered in panic.

"Are you sure?" I whispered back, close to where the pulse in his neck fluttered too fast.

"Well, no, but…" Straightening, he glanced behind him at the furor. "The Ghost would keep his arrival quiet beforehand, no?"

I prepared for everything. Every night, I armed myself with blades and knowledge, ensuring my survival and the survival of my employees. I wasn't prepared for Ghost. Nobody could prepare for that.

Whispers radiated throughout the crowd. *Ghost*, they hissed. *Ghost. Ghost. Ghost.* Some guests fled to safety back inside. Some shuffled closer to the lines of vampireguard. Many just stood and watched in awe.

Some monsters scared the monsters. The overseer known as Ghost was one of those. Few had seen him, but all feared him.

For the first time in a long time, fury burned the back of my throat. Why was he here? Did he know… Did he know about me and what happened in the day? No. No, he couldn't. I was careful. So very careful. He was just passing through. Just another guest.

The carriage doors all swung open at once, hinges squeaking, to deliver their cargo of Dark Ones: demons with barely restrained wings and spiraling horns; lycans with glowing eyes; alien-looking elves; glittering jinn made of smokeless fire; and more. They disembarked from the train and spilled onto my platform, becoming my charges. Tails looped, horns glinted, and eyes drank in the Night Station. It was my job to greet them and entertain them, but I couldn't lift my feet to *move*. Ghost. How was I supposed to manage this?

The crowd jostled, the numbers swelling as the new guests mingled among those already in attendance. So many. My thoughts tripped and stalled. I was better than this. I had to be better than this. Every second I delayed cost me the respect I'd worked so hard to earn. Every moment I hesitated revealed me for what I truly was: a woman in a pretty dress playing with killers.

"Ma'am?"

"Etienne." I still had authority in my voice. I was still the queen of my domain on the outside. Nobody saw the inside. Nobody. I ruffled my skirts. "Have the grand suite made up. Clear the corridors from the lobby to the suite." I swallowed, clenched my jaw, and started forward, boots clipping the platform. "And find out if he has a damn name."

The crowd parted ahead of me, as they should. Good. I was still untouchable. They didn't see my fear, or taste it. My armor held. I had to reach the vampireguard. I had to be the one to greet Ghost. Any other outcome was unacceptable. The people peeled back, sensing my approach. Even demons and monsters far more terrifying than me stepped aside.

I have the power here. I kept my chin up, eyes forward, and walked like I fucking owned this tiny corner of the worlds.

"You must believe or they will not," Gerome had told me. *"We are not powerless. They surround themselves in illusion. We can too."*

"But we don't have magic," I'd said.

He'd patted my head. *"Everyone has magic,* mon chère."

A well-dressed solitary man blocked my path. He stood proudly, his hands clasped atop a silver-tipped cane, his chin down but his gaze up, peering through dark lashes.

I jerked my chin. "Kindly move, sir."

His cheek twitched. "Of course." He bowed slightly and gestured for me to pass. I glanced back once—it was all I could afford—but the crowd had pooled in behind me, swallowing the figure. Something about him had snagged my attention. Another time I'd have sought him out, but Ghost's arrival took precedence.

I reached the line of vampireguard. They were all watching the carriages, blocking my path. "Step aside, please."

"And you are?" Like all vampires, this one looked down his nose at me and saw bloodslave. Those thoughts were as clear as day in his cold, silvery eyes. He'd slaughtered many. If he'd served in the war, as most had, he'd killed unchecked, and here I was, a cow asking a king to move aside.

"Excuse me?" My words were polite, but my tone was not.

The vampire beside him nudged him in the arm. "You'll want to step aside, Caine. That's Miss Lynher Aris."

My name was usually enough to settle things, but Caine's gaze reflected none of the respect it should have. His attention trawled lower and lingered on my neck. My high-necked jacket was buttoned up tightly, preventing him from seeing my pulse beat, but he heard the thump of my blood all the same. For all their rules and profound sense of loyalty to their queen, Caine, like the rest, was a creature driven by need. Had he been able to see my delicate neck and the blood pumping beneath, he'd have fixated on it. While he'd be a fool to try to take *me*, some didn't possess enough control to resist the bloodcall. Perhaps he wasn't one of the old guard, but one of the new, hence his inability to rein himself in.

I switched my glare to his comrade, who posessed more sense.

"Get your shit together," Caine's friend said. He grabbed his forearm, snapping him out of his thrall. "Now is not the time to start trouble."

Caine grunted and rolled his shoulders, shaking off the hunger. He yanked out of his companion's grip, baring a hint of sharp teeth.

He could posture all night, but I had a guest to greet. With Caine's glare burning between my shoulders, I stepped into the space the vampireguard had opened and faced the carriage, trying not to think about how a dozen of the guard, those like Caine, stood within striking distance. I wouldn't see an attack coming. A few drops of their venom would see me lost to their control. But they wouldn't attack, not here. The Night Station's delicate balance assured my safety, as long as I stayed behind the platform's white line.

The train engine huffed, the iron beast restless to be chomping up the rails once more, but it would wait. If this passenger was Ghost, the whole damn world would hold its breath and wait.

A figure moved inside the carriage. Just one. Alone. I expected an overseer to be neck-deep in guards but quickly reassessed my assumption. Having guards would make him appear weak and unable to protect himself. No. Ghost *would* be alone because nobody dared to touch him. Not here. Not anywhere.

I'd never entertained an overseer.

In two years, no one and nothing had tested me like this.

A vampire stepped into the carriage doorway. The station lamps tried to warm his face and failed. I wasn't sure what I'd expected, but it wasn't... *him*. He looked chiseled from stone. Sharp cheekbones accompanied sharper eyes. His mouth was a cruel, pink slash across pale skin. His dark hair, cropped short at the sides and slightly longer on top, spoke of his cutting edges and angles. He appeared no older than me, but vampires didn't age. He could be twenty-three or twenty-three hundred. Some—nay, most would call him handsome, even pretty with those cheekbones. All I saw was a beast with the blood of a billion people on his hands—hands clad in silk gloves. This beast commanded legions. He made rivers of blood flow. A flick of his wrist and thousands died.

Rage heated my veins. The vampires would all sense it on me, but combined with my pinned smile and coy glances, they'd assume I was aroused. And I was, but not the way they all took for granted.

He descended the three carriage steps and paused on the platform to straighten his cuffs. His black shoes gleamed. His expertly tailored suit fit his tall, imposing frame, wrapping the vampire in sophistication and poise. Did he feast on his tailors after they'd dressed him?

His gaze lifted and silence befell the platform. Even the train's hissing faded into the nowhere space between one moment and the next.

I should have looked down, should have knelt and averted my eyes, but I made a mistake. I stared back. His gaze ravaged mine, as though he had somehow buried himself inside my mind without so much as crossing the platform to greet me. The most powerful of vampires couldn't read minds, but they could sense strong emotions. He already knew how I seethed.

His lips curved into a thin smile.

My pulse thumped its siren, alerting every vampire here to my fear. Still, I stared and felt myself falling, coming undone. No vampire had dared charm me since I'd become a host. This one walked a thin line. An overseer he might be, but we had rules he must abide by, just like the rest of my guests. His silver-touched eyes shimmered and his touch on my mind daggered deeper. A test, to see if the rumors about me were true. Oh, I knew those rumors. Some said I was bewitched. Some called me whore. Some called me temptress. Because, like me, vampires didn't like surprises, and I was definitely a surprise.

I shut my eyes, shattering his charm, and lowered my gaze. He didn't rock on his feet like most vampires did when I slapped away their charms, but he'd have felt the whiplash just the same. Now he knew I could resist him. He'd wonder what else I could resist. He'd wonder many things about Miss Lynher Aris and the Night Station my home.

Fool. I shouldn't have let the game go on for so long.

He stepped forward. Light smoothed over his glossy black shoes. As I glanced up, he flicked a hand and the train whistled, signaling its departure. I was right. The world had waited.

"Kneel."

I dropped, striking my knees on the cold platform. This was not the time to fight.

His gloved fingers sank into my hair and clenched, locking into place. He yanked my head back, and I glimpsed Etienne behind the vampireguard, fear and fury alive on his face. He would need to learn to hide his emotions before they got him killed.

"Next time, you kneel *before* my arrival."

"Yes, Overseer."

"If there is a next time." He tore his hand free and stroked a silk-clad finger down my cheek. "You must know my name?"

"Your name? No. But at the Night Station, we know you as Ghost."

"Indeed." Straightening, he scanned the station frontage and the gathered people, again appearing to be searching for something. "I require three nights' accommodation and a loyal bloodslave. I trust my needs will be met, Miss Aris?"

Another finger flick and I rose to my feet. "Everyone is welcome at the Night Station."

He tilted his head, perhaps wondering if he'd heard a challenge in my tone or if he'd imagined it. He would soon learn I had my own ways of charming vampires, even those as vicious as him. "And the entertainment?" he asked.

My smile uncoiled. "That can be arranged, sire."

"Good."

He walked around me as though I were nothing more than a rock in a stream. I fell into step behind him, as was my place, but my hidden blades burned cold against my flushed skin. I could plunge one through his spine and strike at his heart before the guards could stop me. But afterward, as his ashes and mine fell, everything else would fall apart too: the Night Station, my beloved staff, and the countless human lives relying on me to save them.

No.

There were other ways to kill an overseer, and I had three days to make it happen.

29

NIGHT

I tore off my jacket. My heart thumped as fast as my boots struck the corridor floorboards. I needed to breathe, to think, to clear my head. I couldn't disappear in the middle of my night shift. Especially as the Dark Ones would be watching more keenly with an overseer among us. My staff needed reassurance. Everyone needed reassurance. Not even the Dark Ones were immune to an overseer.

Plucking a small piece of paper from a hidden pocket in my dress and a pencil from another, I scrawled a note. I returned the pencil to its snug hiding place and folded the piece of paper into a tiny square. There had been a time when messages had been sent and received via electronic devices, but old technology didn't work so well in the new worlds, and those that did were liable to be hacked. In the new beginning, the vampires had used human inventions against us, and so we'd sabotaged our communication networks.

Gerome had once told me of how satellites had fallen to Earth, streaking across the sky like hundreds of falling stars. Those falling stars had signaled the end of the old world and the beginning of the new, where pen and paper were safer.

I nodded at a couple gliding down the corridor, smiled at a gentleman, careful to keep my gaze from the forked tail poking out from under his coat, and kept on walking the corridor. Some parts of the Night Station weren't open to guests. Some parts weren't on any maps and didn't have doors to reach them. Hidden parts. Secret parts. Walls with eyes. Spiraling passages to nowhere. The station was known to devour unwanted guests, their bodies never found. I wasn't visiting any of those places now. I had another destination in mind. But first...

I lifted an old pitcher on its display pedestal in an alcove, set the small piece of paper on the stand, and replaced the jug, taking no more than two seconds to complete the drop.

People crowded the corridor, wall to wall, outside the old library—now my office. They weren't in uniform yet. Out of the purples and blacks, they appeared so vulnerable. I wanted to gather them up and hold them close.

"All right, I assume you've all heard. The arrival of an overseer need not be cause for concern."

"Is it true, Lynher? Is it Ghost?" a young woman, one of the most recent orphans to find her way to me, asked. The vampires had made orphans of us all.

I nodded and let them gasp and chatter before gesturing for them to settle. "Quiet now. You are all here because you know how to do your jobs, and we will continue to function exactly as we always do. For fifty years, the Night Station has straddled both worlds with grace and professionalism. We will continue that tradition." My words echoed Gerome's, and I fought back the memories before tears pricked my eyes. "The overseer is with us for three nights. After that, he will move on"—*or disappear inside these walls forever*, I silently added—"and everything will return to normal."

Hands clutched at one another. Teeth worried lips. I trusted these people like I trusted my own blood. I knew every single soul, because the Night Station had saved them, same as it had saved me twenty-three years ago as a babe.

"We are protected," I reminded them. To prove it, I lifted my forearm and pulled my sleeve down, revealing the embellished x-shaped tattoo. We all had the same mark, put there by the Night Station itself after it had claimed us. Some glanced at their wrists, taking comfort in the simple symbol that meant so much. "For the next three days, we operate to the best of our ability. Bee will see to your daily queries, while I… while I entertain the overseer." If they'd heard the hitch in my voice, they didn't show it.

Slowly, they filtered back through the station corridors. I watched them go, lingering outside my door to answer any questions. They asked none.

Thirty staff managed the Night Station with me.

Thirty lives in my hands. It was my duty to protect each one.

From a third hidden pocket, I plucked my skeleton key and clunked the library lock over. The door gave with a familiar groan and allowed me inside. Almost instantly, the pressure of having to constantly act the part fell from my shoulders. The library's gloom felt safe and quiet and warm. It felt like home.

I clicked my fingers. Tiny flames puffed to life on half a dozen wall-mounted candlesticks, chasing the dark into the farthest corners.

Two steps in I jerked to a stop.

A man leaned against my desk.

I blinked. He was still there.

Not real. Not possible.

I had the only key, still in my hand. The door had been locked.

I looked at the key, wondering if I'd been tricked, and then looked back at the man.

He folded his arms and waited like he had all the time in the worlds, like his presence was perfectly acceptable and not utterly inappropriate and wrong on an entirely different level to everything else I'd seen tonight.

A cane rested against the desk beside him, and something about it made me want to snatch it up, snap it across my knee, and set it on fire. Then maybe I'd throw the ashes onto the tracks and wait for a train to thunder by, tossing those ashes far and wide.

The cane plucked a memory to the surface. The man from Platform One. The one who had stood in my way and then vanished in my wake.

His gaze snagged mine. I lifted my chin. Was he a magician? He had to be *something* to have gotten through locked doors.

Silver flashed in his eyes. Or had the dancing candlelight tricked me? Because now his eyes appeared to be a less vampiric shade of hazel. Was he a vampire, or was I grasping at any explanation for having found him inside *my* personal space, behind *my* locked door?

"Hello, Miss Aris," he said. I hadn't noticed his accent on the platform, but in the library's muffled quiet, a definite hint of *foreign*, perhaps English, hit my ears. As the station was situated on the outskirts of the old world's ruined city of Boston, I mostly heard some mix of American on my guests' tongues.

I should reply, I realized. If I'd learned anything over the years, it was to never let anyone see you on your back foot. Weakness killed. "Hello, Mister…?"

I moved forward, maintaining my poise and grace, as though his being here were a pleasant surprise and not something that would feed new nightmares. As I slipped around the desk, I discreetly popped the key back into one of many hidden pockets.

"Jack," he said, turning to follow my path.

The desk was the size of a dining table, with clawed feet and scrolled edges. Like everything inside these walls, it had always been here. I used it like a safety barrier.

"Mister Jack?" I added a teasing lilt, turning on the charm and hoping he hadn't noticed the seconds after I'd entered where I'd completely lost the ability to speak.

"Just Jack." He tucked a charming smile into his cheek.

Well, wasn't he a peach. Now that I was closer and my shocked thoughts had stopped falling over themselves, I got a good look at *Jack*. He'd worn a tailcoat in the platform, but it was missing now. Rolled-up shirtsleeves revealed bronze-skinned forearms. That sun-baked skin belonged to the West Coast, but something about the attire felt off, just like his name felt off—because it was a lie. I'd seen his black pants and how they hugged a tight ass on my cruise around my desk. No lace, no velvet, no embellishment. His dark hair, long enough to run his fingers through and sweep out of his eyes, hung loose. He was underdressed for the Night Station. He was, in fact, *unremarkable*. I wasn't buying it. Nobody unremarkable broke into my office. Nobody unremarkable stepped in front of me on Platform One. And nobody wore *unremarkable* so damn well.

"As you can imagine, I'm exceedingly busy. I only have a few moments before I must return to my duties. So, what can I do for you, Just Jack?" I spread my fingers on the desktop and looked him in the eyes.

Old vampires could hide behind a human mask, but it was frowned upon. Pretending to be human was beneath them. Besides, Just Jack wasn't exhibiting any of the classic vampire attributes, like being a child-murdering, sociopathic, psychotic mass murderer. But there was still time for that.

"Well..." He tucked his hands into his pockets and wandered backward to admire the floor-to-ceiling bookshelves behind me. "I was looking for the washroom when I happened upon your open door."

No vampire was this shit at lying. "So you thought you'd wait in the dark for someone to come along instead of turning around and continuing your search?"

"The door closed behind me." His eyebrow arched, as though questioning whether I believed him.

"It did, did it?" Unfortunately, his story had the potential to be true. The Night Station played its games just like the rest of us. It could have taken a liking to Just Jack and sent him on a merry chase. If that was the case, he was lucky he hadn't stumbled upon the less savory aspects of the building.

I smiled my sweetest smile, came out from behind my desk, and offered him my hand. "I'm sure I can escort you to the washroom, sir."

He hesitated, which struck me as odd. He didn't remove his hands from his pockets and didn't step forward to take my hand. In fact, he looked at me as though I'd told him I'd take him to his death. Something withered behind his gaze, and his smile lost its hold on his face. "Are you well, sir?"

"Of course." He snapped himself out of his reverie and folded my hand into his. His touch was warm, if not rough. Worker's hands,

I assumed. But like on the platform, my instincts prickled. Did he need help? Was that why he was here?

"What brings you to the Night Station?" I asked, guiding him back into the hallway.

The library door clunked closed behind us.

"I'm just passing through."

"Everyone is just passing through, sir," I said in a way that might summon his smile again, but something had changed in him. He seemed disinclined to smile, and his gaze had drifted far down the corridor.

Had the station deliberately brought him to me? It would fit with his story about being guided to the library and shut inside, and it wouldn't be the first time either. Those who were lost became found again in our walls.

Back in the main hall, heads turned toward me, as they always did. The weight of that same attention fell onto my companion as well. Jack stiffened.

"You are a wanted individual, Miss Aris." He plucked his hand from my grip and dipped his chin. "I must beg your leave."

He retreated into the crowd, but before he could escape, I called, "Jack…" He pulled up short. "Are you staying with us?"

He hesitated, his back to me, and then turned his head. "I am," he admitted, his jaw firm.

"For how long?"

"For as long as it takes." He left, and nothing else I could say would keep him here.

It wasn't until he'd disappeared and the chatter from the crowd had spilled over me once more that I realized he'd left his cane in my office. The guest book would have a record of his room number. I'd have it returned to him later.

"Ma'am," Etienne said, steering my attention back to the task at hand, "the overseer is asking after you."

Distracted by Jack, I'd almost forgotten I was hosting a monster. "Is he happy with his suite?"

"I believe so." He gulped.

I noticed the top button on his jacket gaped open. "Best button yourself up tight, Etienne, lest you broadcast yourself as prey."

He hastily obliged, paling with every second.

"Does he have his... bloodslave?" I asked, scanning the crowd to make sure all behaved and smiled. Everything was calm. I doubted it'd stay that way for long.

"I sent five to his room, but he sent them away... undecided."

I sighed and found Etienne's darting expression again. "I'll deal with him. You are to assume I'm otherwise engaged for the next three nights. Don't worry about my well-being." I held his gaze so he knew I'd seen his face when the overseer had forced me to kneel. "I'll be all right."

He nodded tightly. His concern was sweet but unnecessary.

"Oh, and see what you can find out about a new guest called Jack."

"Jack...?"

"Just Jack," I said, wondering if there was more happening inside these walls than I could see. But the station saw everything, and if it wished it, Jack would find me again—or I'd find him.

3

NIGHT

The grand suite dominated the entire fourth floor of the central building, right over the station's beating heart, the Grand Hall. The building's vast wings stretched to the east and west. Most guests enjoyed luxurious accommodations in those wings. Overseer Ghost was not most guests. No other room but the grand suite would do for the VGs most esteemed vampire.

I opened the outer door, passed through the inner hallway under thick tied-back drapes, and knocked on the white-painted, gold-leafed inner door.

I had a key that opened every door, but it would be best to keep that secret to myself, especially for what would come later. For now, I had a role to play.

"Come."

I gathered my wits like I gathered my skirts and opened the door.

I'd seen the room before, that morning in fact, but now it was occupied and it had *changed*. Black and red threatened to swallow me whole the second I stepped across the threshold, from the white light of the inner hallway into the dark. The Night Station's magical touch shivered through me. Sometimes, not often, but sometimes, when the world got busy, I forgot the station was alive. At times, it gently reminded me. Just this morning, boxes and dust had cluttered the suite, and now it was dressed to the highest standard. My staff had not done *this*. Plush carpet, of a red so dark it would hide spilled blood, softened my footfalls. Black panels hugged the walls, while gold-leaf frames swirled and traced delicately sweeping waves and filigree. Furniture led the gaze on a chase around the huge space. And this was just the suite's lobby. Beyond the closed doors was the master bedroom, with its dressing room, complete with a selection of the Night Station's outfits, each uniquely tailored to fit every guest's dimensions. A sumptuous bathroom with a sunken bath waited to embrace the tired guest. And so much more.

Black windows beckoned me forward. The outside was so empty it might be another world. I saw only myself in the reflection, hovering like a real ghost, dressed in my layered gown and so easily assumed to be the epitome of grace, when in fact the dress—my first gift from the station—held lethal secrets. Just like me. In the day, shutters would seal those windows so tightly that not a single shaft of light could squeeze through.

"Did I not tell you to come?" His stern voice grabbed at me from the dining room.

I had already displeased him tonight. Now was not the time to dither.

The dining room was no less impressive, featuring massive candelabra and shining silver cutlery, but the grandeur lost some of its luster when my gaze fell on the overseer.

He stood at the end of the table, the fingertips of one hand resting on the glossy tabletop while the other was neatly tucked into a pocket. Black velvet swirled at the edges of his black suit jacket. His burgundy shirt gaped at the neck, flaunting a freedom no human had. He was a vision of lace and silk and velvet.

"Look at you." He snorted a humorless laugh. "Wrapped up so tightly it's as though you seek to hide yourself inside all that fabric." His voice had a rumbling smoothness that he'd likely perfected over the decades. He wielded it the same as he did the power in his gaze. Like all weapons they had at their disposal. Venom. Charm. Strength. Viciousness.

"Do you find the accommodation to your liking?" I asked, entering without permission. I ignored the dress comment, finding it too close to the truth to dwell on.

He arched an eyebrow at my approach, unacustomed to anyone being so forward.

"It is… adequate."

Adequate. He was lying. He was impressed, and we both knew it. "The attire is striking on you, sire."

His eyes narrowed. I'd displeased him. I made a mental note to veer away from mentioning his appearance again, at least in a good light. Perhaps he liked to hear he was ugly. I'd soon learn his quirks so that I might use them against him.

"Your reputation precedes you, Lynher."

"My guests refer to me as Miss Aris or Ma'am." I hadn't told him he was wrong, and he hadn't yet agreed to behave like a guest. This was a game. He'd win, but no game was worth playing if the outcome was set.

I'd moved on, stepping behind him and taking in everything about the room and him. Every glance told me more. He believed he had the power here, and he wore his confidence like a second skin. Decades might have passed since someone had surprised him. Longer since anyone had challenged him. An overseer as feared as he was often found themselves surrounded by yes-givers. Liars. While I could lie, and would lie, I also planned on telling him the truth. He likely hadn't heard it in a while.

He watched me walk around his room, his minnow swimming in his ocean. Or perhaps a better analogy here would be snakes, as he'd been the first to mention them. He was fast and lethal, and a single drop of venom or his teeth in my neck and I'd be his. But I was a small thing, a nothing thing. A garter snake with no bite. Or so he believed.

"You asked to see me?"

"I was expecting you to be here, waiting for me," he said, his tone guarded.

I laughed, startling him, but his widened eyes turned back to razor-thin slits.

"You find me amusing?" he asked.

"I have a thousand guests on any given night and all believe I should be waiting on them." I let that sentence dig in before adding, "You'll have to be patient, sire. There is but one of me."

He breathed in, a sign I was getting beneath his skin as he didn't need to breathe at all. "You play a dangerous game."

"You refused our bloodslaves?" I asked, changing the subject to distract him from my game-playing. "You have my assurance they are all clean and well *behaved.*" The words tasted bitter.

"And what if I don't want well behaved?" He smiled like he knew the question would rile me.

He'd been in the war. He'd hunted down his prey. I was too young to remember anything, but Gerome had seen the vampires kill in the thousands. I'd found him crying alone once, and he'd told me it wasn't magic that had almost wiped out humans; the vampires had done that.

"I can have that arranged." I stopped at the foot of the table and looked up to find his silver-eyed glare pinned on me. "You merely have to ask and it will be arranged."

Three days. That's all I needed to wipe this monster off the map. But I wouldn't subject any of my staff to his barbaric whims. It would be me, if it came to it. "What can I provide to make your stay more pleasant, Overseer?" Every word tasted like ash on my tongue. I swallowed, but the taste lingered.

He considered my words as carefully as I'd constructed them. He knew I'd resisted his charm. What else of his could I resist? For someone like him, I was something new, something of a challenge.

He waved my question away and seemed to reset his thoughts at the same time, as his gaze softened. "You'll accompany me on a tour of this fine station."

"Very well." I approached and offered my arm.

When he looped his arm in mine, a tic started at the back of my mind—a very human instinct to recoil. Every inch of my skin wanted to crawl off my bones and hide. *Predator*, my body screamed. I smiled at the monster beside me and shoved all the fear far, far away. I could scream and cry and rage at daybreak, but not yet. NOT. YET.

His fangs gleamed their threat and their promise. We both knew I wouldn't make it through the next few hours without him trying to breach my defenses, but for now, he was content to play. While he played, I'd learn all about Ghost and how best to make sure he didn't leave my care alive.

Ghost appeared not to notice how the corridors had miraculously emptied prior to his arrival, or how all but the vampireguard were deep in conversation, or how guests averted their eyes as we entered the Grand Hall. By now, everyone knew I was entertaining the overseer. They all wanted a look at the vampire with the fiercest reputation, bar the queen herself, but few ventured too close.

I traded smiles while the vampire on my arm marked each soul we passed by, the shimmer in his eyes seeing deeper than the superficial. He'd paid attention during the tour, absorbing every detail about the Night Station and its peaceful role in these troubled times. I'd told him the myth of how the station had appeared at the same time as magic, when a dark-matter experiment buried in the Alps had gone so very wrong and torn the human world open, inviting in all the bad things. I'd told him of how the station *moved*, and he'd laughed, like such a thing were fantasy. For a being made of magic at his roots, he was surprisingly blind to it. I saw it all around him, as shifting and alive as candlelight. It was corrupted, as magic always was with the Dark Ones, but there all the same.

I'd also told him about the lore that claimed the arrival of Ghost was a death omen. He didn't laugh that time, but held my gaze before leaning in and brushing his reply against my cheek. "Only my enemies need fear me, Miss Aris."

Even after he'd withdrawn, the touch lingered across my jawline. The touch had been no mistake. Vampires weren't careless with their touches, unlike humans. Instinct demanded I shove him back and run far away from this monster in velvet and lace. Even as screams filled my head, I angled my face toward him, snaring his gaze before it could drop to my neck. I had my coat back on, buttoned up to my chin, but this close, he could hear my blood pumping, and like Caine on the platform, he only had a finite amount of control.

"Why are you really here?" I asked as we performed a slow side-step around each other, the crowd forgotten.

"Ah." He breathed in and straightened, cutting off the intimacy. "I was going to discuss this with you tomorrow, but as you've asked..." He took my hand and guided me to sit at a nearby occasional table, then settled in the opposite chair. We'd found a nook at the edge of the Grand Hall, tucked in shadow. Alone yet surrounded by hundreds. Intimate but exposed.

A face in the crowd caught my eye, mostly because he wasn't laughing or chatting like the others. Jack stood on the other side of the Hall. Impossibly, a line from him to me had opened through the crowd, as if everyone had known when to step aside to reveal him.

He didn't blink. Didn't smile. And in that second, I could almost feel his rough hand in mine.

"... high-value cargo..." Ghost was saying.

I blinked. The crowd pulled together, flooding the inexplicable gap, and he was gone. Was it the Night Station's influence that kept bringing us together or fate?

"He must be quite the man to pull you from my presence."

Danger lurked beneath Ghost's wry tone. I smiled, giving him all my attention again, and boldly placed my hand over his on the table. "Just another guest. My apologies, sire. You were saying?"

His brow pinched. "On the second day of my stay, at exactly zero-five hundred, an inbound train will stop at Platform One to take on water and fuel." He lifted my hand, leaned an elbow on the table, and brought my loose fingers to his lips, as though to kiss them. A more civilized guest would think it a polite gesture, despite the intimacy of it, but a kiss was not his intention. His grip turned to steel and clamped closed, trapping my fingers in his vise-like fist. Pain radiated through my hand, trying to twist me to his mercy. I pulled, but there was no use fighting him. If he wanted, he could throw me down onto this little table and snap my neck before I could draw enough breath to scream. The station would stop anyone else, but was he different?

"If anything should interfere with this train and its cargo, I'll hold you personally responsible, Miss Aris." He hissed my name, revealing fully extended fangs.

"Naturally, sire." I breathed too fast and smiled thinly.

His fist opened, freeing my trembling hand. He tracked every movement as I pulled my hand to my chest, his black pupils blown wide.

I could still walk this back. I fluttered my lashes and smiled. "As formidable as you are, this is my sanctuary, and any harm that comes to me or my guests shall be met with equal force." His top lip peeled back in a snarl. "Trust me when I say you do not want to do this here."

A glance to my right revealed we had garnered quite the crowd. The alien-looking elves with their big, oval eyes and pointed ears openly observed, while others were more careful with their glances. They didn't care for me. They were more curious to see what *could* happen in this sacred place so they might later do the same.

I didn't see Ghost move from his chair or stop beside mine, but I felt his hands grab my wrist and shoulder and yank me to my feet. The sudden jolt whipped through me until all I could see were those black eyes and shining fangs.

This confrontation had been building since he'd tried to charm me on the platform and I'd brushed him off. It seemed our overseer needed a lesson in Night Station etiquette.

I let him think he'd caught me, allowing his killer instincts to ramp up, and then I twisted my trapped wrist enough to clutch his arm. Power shocked through me and into him where my hand touched his arm, snapping, hissing, sparking. With a shout, he tore himself away. Lazy smoke trails drifted upward from the singed patch on his immaculately tailored outfit.

I rolled my shoulders and righted my jacket by pulling on the lace cuffs, hiding the now-blazing x-symbol. "Kindly refrain from threatening me and your stay will be far more pleasant." A step closer brought me within whispering distance. Furious silver sparks blazed in the overseer's dark eyes. His fangs—fully on display—leaked debilitating venom. It was my turn to lean in and whisper against his cheek. "Sleep well under my roof, *Ghost*."

Turning on my heel, I left him there, my last words ringing in his ears. In less than an hour, the sun would rise. Day would break, and Overseer Ghost would find himself in my care until the realm of Night returned. The bastard wouldn't be sleeping well.

4

DAY

High-value cargo.

My boots struck the corridor floor in time with the words repeating over and over in my head, as though hammering nails into my soul.

High.

Value.

Cargo.

I veered through a door and into an inner passage, took a sharp left turn through another door, slinking through the station's service sections like a snake through tall grass until I was sure no one was following me. Plucking the key from my pocket, I stopped outside the last door at the end of a long narrow passage. A nothing door. It could have been a closet for all its dullness. I listened, waiting for any sign I wasn't alone. Warm morning sunlight filtered through the window blinds. I didn't look outside. Nothing changed out there. Empty buildings. Empty streets. Looking outside reminded me of why we were in here, living the illusion of freedom.

An extra few moments, just to confirm no one was observing me, then I slipped the key into the lock and turned it over.

Inside, stairs spiraled downward. Down and down and down. I ran my hand along the high-gloss wooden banister. Candlelight rippled over lavish gold- and green-patterned wallpaper. *Down* into what might as well have been a different world.

I emerged into the mirror image of the Night Station, complete with long corridors, high ceilings, and polished paneled walls. Only here, the entire front section of windows had their shutters thrown open, inviting sunlight in. My steps lightened, relief lifting the weight of responsibility off my back. It was day, and things were different now. So *very* different.

Platform One still ran the full thousand-foot length of the station's frontage, but nobody gathered there. Any creature looking in from the outside would assume the station was as deserted as the surrounding crumbling buildings. The station was only seen by those it wanted to be seen by.

Pulling off my jacket, I unbuttoned the first few gown buttons, freeing my neck and shoulders to the air's cool kiss.

The library here glittered with books, all lit by sunlight pouring in through vast arched windows. It smelled like warm books too, like home. But this home truly was my sanctuary.

Sprawled in the chair at my desk waited a man I sometimes hated, often admired, but always loved. Kensey Aris. My brother had kicked his boots up on the edge of the desk, raining dirt on the desktop and floor. He'd managed to tie his unruly dark hair back. Mostly. A few too many curls fell free, stroking his cheeks and jaw. It was a miracle he'd buttoned his shirt up without missing a hole. We were twins. You could tell by our eyes and in our cheekbones, if we were standing next to one another, but that was where our similarities began and ended.

He looked like he'd fallen out of bed and into that chair. He didn't need to care about his appearance. He didn't need to put on an act to survive each night. His life wasn't like mine. Like our roles dictated, we were as different as night and day, but he needed me and I needed him. There was no Lynher Aris without Kensey Aris. I was his secret and he was mine.

"I got your note." Worry pinched his dark brows. He set his boots down and leaned forward. "Are you all right?"

Was I all right? I'd spent all night entertaining a creature infamous for genocide and he was asking if I was all right? I waved off his concern, dumped my jacket on the desk, unlaced my boots, and kicked them off, leaving them where they'd fallen. From behind an old book title, I pulled a tarnished bottle of whiskey and poured myself a glass, then took the glass and the bottle to the desk. I didn't drink. Just stared.

"Did he hurt you?" my brother growled.

I turned my head and regarded his scowl. His gaze dropped to my neck, now exposed, looking for bruises or swelling. If Ghost had hurt me, there was nothing Kensey could do about it.

"Say something," he urged.

"No, he didn't hurt me." *Yet*, I added silently. "I'm dealing with him." I picked up the glass and downed the drink in one gulp. The burn radiated through my chest, making me feel some way to human again. I needed to get out of these clothes, needed to eat, to sleep, to do all the human things the Dark Ones didn't need. I needed to fall into a bed and wrap myself in safety so I knew there was something worth getting up for every night.

"Can we get to him?" Kensey asked. His eyes had hardened, turning cold.

"I think so." I poured another drink. "But there's more. In two days, he's expecting a train with *high-value cargo*."

Kensey's face crumbled. He stood, stole the drink from my hand, threw it back in one, and hissed as it scorched his middle.

High-value cargo meant only one thing to the vampireguard.

Kids. Carriages full of them. Orphans. Just like Kensey and me.

He handed the glass back, still wincing from the heat of the old alcohol. "We're stopping that train."

"Yes, we are."

His gaze tracked to the windows where dust danced in the warm sunlight. I knew what he was thinking. All the times we'd failed, all the trains that had passed through without stopping, reaching their final destinations—the numbers we hadn't saved were like those dust motes: too many to count. In a world oppressed by the Dark Ones, we couldn't save them all. It was never enough, but saving just one was better than none. We made a difference. For all his faults, his recklessness, his freedom, I loved my brother for his heart.

He reeled me into a hug, tucking me in close. I hadn't realized how much I'd needed to feel safe until that very moment. I sighed and melted against him. Layers of armor peeled away, one by one. Everything I'd endured in the hours before fell off me, and in my brother's arms, I was just Lynher again. Just a girl in a world gone wrong.

"We can do this," he whispered. "It's just you and me. We only have each other. We *can* do this."

I nodded, fearing the knot in my throat might break any words I tried to speak. As more layers fell away, the truth of me rose to the surface. I did not have any power, not really. No human did.

"We'll get them back for taking Gerome," he said. "For taking everything."

I clutched him close. He'd always been there. When I'd run too far from the station platform as a child and gotten lost in the dark, where monsters ate lost little ones, he'd found me. When I'd fallen from a rickety balcony and broken my arm, he'd wrapped my shattered bones and made the pain go away. When I screamed and cried because I couldn't do the same at night, he listened. Every morning he was here, waiting. And through it all, I did the same for him, picking him up when he fell, holding him down when he tried to do something foolish. Family. The two of us alone in the big world of monsters. Always. Kensey and Lynher. We saved each other, day after night, night after day. If we could save ourselves, how hard could it be to save the world too?

If it wasn't for exhaustion, I wouldn't sleep at all. With day came a reprieve from the Dark Ones and a chance for me to be me again. I fell into bed and slept longer than I should have. When the station didn't wake me by chiming the grandfather clock outside my room,

Kensey appeared with a breakfast tray. He perched himself on the edge of my bed as I bit into the toast, savoring the sweet jam. The station gifted us treats like jam. I'd asked Gerome once where all the food came from, and he'd laughed and told me it was from the same place as everything else, which answered nothing. Answers were a rare commodity at the station.

"How's Etienne?" Kensey asked.

I chewed and considered Etienne's first shift. "Still alive." As first shifts went, outside of Ghost's arrival, everything had gone smoothly. Happy guests made our lives easier. I was beginning to think Etienne might do all right.

"Well, that's something. I wasn't sure he was ready—"

"He's not."

Kensey frowned, and like always, his emotions showed in his eyes.

"You can't be ready for the night shift," I explained, but he'd never fully understand.

Gerome had prepared us for very different roles. Kensey didn't encroach on my territory, and I didn't encroach on his. He dealt with rehabilitating refugees. He ferried them far from the edge of the world and to new lives by way of his contacts spread across the land, and quietly, carefully, he threaded those we saved into a relatively peaceful existence. I found those who needed help and got them to him. He moved them on. Neither of us asked the other how we did what we did. It was safer that way, should one of us be compromised—or so Gerome had taught us. Sometimes, I'd want to know what happened to those we'd saved, like the little girl who'd smuggled her ratty old teddy onto the train with her. I'd washed the teddy and discovered it was pink, not gray. She'd laughed. There were many like her. Faces I'd never forget. But I couldn't know their fates. I was not infallible. All it would take was someone like Ghost to find a crack in my armor.

I pushed the tray aside.

"What's he like?" Kensey asked what he'd been dying to ask since waking me.

"Horrible. He made a very public display of having me kneel on the platform."

Kensey opened his mouth.

"There's nothing you can do." I threw back the covers and pulled on a dressing gown. "When his games crossed the line, the station protected me." My sleeve had pulled up and exposed the cross on my wrist. A simple but powerful mark. I pushed the sleeve back down and headed for the shower. "He knows he needs me to facilitate his people trafficking. He won't try it on again."

"You don't know that..." My brother's voice followed me, muffled by the shower-room door closing. "He's not used to anyone standing against him. He might decide you're worth losing a delivery of kids for."

That wasn't likely and Kensey knew it. Vampires needed kids for their bloodfarms. They'd rear them in cages, breed them, and bleed them until they were all used up. Then they'd be slaughtered for meat. A carriage of kids was as precious to vampires as air was to humans.

I stepped into the shower, and hot water pounded on my head, neck, and shoulders, massaging away the aches and the remnants of the overseer's touch.

Kensey and I had been destined for such a farm. We'd likely be dead now had the station not delivered us to Gerome. "Human stock" didn't live much beyond twenty years old.

"I heard from my European connections," Kensey continued. "There's a rumor of a rebellion..." He left the sentence hanging, and I wondered what I was supposed to do with that knowledge. I hadn't heard of any such rebellion. Had there been an uprising, I would know. The VG didn't talk—they were too obedient—but others loved gossip, which meant any uprising had failed or was about to.

"I have connections near New York. It's too late now, but if we'd gotten word of the overseer's arrival, we could have planned ahead, gotten more help, and orchestrated an attack—"

"That's precisely why we didn't hear ahead," I said, talking over the sound of the water.

"I just..." My brother trailed off. I thought he'd gone, but then he added, "I want to do more. I know we can do more."

Doing more meant leaving the safety of the station. Stepping over the white line left us vulnerable, and if he was caught...

Kensey had been gone before. He'd vanished for five days right after Gerome's murder. Five mornings when he hadn't greeted me after the night shift, when I'd thought him dead, when I'd feared I was suddenly alone.

I shut off the shower, wrapped myself in a towel, and opened the door. Kensey stood at the window, bathed in sunlight, thoughtfully gazing through the grubby glass.

"Maybe the European rebellion will succeed and we'll learn from that," I told him. I didn't believe it, but he needed hope to keep him moving forward, and I needed him for that same reason. I'd lie to him all day, every day, if it kept him here, doing what we did best. This was our place. Not outside, but inside, saving every single human we could. And we were damn good at what we did. Changing things was too much of a risk.

"Maybe," he replied.

I gathered day clothes, and when I looked for my brother to ask what he had in mind for the day, he'd gone.

The station in the day was a very different beast from the station at night. Kensey ran a small number of staff. The halls only ever bustled with life after we'd free a delivery of human slaves. Kensey housed them here, and with the station's help, he fed and watered them, cleaned them up, helped them manage their trauma, and worked to rehabilitate them. Etienne had been one such person, but he hadn't wanted to move on to a new life; he'd wanted to do more, as some often did when they learned how the station was different. We declined most help, but Kensey had taken a liking to Etienne. A *strong* liking. They were near the same age. Etienne had been full of tales of the *outside*, igniting Kensey's wandering spirit. If I hadn't accepted him on my staff, Etienne's tales might have lured my brother's desires into the wider world. Once the station had marked Etienne, the decision had been made for us anyway.

The halls were empty now. We hadn't saved any cargo since Gerome's death. That made my brother restless, made him feel as though he was failing. If he could see what happened at night, he'd know our work continued, but he couldn't, and so he rattled around these sunlit empty hallways, killing time. The high-value cargo had come at the right time to keep my brother occupied.

I stood at a huge arched window and admired the empty world outside. Overgrown and forgotten, the tracks were hidden among thick brush. Beyond that, empty skyscrapers clawed at a blue sky. It looked so… peaceful, in the way the dead look peaceful. There was no human life out there. Plenty of monsters, but nothing with a human heart lived free.

It seemed impossible that humans had once filled those huge towers from top to bottom, that humans had once streamed through the streets.

Heat fizzled at my wrist. I lifted my arm and watched the edges of the cross shimmer red. *Trouble.*

My night shift was starting early.

5

NIGHT

Trouble was too small a word for what I saw in the Grand Hall.

I should have expected the overseer to retaliate, and I had, but I'd expected it after dusk, not before the night shift had yet to start. Apparently, he was an early riser.

The dead succubus hung limp and doll-like from the Grand Hall's main chandelier. The fact she was naked wasn't a surprise, but the fact she was dead was. Her leathery wings hung open, their clawed tips dripping blood the long way down to the marble floor, where it gathered in a shiny pool. It took a great deal to shock me. A dead succubus hanging from my chandelier succeeded.

I grasped the balustrade on the landing atop the sweeping staircase. The position of the succubus put her at eye level, about fifteen feet out of reach, and forty feet from the floor below.

Ghost had taken up a spot by the foot of the stairs, the same spot we'd had our little altercation the previous night. Lounging in a chair, legs crossed at the ankle, a glass of blood in his hand, he smirked up at me like the monster he was. I could guess the origin of the blood he was drinking.

It was early. The Dark Ones were still rising. The news would spread like wildfire, but at least he'd produced this display when I had a chance to clean it up. I just needed to get the body down and fast.

The overseer raised his glass to me in a silent toast and drank. He clearly had no intention of moving from that chair while I worked.

He lowered the glass, and blood painted his lips. He licked them clean, never taking his eyes off me. The message was clear: if he couldn't get to me physically, he'd make my life difficult in other ways, and a dead demon did make my life difficult. I was supposed to protect every guest here, and he'd just pissed all over my authority.

"Ma'am…?" Etienne hovered to my right, studiously not looking at the body.

"I want you to pay a visit to Room C-Forty-Six," I said. "Tell them I sent you. Tell them…" I met Etienne's gaze. "… I need to call in my favor."

"Aren't the… the fae in residence in that room, ma'am?" he asked.

"Elves, and yes, they are."

"Oh… all right. I just… I mean… I've heard—"

Had Kensey not taught him anything? "Don't take anything they offer you. Don't enter into any conversations with them. Don't let them touch you. Just relay my message. Can you do that?"

He cleared his throat. "Yes. I can do that." And off he went.

Ghost's smirk told me he'd observed it all. Fucking vampires. Now I'd have angry demons to contend with as well as the overseer.

As for how he'd gotten to the succubus while inside my station, the answer was simple: he hadn't. He'd lured her outside the white line. It wouldn't have taken much for a vampire like him to charm her, and while I wasn't responsible for stupid demons, the fact he'd strung her up in my Grand Hall sent a clear message to all. He thought he had control here. If that message reached too many ears and others fancied pushing back against the rules, I'd have more trouble on my hands than one overseer.

Filling my lungs for the confrontation to come, I turned and stepped straight into Jack. I hadn't heard him approach, and his fingers wrapped around my wrist, the sudden touch startling the breath out of me.

"Ask him if he got her name."

"What?"

He freed my wrist and moved on, the whole exchange having taken less than a second. For any onlookers, it could have appeared as though he'd merely bumped into me and stopped me from teetering in my heeled boots.

I whirled and watched the man walk away, his cane back in his hand, tapping against the floorboards. Who on earth was he, and what was his interest in this? A glance down at Ghost revealed an arched eyebrow. He'd probably heard the exchange too or at least seen something pass between Jack and me.

I descended the curved staircase and planted myself next to Ghost. "There are rules, Overseer. Perhaps you have forgotten them?"

"I make my own rules, Miss Aris." He gestured across the table. "Sit. Won't you have a drink with me?"

"In case you hadn't noticed, there is a succubus hanging from my chandelier. I'd like to see her body removed before drinking with you, sire."

He leaned forward in the chair and looked up. He kept his face blank, which made his next words cold. "I hear the derision in your tone. I sincerely hope you're not suggesting I had something to do with that creature's death."

"Of course not." It wasn't a suggestion.

With a gesture, he dismissed the dead demon. "Keeping succubae around vampires is likely to result in this. It's a foolish mistake on your part. Frankly, I'm beginning to wonder if the rumors of your"—he raked his glare over me—"professionalism are overrated."

"And I see rumors of yours are not."

His gold-touched dark eyes flicked up and narrowed. "Be careful how you address me, or you may find Etienne's carcass hanging from the next chandelier."

Oh, to threaten human life with such a silver tongue. I'd be sure to cut that tongue out when the time came. The daggers against the small of my back warmed at the thought. I thought of Kensey too. He saved people. In his heart, he was good. In mine, darkness coiled, waiting to strike. A large, ruthless part of me wanted to see the overseer hanging from that chandelier. If it were up to me, he would hang, but there were too many here relying on my so-called professionalism to keep them alive. If I strung up an overseer, the VG would come down on me and the station, leaving nothing standing.

I sighed through my nose while Ghost watched me struggle to rein back my desire to stab him in the heart. Plucking a smile out of my armory, I plastered it to my face and stepped closer, deliberately brushing my knee against his thigh. As he remained seated, I looked down on him. "You look at me, sire, and you see weakness. That is a mistake. We'll call your indiscretion a mistake also. Young succubae can't resist vampires. They really should know better than to seek one out, especially one such as yourself. I trust, next time, you'll control your bloodlust in a manner becoming of your position."

He downed the thick syrupy blood, set the glass down, and got to his feet, bringing him almost chest to chest and eye to eye with me. "What happens when it is you who steps over the white line, Miss Aris?"

Rage only covered so much. Fear snatched at my breath, and he heard.

"I thought so." He smiled and stepped out from our discussion, intending to leave.

I should have left it at that, but for all the people who didn't have a voice and all the souls he'd destroyed, I couldn't let him walk away. Remembering Jack's words, I asked, "Did you get her name?"

He stopped. His shoulders tightened. Slowly, he turned his head, showing me his handsome profile and twitching cheek. "What did you say?"

He'd heard me. "I asked you if you got the demon's name… before you killed her. It's a simple question."

A shrug. A flick of the hand. "A worthless thing like that? Why would I care for its name?"

Jack's words had affected him, and for the life of me, I didn't understand why. What did it matter if the overseer had asked the demon's name?

He left the Hall, his heels striking the marble floor like the second hand on the Hall's ticking clock. Looking past the hanging demon body, I searched the landing for Jack, but others had gathered there to gawk at the grotesque display.

This wasn't over.

The overseer would continue to assert what he thought was his authority under my roof, unless I could stop him. Jack knew what screws to tighten, but how could he? It was time I paid more attention to Just Jack—right after I'd cleared up this mess.

An elven couple glided across the floor, the pair wrapped in flowing pastel-colored gowns. They appeared mild and shy, with their big eyes and quiet nature. Like most guests here, it was a lie, camouflage, or even armor, just like mine. Only the vampires and the permanent resident of Room 3B frightened me more, but these two owed me.

"Your problem?" the female asked, gesturing at the dangling body. Her name was Aoife. I'd seen her rip the face off a lycanthrope using just her nails. I'd seen her sob as she'd handed her child to me, so the vampireguard wouldn't take it away. She'd never asked what had happened to her child. She didn't need to. It was better that way.

I nodded at the demon carcass. "Yes."

She swallowed and glanced at her partner—Connaught. He raised his pale eyebrow in silent comment, either at my daring to ask anything of them or at having his partner perform in public. But he wouldn't object. For all their manipulation and lies, elves adored their children. Knowing theirs was safe was priceless.

Aoife clapped her hands. A glittering cloud drifted in through the open platform doors, as beautiful and surreal as a rainbow amidst a rainstorm. I'd never seen a storm of pixies before, but I'd heard other Dark Ones call them piranha with wings. The cloud wrapped around the demon and devoured it within fifteen seconds. The delicate cloud drifted out the way it had come, and I reminded my heart to beat again.

Aoife smiled her most pleasant smile. Pixies ate the living too. "Our debt is settled, Miss Aris."

A nod and the deed was done. The pair melted back into the crowd, leaving me to examine if anything was left of Ghost's macabre display. Even the blood had vanished. It was a shame he hadn't stuck round to admire the clean-up; he might have learned a thing or two.

With that done, I had the demon ambassador to find and a small war to avert, all in the name of reluctant peace.

The sun had just set when I stood outside Room 19 and rapped on the door. It was going to be a long night, but I needed to control the fallout of the overseer's actions.

The door creaked open. Sweet floral scents swept into the hallway. I'd only ever been inside the demon ambassador's room once, and that hadn't been by choice. Gerome had found me days later, wandering the halls, my memory in pieces. I'd remembered enough to tell him a single name, and I'd learned enough to know I never wanted to return.

Pushing open the door revealed a dense grove of tropical plants. Water dripped onto shiny banana leaves and flowed in rivulets alongside a muddy path beckoning me deeper inside. Where it went, I tried not to think on. It wasn't always like this in Room 19. I'd knocked once and opened the door to an old-world-style high-rise with a sparkling cityscape view through windows that didn't exist. I hadn't entered then, despite the view singing to something of the old world in my human soul. I'd asked Gerome how such a thing were possible, and he'd told me it was best not to think too long on it, lest the evasive answers drive me crazy.

Nobody had ever explicitly said the station was good or evil. It was poised between the two, which was why it wouldn't fling open the overseer's shutters during the day and burn him to a crisp. Everyone was "safe" here, including the demon I was about to meet.

I stepped across the threshold. Sticky heat clung to my face and tried to soak through my dress. A few more steps and a bright pink flower bloomed alongside the path ahead. It looked friendly enough. But knowing its owner, it was safer to assume everything here would try to kill me eventually.

A click sounded behind me: the door closing.

Wonderful.

I had my key. I could leave at any time. But I didn't run from monsters.

The path tangled its way through the thick undergrowth. Branches clawed at my hair and dress. I glanced back. The path had grown, hadn't it? I'd lost sight of the door. This was far enough. I planted my boots and breathed in, tasting warmth and wetness. A dribble of perspiration trickled between the blades hidden at my lower back.

I didn't need to wait long.

Some demons could appear human for short periods, and it was said the ambassador sometimes liked to walk the platform unnoticed. The demon that emerged from the greenery blended in perfectly with it. She wasn't human now, although she had a humanoid design about her. The bone arches of two vast wings towered over her shoulders. Her wings were clamped shut. Horns spiraled from her head. Her skin was all black, with a glittery shimmer that looked like dust. The demon ambassador, Lilith, was beautiful.

"Why do you not bring me the gift of the overseer's head?" Her voice scratched at parts of my brain designed to trigger me to flee.

So, she'd heard about the death. I shouldn't have been surprised. News traveled faster among demons than any of the other Dark races.

She moved like liquid, her hips and breasts carrying a seductive sway. I blinked myself from her thrall and met her stunning eyes. Dark slits cut through luminous green irises, like cat's eyes. "The same reason you haven't killed him yet."

I wasn't sure if she could kill him, but she'd certainly thought of it.

Her double eyelids flicked. "He charmed Sonel outside the station boundaries. She was young and easily manipulated. Had I known the overseer was arriving, I could have prepared her." She held a glass jar, and inside the jar, a colorful butterfly flitted and jerked, struggling to understand its invisible prison. She admired the poor creature, turning the jar this way and that. I'd seen her collect others in similar jars, but rarely saw the same butterfly twice.

"His arrival was unannounced."

Wedging the jar in a tangle of tree branches, she then slunk behind me, moving silently through the sweating plants, and circled to my left, eyeing me like I was a piece of fine meat strung up on a hook. Fat leaves stroked over her naked thighs and hips. Her skin glistened. "Why is he here? What does he want?"

"He has cargo arriving. He'll be gone after that—two nights from now."

"And this cargo is special to him, else why accompany it himself?"

Demons didn't abuse human children the same way vampires did, but they weren't known for their kindness either. A trainload of orphans was a valuable prize for any number of Dark Ones and valuable leverage should a demon want to bargain with vampires.

"Do you know what this cargo is?" she asked.

"Yes." Liars knew lies when they heard them.

When she smiled, her green eyes glowed red at their edges. "Of course you do, little Lynher."

I expected her to ask what the carriages carried, but she tapped a claw-like nail against her chin and breathed in instead. Her wings rustled, flexing outward a few inches before sealing closed again. I'd never seen her fully open them. She could ask about the carriages, but she knew I wouldn't tell her. We had something of a mutual understanding: I ran the Night Station and didn't interfere with her business, and she made sure her demons behaved while on the premises. As I'd said to Ghost, getting along made everyone's lives much easier.

"I want to see this overseer for myself. I think it's time I socialized." She eyed my clothing. "Is that *garment* the current style?"

"Purple and black are Night Station colors, but otherwise, silk and lace are generally considered appropriate."

"Hm." A twist of her lips and she said, "I'm sure I can rustle up something suitable." She sensed my reticence and approached my side, leaning in intimately close. Her tropical sweetness tingled on my lips and tongue. "Darling, no vampire can charm me. They were once ants scurrying around my feet. The sands of time will shift again, and it will be his carcass hanging from the chandelier."

It seemed our thoughts were aligned, which perhaps said more about me than it did her. I didn't doubt her conviction, but when a creature as powerful as Ghost faced the oldest known demon to still walk this earth, I'd be the one picking up the pieces.

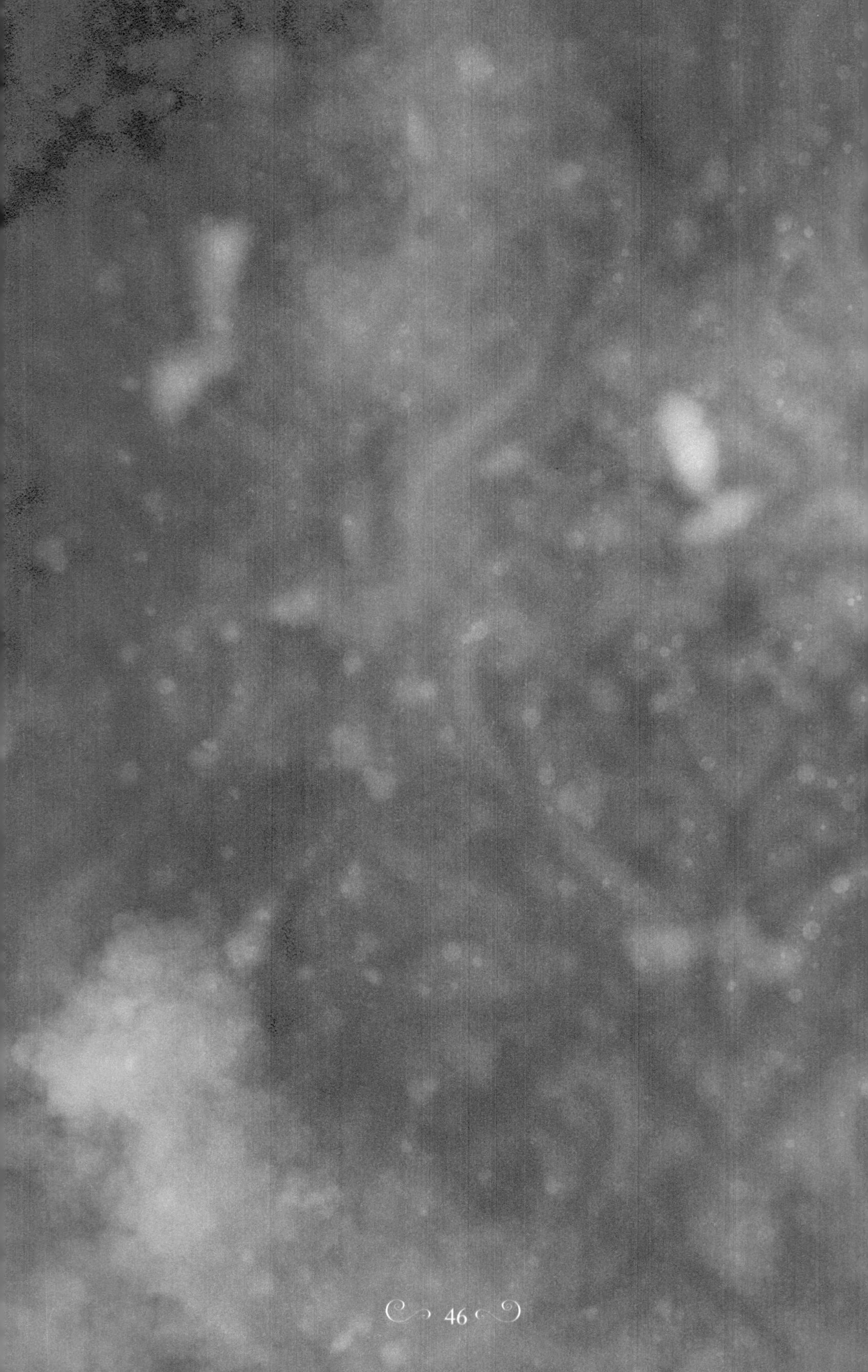

6

NIGHT

I might be human, but I wasn't helpless. I had other weapons at my disposal besides the obvious, and I planned to wield them to bring down Ghost and save his high-value cargo. Kensey was working on securing futures for the cargo, once I'd ferried them safely through the night. I just had to arrange for Overseer Ghost to be elsewhere when his train arrived.

Gerome had always told me the Night Station's cogs were sometimes like a huge game of chess. Secrets and favors were traded like currency. As long as I was thinking several moves ahead than those around me, the cogs would keep turning and the game would go on. It sounded easy. It wasn't.

One cog who had me stumped was Jack. He was not some unassuming fool who had stumbled upon my library office, but he was trying very hard to be. He had an interest in Ghost, and that made him interesting to me.

Etienne was dealing with the identical Corvus sisters as I approached the sweeping half-moon reception desk. Staff milled about behind, dealing with the minute-by-minute requests of our demanding guests. Ghost would summon me soon, and we'd start our dance all over again, but before he did, I needed to know more about the elusive Jack.

The leather-bound guest book noted every single station resident, spanning the station's fifty-year history. As a child, I'd sit with the huge book cradled on my crossed legs while Gerome stood at this very desk. My memory conjured him now, politely greeting the next waiting guest. He'd had a natural charm and a way with words that few could resist. Sometimes, I wondered if the flickers of his ghost were real. I'd lost count of how many times since his death I'd *known* he was behind me, his hand gently guiding my shoulder, only to turn and find myself alone.

I blinked the memory clean. Pushing aside the hollow sense of grief, I skimmed down the recent entries in the book. Human hands didn't write the swirling, elaborate names. Each name appeared as soon as a guest stepped across the white line, and there were thousands of entries.

As I read, the Corvus sisters—ravens in their natural form but human now—chittered about the evening's entertainment. They disliked violins and wanted all string instruments removed from the show. Etienne politely told them we couldn't change the entertainment to suit every individual's need or we wouldn't have any musicians left. They then proceeded to complain about a missing boot and some other various items. I allowed myself a small smile at my assistant's polite wrangling and flicked the book's pages, running a finger over each entry.

The station had seen a large influx of visitors these past few days, and more appeared to be staying longer too. Perhaps Kensey's contacts were on to something and there was unrest on the outside? As the only sanctuary and neutral ground on the east coast of America, this station was a desirable breathing space for many. But such things were out of my control. My world was inside the station walls, not beyond them.

Race wasn't noted in the book, but I recognized the style of some names as belonging to the Dark Ones from all over the world and its realms.

Ghost's name was on the list, simply written as *Ghost*. Perhaps that was his real name? Some things even the station didn't know or chose not to show me. Predictably, *Just Jack* and his average-sounding name wasn't listed among the new arrivals. I was fairly certain he'd arrived on the same train as Ghost. I'd first seen him on the platform, blocking my path, but that only narrowed him down to one among eighty-three new entries. It appeared I'd have to wait until he showed his face again to get my answers.

"Goodness, they are hard work," Etienne mumbled. He'd sent the sisters off, apparently happy, although it was difficult to tell by their breathless chatter.

"You did well."

He smiled shyly. "Thank you. I… I've been trying to remember everything Kens—"

"We don't say that name here." Ice spilled into my veins. I kept my smile but sharpened it. "Remember?"

His grin spluttered and died. I almost felt sorry for him. He'd been doing so well, but if he mentioned my brother's name, I'd send him away before the next shift. Kensey's name was not to be uttered at night. Ever. As far as Etienne was concerned, Kensey did not exist.

He cast his gaze downward. If he truly cared for my brother, he needed to get his shit together before he got us all killed.

"I was um… I was hoping I might visit"—he frowned—"*him*?"

The question was ridiculous. Night staff and day staff did not mix. Only I had the key that opened the door between the two. The station's secrets were too vulnerable to be exposed to anyone else. Etienne knew this. He shouldn't have asked, but I understood why he had. Kensey hadn't told me in so many words, but I'd seen the way my brother acted all stoic when he mentioned Etienne's name. He forgot I could read him as easily as a book from my library shelves.

"I asked you to discover more on Jack. Did you find his name in the register?" I asked, ignoring his request.

He hesitated, cleared his throat, collected his professionalism, and peered at the open page. "No, but I did find something interesting." Turning the page forward again, he tapped Ghost's name. "Are there often errors like that?"

I blinked at the page. I'd been so consumed looking for Jack that I'd missed the error beside Ghost's name. The entry should have had him down as staying in the grand suite, but he was listed as staying in Room A4, much farther down the wing, in a small room reserved for standard guests. "No… the station doesn't make mistakes," I muttered.

"Oh, I thought… I saw some pages were missing and I thought errors were normal."

"The missing pages have been gone a long time…" I scanned up the register for any mention of who was staying in the grand suite, and there it was: Felipe Berger, written in beautiful swirling ink. So, was "Felipe Berger" Ghost's real name, or was the vampire in the grand suite not Ghost at all, and whoever was staying in A4 was the real Ghost, as the book suggested?

There was only one way to know.

I started out from behind the desk.

"Ma'am… Lynher?" I turned and raised an eyebrow at the use of my name.

"I'm sorry…" Etienne began, worrying himself into blushing. "*Mon Dieu*, this is so much harder than I thought. I don't know if I can do this. I'm sorry. I try—"

I lifted my hand, cutting off his nervous ramblings. "Etienne…" Returning to the desk, I looked the man in the eye. He was young. We all were. Nobody could be fully prepared for Night. Kensey himself didn't know this life, not really. He knew what I told him, but he'd never lived it. Etienne was woefully underprepared. "You're here because the station wants you here. That is no small thing. Now, get back to work. We have guests to accommodate."

"Just… Miss Lynher, please, if you're going to Room Four A… be careful?"

Careful? I smiled, which probably wasn't the reaction he'd hoped for. I wasn't Kensey. Careful wouldn't get anything done here. Careful would see me eaten. Day was the time for careful; night was the time for calculated recklessness. "If the overseer summons me, distract him."

Etienne's frown tightened. "Distract the overseer?"

"I won't be long..." I turned and started down the inner hallway, heading toward whoever the station register had deemed was really Ghost. While there, I hoped to discover why an imposter might be staying in the grand suite, taking it upon himself to kill succubus and drape them from my chandeliers.

The door to Room A4 looked like all the others in this wing, its deep mahogany wood warm to the touch. Nothing obvious suggested the most feared vampire overseer might be staying inside.

I eased my skeleton key into the lock like I had every right to enter a guest's room and slipped inside before any of the numerous guests noticed who I was. My dress and reputation often made subtlety difficult.

Thick darkness inside the room tried to swallow me down before I could get a good look at anything. I clicked my fingers, signaling the station to light the gas lamps. Warmth flooded in and over a naked body lying facedown on the bed. Very obviously male. He was either out cold or dead. He wasn't moving. Maybe Ghost had killed him?

This was... unexpected.

I'd dealt with dead bodies. Hours earlier, I'd had the elves dissolve a demon. But this felt different. My skin crawled, like whatever this was, it wasn't meant to be seen. Like I'd stumbled upon something bigger than me, bigger than the station, even. I couldn't quantify this feeling. It made no sense. The weight of wrongness crawled over my skin and tried to push me back out the door, as though the station had also realized its mistake and wanted me gone.

The man's body was a map of black ink from his ankles, up his powerful thighs, over his rounded ass, and across his back. The swirls held no discernable pattern, like he'd been wrapped in brambles and his skin had absorbed their rope-like embrace.

I inched closer. His skin had a caramel glow, darkened by the spluttering lamps. As I drew closer to the bed, his breath stuttered and so did my steps. Not dead, then. That was good, wasn't it? From the glisten on his skin, he certainly didn't look well.

An elaborate cane caught my eye. It rested against the bedside table. I'd seen it on the platform, in the hands of Just Jack.

He turned his head.

Hazel eyes blinked.

"Jack?"

His lashes fluttered, and he blinked again before narrowing his eyes on me, finally seeing. Wherever he'd been inside his head, it hadn't been inside this room. He looked through me, frowning. "Miss Aris?" His hoarse voice cracked.

"Are you sick, sir?"

He swallowed. His throat moved, lips parted. All those things seemed drawn out, as though they took considerable conscious thought.

"I'm fine." He got a hand under him and gingerly levered himself upright.

He didn't sound fine. He didn't look fine either.

"We have healers on staff—" I cut off and quickly turned away as he brought his legs around and propped all of his naked self on the edge of the bed. I'd seen enough to know my brain and body wanted to see a whole lot more. "Do you need their assistance?" Lusting after a sick man was a new low, even for me.

"I said I'm fine," he said, alert enough to sound annoyed. "Why are you in my room, Lynher?"

I let the name slide, thoughts reeling. Was this man Ghost? He didn't seem dangerous, the opposite in fact. My instincts wanted to help, and they were rarely wrong, but what if he was a mass murderer? Gods and spices, I'd eyed him up like he was my own personal feast.

"There was a… a report of a disturbance outside this room." I cleared my throat. "I was concerned about the occupant."

All lies. If the station was right and Jack was Ghost, I needed to rethink everything he'd said to me and all the moments we'd met. This man was trying very hard to be a nobody and wore the perfect camouflage. First, he appeared human but wasn't. Second, he and the Felipe staying in the suite had fooled everyone, including me. If this man was the real Ghost, I could use that.

The bed creaked. "As you can see, everything is well." His voice moved around the room. Clothing rustled.

I stared at the closed door, resisting a powerful urge to turn and see those unique tattoos again. I'd heard nothing of Ghost being marked in such a way, but what did anyone know of him? Just his reputation. Nobody had known what he looked like—until now. I knew, and it was worse than anyone had thought, because he looked *normal.*

The man behind me was a human butcher. He controlled swathes of vampires across the lands, killing for his queen, tearing down humans like they were no more troublesome than wheat in a field, harvesting children for bloodfarms, and cutting out their tongues so he didn't have to hear them cry.

I could not afford to let this creature take me.

I was better than that.

"Was there anything else?" he asked.

I blinked and found him standing to my right. He'd thrown on a shirt and pants. Scruffy hair framed his handsome face, and his eyes were still glassy from sleep or whatever I'd walked in on. The little unassuming smile completed the harmless appearance. I'd faced demons bristling with claws and horns and fangs, vampires turned rabid on bloodlust, but I'd never looked into the eyes of true evil before now. Worse, his eyes were charming, just like the rest of him.

"Nothing else." I headed for the door.

"Lynher?"

"My name is Miss Aris, sir. Don't forget it." I was outside in a few strides and pulled the door closed with a hard *thwunk*.

Anger fueled my strides. I was angry that I hadn't seen it sooner, angry that I'd looked at him and *liked* him. Felipe Berger had had me on my knees, with his power probing my mind, and I would have done more to protect my staff, might have to if I wanted to save the children on that train, and he wasn't even Ghost; he was just a vampire general, a grunt, albeit a powerful one. They'd both played me.

But I knew the truth. The station had shown me. I still had power here, and I could still save lives.

A demon poofed into the hallway to the squeals of nearby residents. The pop of air pressure and scattering of sparks wasn't subtle, but neither was the demon the display belonged to. As noncorporeal travel was forbidden inside my walls and I wasn't having the best night so far, I plucked a throwing knife from its hidden place against my lower back and flung it true, right between the demon's mismatched eyes—one blue, one green. Unfortunately, not only did the demon know to expect a blade, but he also knew it was my opening gambit. He snatched the small knife out of its spin, as easy as picking a flower from between the platform cracks, locked his gaze on mine, winked, and poofed out again.

I whirled, my second blade free, plunged my hand into the gathering cloud of sparks, grabbed his now-corporeal throat, and shoved him against the hallway wall.

His sparks rained around us, bouncing off his bare shoulders, scruffy hair, and horns. He'd tucked his wings behind an illusion, but being shoved against a wall still wasn't a comfortable way to start his evening.

"*Rafe*," I greeted. "There are rules."

"Darling, you know I live to break them," he purred, or rumbled, or whatever the sound was that demons made, especially this demon. He had a voice made of liquid chocolate. It flowed and spilled and found all the little crevices to worm its way inside. "Hurt me some more, Miss Aris… exactly how you know I like it."

A hard touch pressed against my leg, beneath my dress, and snaked its way higher, looping around my thigh.

I pressed into Rafe, holding the small knife against his neck. He tilted his head back, allowing me access. Like a vampire's invading charm, Rafe's brand of magic tried to coil around me and lure me into his embrace. I wasn't immune, but I recognized the signs. I could mostly shrug off his incubi allure, and he knew it, which was why his tail was taking liberties when the rest of him could not. "Quit it or I cut it off."

We'd attracted a crowd, and in games like these, I had to win. Rafe knew that too. Some days, he knew too much.

His tail unraveled from my leg while the incubus's two-tone eyes read the intent on my face, his smile growing with every second I kept him pinned. "I submit in every way. Will you punish me…?" he purred and layered on the charm. "Please?" He said it loud enough so that everyone heard. His submission was bullshit. He lied like he breathed. But only the station regulars knew that. To these onlookers, I'd subdued a naughty demon, repairing the equilibrium.

With a flick of his wrist, he produced a black origami swan and offered it to me. He liked to craft whimsies out of paper and leave them all over the station—reminders of how he was never far away.

Shoving off him, I slotted my knife home and held out my hand for its twin. He rolled his pretty eyes, hoping I'd forgotten he'd taken it, and then magicked it out of thin air with another hand flick.

"The ambassador has summoned me," he said, handing out the blade while tucking the swan back into his pocket.

I took the blade, ignoring his smug look. "Then go to her."

Rafe was Lilith's lapdog, assistant, pet, soldier, her everything and nothing, as far as I could tell. When she called, he appeared and made a pest of himself.

The crowd dispersed now that the fun was over. Rafe watched them go while he straightened his waistcoat. He wore nothing underneath the waistcoat and black suede pants, preferring to advertise every lean inch he had on offer. Like all incubi, he changed his appearance to suit the admiration of those looking his way. Whatever their sexual whims, he made it happen, but now he wore the resting form he preferred, at least around me. Probably because he knew I preferred it too. Without his horns, two backward-pointing prongs of black keratin, he might have passed for a ridiculously attractive mid-twenties human male. He wasn't any of those things, besides male.

"Our lady thought you might need my assistance."

Lilith thought I needed him? I laughed him off and started back toward the heart of the station. Rafe trailed behind, his tail menacing any passerby—male, female, or non-gender, he didn't care so long as he got a feel in.

"Stop it," I hissed.

The last thing I needed was Rafe thrown in the mix. He was like a badly behaved ferret that got into everything, leaving chaos behind. Lilith seemed convinced of his uses. I'd never seen any, beyond his ability to distract, like he was distracting me now.

"You are tense this evening." He laughed, and that laugh plugged into all the feminine parts of my brain, switching them to *on*. "I have a remedy for that, you know."

"I don't want your remedy, or you, for that matter. If you could go make yourself useful somewhere else, that'd be grand. I have enough to deal with."

"Like Ghost?" he asked, eyebrow rising.

I veered toward an empty room, unlocked the door, and entered. Rafe followed, confidently striding on past. Now that we were alone, his illusion fell away, and he unfurled his wings like shaking out folded drapes. His wings were nothing like Lilith's. They had the same leathery arches, but his had patterns to catch the light and make them shimmer. His wings were my weakness. He knew that too.

He spotted the large four-poster bed and turned, lifting a wing out of the way. "Straight to the foreplay. Why Lynher, you minx—"

I stepped back, pulled the door shut, and *snicked* the lock, locking him inside, then kept right on walking. Some rooms were magically sealed. This was one of them. He'd have a hard time translocating out of here.

He'd be fine. Rafe was always fine. I did not have the time or energy to deal with a sexually motivated incubus *and* everything else.

Taking a piece of paper and a pencil from my dress, I scribbled Kensey an update and left it under the pitcher, like before, then headed on to find Felipe and continue the dance of death and survival none could admit we were all a part of.

7

NIGHT

A woman danced with Ghost. She wasn't really a woman, and he wasn't really Ghost, but we were all playing along. The pair swirled and dipped and rose to the music, looking like the perfect couple. Lilith wore the body of a tall, stunning human female, her golden hair pinned back from her face but flowing down her back. Her dress glittered and rippled around her ankles. She looked like an angel, if such a thing existed. Felipe—the vampireguard pretending to be Ghost—was her exquisite opposite.

He said something, and she laughed, bright and free, presenting a picture postcard of a date. As I watched from the gallery a level above, I couldn't decide who had snared whom. Both were vicious, cold-blooded killers. Had I still believed Felipe was Ghost, it would have been a close call, but he was likely a general following Ghost's orders, which put him at the same level as demon kibble compared to Lilith. Right now, she was testing him, putting him at ease, letting him think he led the dance. He had no idea he danced in her web like the fly he was.

Did Lilith know he wasn't Ghost? I'd have to meet with her later, right before dawn, to decide how to proceed. Until then, I was grateful for the breathing space her dealing with Felipe gave me. Now, all I had to do was find Jack.

"Not dancing, Miss Aris?"

My blood chilled. The smile on my lips was a mask I wore often, but it didn't feel like enough around Jack, like maybe he could see right under it.

"I'm sensing some… resistance," he said, resting his cane against the banister.

A server passed by. Jack plucked two champagne flutes from the tray and handed one out to me.

"I really can't, not while working," I declined.

"Well, now here I am, looking like a fool with two glasses of champagne."

I took the glass and averted my eyes to the dancing crowd below. The sip turned out to be a gulp. The champagne wasn't nearly strong enough, so the rest went down far too easily until I'd drained the glass.

Jack flicked his gaze up. "Do you ever not work, Miss Aris?" he asked. "In the day, perhaps?"

He'd been watching my throat. "Yes. Now, if you'll excuse me—" I pushed off the banister, heart fluttering like a trapped bird.

"Miss Aris?"

I stopped, wore my wooden smile, and turned. "Yes, Jack?"

He stepped closer and took the empty glass from me, his fingertips brushing mine. It wasn't right that he should look so… nice. Perhaps this was why they called him Ghost. He blended in, went unnoticed, and anyone who figured out his secret didn't survive to tell it. But I'd survive him. I had to, for the train's cargo, for everyone who called this station home, for my brother, for hope in a ruined world.

"Have I offended you?" he asked, laying on the innocent act so thick it was a miracle he didn't choke on it.

Only genocide. "Of course not, sir."

"Will you dance with me?" His words surprised him, and he smiled at his foolishness. The server passed by again, taking the empty glasses. He even thanked him, like a gentleman. An act like his could break a thousand hearts. "I'm leaving soon and I don't know when—if I'll return," he said, his attention back on me. "It would be my pleasure." He offered me his hand.

So honest, like he truly cared, but a creature like him had no soul. He didn't know how to care for anything other than his queen. Even his love for her was fake, built into his design. For some reason, my gaze found his cane and its beautiful carving.

"I can dance without it, for a while," he explained, assuming I was concerned for him. "So, shall we dance?"

I might have, if the station hadn't shown me his ugliness. "No, sir. We shall not."

I couldn't. I couldn't hold his hand or stand close to him and dance and smile and pretend everything was all right. I wasn't Lilith. I couldn't dance with a monster. I dropped my smile. It had been a dead thing on my lips anyway. He saw the horror in my eyes and the disgust in my downturned mouth, and his expression changed too. His smile cracked, as did his gaze, and some of the truth glared through from deep inside. A hungry coldness leaked from inside. It reached for me, made me stagger away, made the mark on my arm sizzle to life. Something old and dark and dangerous inhabited this man, and it had me in its sights.

A scream shattered the connection.

More screams rose from the ballroom. Glasses smashed. The smell of burned rubber tainted the air—the smell of demon magic.

I should have looked, should have dealt with it, but Jack's coldness had its grip on me, trying to consume me. I'd never felt magic like it, not from Lilith, not even while passing by Room 3B. This thing standing in front of me was more than a vampire, more than all the Dark Ones put together, and he was looking out from behind human eyes, seeing deep into my soul, turning me out, ripping me open.

Sparks fizzled to my left. "Excuse the interruption." Rafe inserted himself between Jack and me, breaking the spell. He leaned against the banister and peered down. "But we're all fucked…"

Jack withdrew, having the nerve to look stunned, like I had poured ice into his soul. He wobbled against the banister and grabbed for his cane, needing it.

"Lynher, what do we do?" The incubus turned to me, his two-tone eyes wide. I'd never seen him shocked. *Nothing* shocked Rafe.

Jack limped along the gallery, and I let him go, hiding my tremors as I leaned against the rail beside Rafe and tried to make sense of what I saw below. Blood. So much … like a red star had exploded in the center of the dance floor. At its center stood Lilith with not-Ghost sprawled on his back on the floor. The gaping hole in his chest likely had something to do with the heart Lilith was eating out of her clawed hand.

"Shit. She wasn't supposed to do *that*." It shouldn't have been possible. The station should have intervened.

A whistle sounded, and the red-and-black vampireguard poured in from all doorways. Lilith dropped all pretense of being human and shifted to an eight-foot-tall, black-skinned demon with eyes of fire and wings dipped in lava. She whirled on the spot, throwing open her enormous wings, and screamed. The noise tore through the air like a physical wave. The station's wall of windows exploded, raining glass.

I clamped my hands over my ears but heard Rafe say, "Oh, fuck no." His arms looped around my waist. He flung open his wings and threw them around me, muffling Lilith's scream.

Air pressure rushed outward. My ears popped and my lungs ached and just as my thoughts had caught up with what Rafe was doing, he let me go.

I shoved at his chest, needing space, and instinctively freed my knives. "Stay back!"

The mark on my wrist burned brighter. A warning, a protection.

Rafe bared his teeth. "Try a *thank you*, Lynher." He flicked his wings out, realigning them and drawing my eye to our silent surroundings.

Trees. Bushes. All painted in shades of black.

No, no, no…

The breeze on my tongue tasted like metal and death.

The night sky hung over us, its stars winking.

We were outside the station. Beyond the white line.

"Take me back." Cold and fear robbed me of all sense of safety and warmth.

"Back in there?" He flicked a thumb over his shoulder toward the station. "Lilith is about to remind those vampricks why they don't mess with demons, and she wants you out of the way. You're staying here."

I bolted for the brush behind him, dodging his attempt to grab me, and plowed into the bushes.

Branches clawed at my face and pulled at my dress. I had to get back. I couldn't be outside the station. I couldn't be beyond the white line. The station needed me. My friends, my family. The vampireguard would come. They'd hurt them for Lilith's actions. I had to get back there to stop it.

A wall of wings and reaching hands blocked my path.

I skidded and slashed wildly at Rafe, opening a thin bloody line through his waistcoat. He hissed and reeled, more surprised than hurt.

I ran again. More branches snagged my clothes, so I took the knife to my skirts and cut them free, then ran out of the brush and across open asphalt peppered with weeds and spindly trees. I'd lost my shoes but I had no time to care. The station platform lay ahead, its one-thousand-foot facade of windows beacons in the night.

I had to get back inside. It needed me.

My heart raced along with my bare feet on the cracked road.

Get back behind the white line…

Something in the sky screeched. Rafe maybe. Maybe not. Out here, I was prey. The white line… I just had to make it over the line.

Smoke swirled ahead. It coalesced between me and the station's lights. A black figure grew from the smoke. *A phantom.* Soul suckers. Screamers. The VG had many names for them. They didn't bother the vampires. Why would they? It was souls they fed on. They'd bother with me.

I had nothing to fight it, just my knives.

The phantom's outline wavered, grew, and straightened. It had seen me. No… nothing would stop me from getting back. Not Rafe and not that *thing*, pulled from one of the otherworlds and dumped into this one.

I ran harder, knives locked in my fists.

The phantom unleashed a horrid wail that shook my soul in warning. Then the train hit it. The iron engine made of fire and smoke annihilated the phantom, blasting it into pieces. I slowed to watch the iron beast thunder on. It roared and whipped up dust, tainting the air with the ashes of a dead world. When the train had passed, the platform waited just a few strides ahead.

I stumbled over the iron tracks, breathing too hard, heart trying to hammer free of my chest.

A phantom's scream cut through the new quiet.

It wasn't gone. Or maybe this was a different one.

And now it was pissed off and moving in fast.

I twisted, stumbled backward, my little knives out like they could protect me, and stared into its hollow, hungry eyes. If I died here, more than my life would end. The station would end, and I could not allow that to happen.

The phantom stopped a few strides from me. Its torn outline swelled as it turned itself into a churning storm of blackness. I had the platform at my back, its edge against my shoulders, but I needed to climb up and over that edge to reach the white line, and there wasn't enough time.

Gods, it was really over.

I'm sorry, Kensey. I tried. I tried so hard… but in the end, I was just a little girl in a silly dress, playing with monsters.

Wings and sparks filled my vision. I blinked, noted the pretty shimmer on the leathery membranes, and realized, with gut-dropping dread, that Rafe was here.

Most vampires were unnaturally spawned by their queen and therefore soulless. Demons were not.

Rafe roared at the shadow. His wings opened to their full span and his tail lashed—its spiked prong a weapon. He seemed more beast than man.

The phantom rushed in and tore *through* him.

He staggered and almost fell against me. Smoke flowed from his skin, dragging some vital essence, and then the phantom soared into the sky, vanishing among the stars.

Rafe toppled forward, dropped to his knees, and fell facedown across the tracks, one wing flapping, then falling still.

Silence had never sounded so complete.

"Rafe…?" I dropped beside him, avoiding his wings so as not to further hurt him, and brushed his hair from his face, tucking it behind a horn. His eyes were open, his lips parted. He wasn't breathing. But he'd be okay… He was always okay. I'd known him since he'd found me outside the line, toddling off somewhere like silly humans did, and he'd brought me back onto the platform, back to safety. "Our secret," he'd said, his finger pressed to my lips. I hadn't been so scared of demons after that. He'd been a constant, like Gerome, but facing his motionless body, I realized I couldn't lose him too.

"Rafe?"

His cheek felt cold. He was *never* cold. He was smiles and motion, laughter and lust, and now he was… dead? "No…"

He was always all right, and he'd be all right again too—if I could get him across the line.

I hooked my arms under his and dragged him off the tracks before a train could truly finish him off. Heaving and shoving at his dead weight, I propped him against the platform wall and scrambled up and over its edge. Reaching down, I got a grip around one arm and tried pulling him up, but his wings flopped, lodging him beneath the platform's lip. Reaching even farther, I looped an arm around his waist, but his weight slipped and pulled me over the edge. We both ended up in the dirt. *No, no, no…* Sanctuary was right there! Tears wet my face, tears for a pest of a demon who should never have taken me outside the white line. What had he been thinking?

"You idiot creature." I thumped him on the arm and then rested my hand on the same spot, stroking away any hurt. "Why!"

This was too much. It was all too much. Lilith, the dead vampire, the phantom… Lilith had killed Felipe in my station. The VG would not forgive that. Was everything falling apart? Was it all over?

I ran my hand down Rafe's limp wing. I had to leave him to get back inside. He was just another demon, and the station was more important than any individual. "I'm sorry—"

"Miss Lynher Aris," a stern male voice declared.

I looked up, straight into the cold eyes of a vampireguard.

"Come with us."

They were everywhere, spilling down the tracks and coming in fast. Hands gripped me under the arm and hauled me onto the platform, finally behind the white line. It took four of them to heave Rafe's awkward body onto the platform too. Under the station's flickering lights, his skin looked gray, his left wing bent at the wrong angle.

"Is he dead?" I asked, but nobody was listening. *"Is he dead!"*

They ignored me. Cold, rough hands pulled me in through the station doors. The guests looked on, so many they had to jostle each other to see.

Etienne pushed through the crowd and pulled up short, his face stricken. I shook my head. He'd panic and try to contact Kensey, putting my brother in danger. That could not happen.

My reflection ghosted the hallway mirrors. At first, I thought the glass was cracked, but it was me who was broken—my dress torn, legs cut up and bleeding, hair pulled and yanked, and the tracks of tears staining my face. The VG, the Dark Ones, my staff, everyone—they all saw me. The real me. Just a girl. In a dress. Playing with monsters. And now everything would change.

8

NIGHT

Three VG accompanied me to a room I'd never seen before. It didn't have windows, just a single chair and a white-tiled floor with a small drain in the middle.

They dumped me in the chair but left me unrestrained. My only way out was through the one door behind three vampires, two males and one female, each one as cold and uncaring as stone. Their black-and-red uniforms were spotless. One I'd seen before: Caine. He didn't have his sensible friend beside him. He'd seen me defy Ghost, seen me kneel to Ghost too, and now that fake Ghost was very dead, his heart eaten in a public display should've been impossible. There was no coming back from that. It didn't matter that Felipe Berger wasn't the real Ghost, or perhaps they didn't know either, which meant I was in for a whole world of hurt for failing to protect their infamous overseer.

I waited, time stretching on. It would be day soon. Kensey would be waiting. I'd never missed a day before.

"You must think us fools?" the female asked. Broad-shouldered and with cropped bloodred hair, she looked as mean as her black-and-red uniform suggested.

I lifted my chin. "You need to let me go. The station must—"

"You're not going anywhere."

"You can't keep me here."

She folded her arms. "By all means, try to get past us."

Caine straightened, suddenly invested. He wanted me to fight so he'd have an excuse to tear my throat out.

In my torn dress, knees all banged up, it was difficult to maintain the act that I had any power here. "If you hurt me, the station will react."

"Maybe, but the rules don't apply to some, do they? And you'd still be dead." She came forward and crouched to my eye level, like this was just a friendly discussion. "Ghost was killed on your watch, Lynher Aris, and as you so often say, everyone here has sanctuary. That makes his death your responsibility. So, would you like to explain how a demon was able to rip out a vampire's heart in your so-called sanctuary?"

"I don't know." The only way it could have happened was if the station had allowed it, but exposing such a huge loophole would put everyone at risk.

"Give her to me..." Caine said, leering. "I'll make the bloodbag spill her secrets."

The female smiled, but it was out of place on her hard face and full of bright, perfect teeth. "Do our kind have sanctuary here? Because if we don't, we'll see these premises burned to ashes like every other human stronghold."

My heart fluttered. "They do—you do."

"So, how then—"

"I said I don't know."

Her hand shot out and her iron fingers wrapped around my throat. The mark on my arm stayed quiet. She wasn't hurting me so much as threatening me. A twitch, though, and I'd be dead. How fast was the station? Usually, my mark would have started fizzling by now. Maybe something was wrong with it and that was how Lilith was able to kill the vampire?

"Do you have an affinity for demons, Miss Aris?"

"No." I held her gaze as her charm probed my thoughts for a way inside.

"You were seen with one prior to the overseer's death. An incubus known to frequent the ambassador's rooms. You were then discovered outside, next to his body. Did you think to perhaps dispose of any incriminating evidence beyond the white line, where sanctuary does not apply?"

Then Rafe *was* dead? It hurt inside like it had hurt when a vampire had appeared at the reception desk and told me Gerome was dead. It hurt like something vital had been ripped out of me. My thoughts tried to collapse in on themselves and bury me under grief, but I couldn't let them see me broken.

"No. Rafe is..." I licked my lips, and her gaze fell to the movement. "This is a waste of time. I didn't do anything. My job here is to make sure the station runs smoothly for everyone, including the vampireguard. I serve you as I do all Dark Ones. What happened was a travesty, and I'll see it's dealt with—"

"The little human thinks she can *deal* with this?" She laughed and turned her head, seeking Caine's attention. His eyes glowed, losing all pretense of humanity. Twin curved fangs glinted from behind his smile.

"Maybe if your Ghost hadn't killed a succubus, we wouldn't be in this situation," I said. "Perhaps that's why Lilith was able to kill him, because the station deemed it fair. I really don't know. I'm human, as you pointed out. Why would I know anything? I have guests to see to, trains arriving, and many Dark Ones wondering why they aren't being entertained. The overseer made a mistake and paid for it. We should all move on, including you. Isn't that what your queen would wan—"

I didn't see Caine move or feel his teeth plunge into my neck until I was already crushed against his chest, my neck bent at a painful angle. Power flared through my veins, lighting me up with ten thousand volts of Night Station backslap that was more than enough to kick Caine in the mental nuts.

He howled and threw me down.

I staggered to the far side of the room, as far away from them as the walls would allow, my vision misting, thoughts spinning. Caine had bitten me. Cold shivered through my veins, racing toward my heart. I dabbed at the wound, and my fingers came away wet with scarlet blood. My stomach flipped, shock and fear trying to hold me down.

A fifth figure stood in the room, his cane at his side.

"Leave." He didn't shout, didn't growl, but the VG scattered, closing the door behind them, trapping me with a monster worse than them.

I clamped a hand over my bloody neck and stared at Jack.

Venom tingled, plucking on my frayed nerves and smoothing them out so everything seemed perfectly fine. The venom also worked to clot the wound so I wouldn't bleed out, which was convenient, seeing as I felt like sitting right where I was.

I slid down the wall, thoughts swimming.

Well, that proved a theory. The station *did* protect me fast enough to see one of them off, but not fast enough to stop a bite.

Jack came forward, so tall now that I was on the floor, looking up at him.

"You are in a very dangerous position, Miss Aris."

"I know, Jack."

"My name isn't Jack."

"I know that too," I slurred and then realized I'd maybe said too much. My hand shot to my mouth to seal in the secrets. "Is Rafe dead?" I mumbled, and my heart hiccupped. That damn demon had been a nuisance my whole life. I'd wished him gone a thousand times, but now that he was, I wanted him back. I was going to cry again, for Rafe, for Gerome, for me. I wasn't ready to be a host. It wasn't meant to happen yet…

The real Ghost crouched in front of me, his eyes impossibly kind. He had to be the real Ghost for the VG to scurry away like they had. I wanted to fall into his arms and weep. That was the venom. It made humans pliable, made them weak, and made feeding from them so much easier.

"You are very nice to look at." That seemed like the wrong thing to say too, but I couldn't imagine why. He had looked quite delicious sprawled on his bed, buck naked. My mind hung on that image, finding it fascinating but also important, as though I'd missed something while seeing him stripped of all his pretty lies.

Ghost pulled a handkerchief from his pocket and pressed it to my neck. "Hold this here."

I obeyed because he'd asked so nicely. "My brother will be missing me…" Oh, that was bad. Very bad. I didn't have a brother. I couldn't. "I don't want to speak to you. You're one of the bad ones."

"That"—he took my hand and straightened, gently lifting me with him—"is the truth."

I liked his eyes, as deep as they went, two pools into worlds I didn't know and didn't want to. Then I remembered all the lives he'd stolen, and the children he'd raised to feed his army, and the queen he served, sitting at the center of a nest of monsters somewhere far away, and I plucked my hand from his.

"When this venom wears off, I'm going to make you wish we'd never met, *sir*."

Then the venom pulled me down to where the hurts all went away.

DAY

Most people didn't wake up from a vampire bite. It sure felt like I shouldn't have. It was day, and sunlight streamed in through my window. *My* window. I blinked and jerked upright. I was in my bed. During the day. How? My torn dress lay over the back of the vanity chair. Oh gods, someone had undressed me and brought me from night to day. Please let it not be the murdering asshole… Shit, I'd said some things—Kensey!

I threw off the covers, tossed on some clothes, and dashed from the room.

"Kensey!" What if Ghost had found the key in my dress? What if he'd brought me here and found Kensey? What if he knew everything? The resistance, the lives we saved in the day? I tried the library, found it empty, then tried the old reception, now moth-balled and dusty.

"Damn you, Kensey. Where are you?" I ran into the ballroom, with its dust-sheet-covered piano and scattered furniture, and there he was, standing by the window, draped in sunlight, talking to Etienne, the pair a hair's breadth away from each other. Relief turned to rage. Etienne was *here*? "Did *you* bring me here?"

Etienne stepped away from Kensey as if he thought I didn't already know they were lovers or wanted to be. "I-I—"

Kensey grinned. "Lynher, you're awake."

I ignored him and went straight for Etienne. "You can't be here."

Kensey held out a hand to stop me, while Etienne shrank back. "Calm down, okay? I met him at the door. I told him to come through with you. He wasn't going to, but I asked him. I needed to know what happened, and I'm glad I did."

My brother reached out to touch my neck. I batted his hand away and touched the small bandage there instead. "I'm fine. It's nothing."

"It's not *nothing*." Kensey's tone made me feel small again. "What the hell, Lynher? You asked the ambassador to help you? What were you thinking?"

"I told her about the succubus and she volunteered. I didn't know she would kill him like *that*." I dropped into a sheet-covered chair, sending clouds of dust into the sunlight. "Does the VG have her?" I asked Etienne.

"No, I don't think so. They demanded the visitor book and all the files and—"

"You gave it to them?"

"Of course he did," Kensey answered for him, his lips twisting at my tone. "He did a good thing bringing you here. You're both safer here."

"I have to go back." I leaned back in the chair and sighed. "It's a mess, Kensey. And the train is tonight. And Ghost… Ghost is not dead. He's…" I touched my neck again. He'd handed me his handkerchief and helped me to my feet. What had happened after? "How did you find me?" I asked Etienne, hating how small and weak my voice sounded, especially in front of him. My brother knew me. He knew I wasn't the woman I pretended to be, but to Etienne, I was the infallible hostess. That act was over. He'd seen the VG march me in, seen my tears too.

He swallowed, glancing between my brother and me. Kensey nodded, urging him to answer, and it irked me some more that

Etienne would defer to my brother over me. "The guest, Jack, summoned me to his room. You were on the bed, out cold, bitten. I didn't know what to think or what to do… but he said I should… look after you."

I groaned and buried my face in my hands. Jack knew about Etienne. Or maybe he didn't. Maybe he assumed Etienne was my assistant like everyone else did. What else did Jack know?

"Who is Jack?" Kensey asked, leaning back against the window frame.

"Jack is the real Ghost."

Etienne uttered a curse in French, and my brother's expression hardened. "And he *helped* you? Why?"

"He's… I don't know. He's pretending—hiding who he is. I can't figure him out." Why had he helped me? Why hadn't he let Caine have his fill so he could deal with his high-value cargo and move on? "Did he say anything to you?" I asked Etienne. "Anything about what happens during the day or Kensey?"

"Just that you were unwell and needed to rest. Nothing else. I swear, ma'am."

Okay, that was good. Jack was still in the dark—literally. We had to keep it that way. He'd fooled me with his act, but the station had seen through it. And since Ghost wasn't actually dead and Lilith had only murdered a vampire general, maybe the VG wouldn't come down on us too hard.

"And you don't know if they caught Lilith?"

He shook his head. I dared not mention Rafe, not with Kensey watching. He suspected Rafe and I had had more than a passing interest over the years. We hadn't, but it was best not to mention Rafe at all.

"Can phantoms kill demons?" I asked instead. Etienne would think I was asking for Lilith's sake.

He looked at Kensey, who shrugged. "Don't they just take souls?"

Which meant Rafe might be alive but hurting. That couldn't be my problem right now, not with everything else going on. He'd taken me outside the white line and shouldn't have. I'd get to the problem of Rafe after I figured out how best to save the high-value cargo.

"What were you doing outside the line?" Kensey asked, cheek flickering. Draped from behind in sunlight, legs crossed at the ankles, arms crossed over his chest, he seemed so solid and real and untouchable. He was my brother and I loved him more than anything in this world, but some things he didn't need to know.

"I..." If I told him a demon had translocated me out there, he'd ask why, and how was I supposed to tell him an incubus had been trying to keep me safe?

"The VG arrested her on the platform," Etienne answered neatly for me, either sensing my reticence or *knowing* it because he'd heard me begging to know if Rafe was alive. "Lots of people were running outside. Miss Aris was helping them."

Did Etienne know he was lying for me, or did he believe his own words? Either way, I appreciated it. Arguing with Kensey was the last thing I needed.

Bowing my head, I combed my fingers into my hair and locked them there. All that mattered were the kids. The cargo. The plan was the same. Ghost was a cog in the machine, a big one with nasty teeth and perfect camouflage, but so was I. And so was Kensey. We could do this.

"With any luck, the VG will write this off as interspecies vengeance. The ambassador can handle herself." Looking up, I found the pair watching me. Kensey's brow was pinched with worry. He'd have worried a lot more if Etienne hadn't brought me in today. "Thank you, Etienne."

Etienne's fluttering smile broadened. "Anytime, ma'am."

Kensey's frown eased. "You can call her Lynher during the day, you know. She's different here."

I could allow him that, I figured, and nodded. Etienne tucked his flighty smile into his cheek, and I could see why Kensey had fallen for him. He had a good heart too, and maybe he was growing on me—like a rash.

"Are you ready for tonight?" I asked my brother.

Kensey nodded. He was always ready to save lives. Always had a plan. Once the train arrived and I got those kids off, he'd take them into day and keep them safe. He might act like he didn't have a care, but in many ways, that was his mask. We all wore them.

I sighed, trying to ease the growing weight of responsibility. That carriage was coming, and inside, there might be fifty little lives needing us to save them. Everything else was inconsequential. "I just need to figure out a way to distract Jack before the cargo arrives." Lilith had been my plan for that, but with her in hiding, her participation looked unlikely. The VG was hunting her, and they'd do just about anything to get her. She hadn't left the station in years. She'd be inside its walls, but she knew how to hide, and if the station supported her actions, as it appeared to, it would help her. But there was one way to find her.

"Have you eaten?" Kensey asked.

"No." The venom had all but cleared from my system, leaving me ravenous—a side effect to ensure a vampire's prey looked after itself for the next feeding. My skin crawled at the thought of Caine's teeth in my neck and what *could* have happened. But the station had protected me. Millions of humans hadn't been as lucky.

"C'mon, both of you," Kensey urged, his smile infectious. "While you're here, let's make the most of it." He sauntered across the ballroom, leaving Etienne waiting for me.

"Are you all right?" he asked.

I nodded. "I will be."

Maybe Night was too much for him. I should send him back, but there was no guarantee the station would keep him in a day role. If he left, it would break my brother's heart. Kensey only had me, like I only had him.

"Don't think it," he said, guessing the direction of my thoughts. "I can do this."

"Etienne, I don't want you to get hurt, and Jack is… aware of you."

"I can handle it. I just needed to be here for a little while. Night is… hard, but I'm getting used to it. I can do this, Lynher. I want to be part of this. It's important."

It was harder for him. I'd grown up with Gerome at Night, surrounded by Dark Ones. Having the truth of Night thrust upon him after a lifetime of day couldn't have been easy. "C'mon." I stood and waved him on. "Kensey makes the best pancakes."

He smiled, and I realized he likely already knew that.

10

NIGHT

The day with Etienne and Kensey went by too quickly. We ate and rested, and Etienne told Kensey all his near screw-ups to my brother's amusement. Only Kensey could laugh about the dangers I faced every night. Then Kensey told Etienne all *my* mistakes, and I'd made plenty while under Gerome's watchful eye. Etienne was too kind to laugh outright, but he chuckled all the same, and maybe I did too.

It hadn't escaped my notice how Kensey leaned into Etienne when they spoke. Their hands occasionally brushed, and Etienne's smile warmed the more time they spent together. Would I ever find a love like theirs? It was good, seeing hope and kindness, the important things Kensey and I fought for. On bad nights, it was too easy to forget the good.

Near dusk, I left them to wander the hallways, breathing in the smell of old wood and warm drapes. The station was quiet and comforting in the day, and at dusk, it settled on its old foundations. Running my hands along the paneled walls, I listened to the building sigh. If the walls could talk, what would they say? Most days and nights, the station helped us, but sometimes, like when Lilith had killed the imposter, its help left much to be desired.

I'd tried to find the station's heart once. I'd listened through Gerome's office door and heard him speak of it. Insatiably curious, I'd set out to look for this elusive heart. Gerome had later found me in the cellar, digging my fingers into cracks in the walls, looking for secret doors. He'd taken me by the arms, looked me in the eye, and warned me never to go looking for it again. It was the only time I'd feared him.

"Will you help me?" I asked the empty hallway.

Nothing replied.

In my room, I found my tattered dress replaced by a black and red ensemble, complete with black suede pants and lace bodice. I picked up the crushed velvet tailcoat and stroked its fabric. It was gorgeous but heavy, and it was *black and red.* Vampire colors.

"Really?" Arguing was pointless. If I opened my closet, I'd find similar garments inside, all the same color.

The outfit was a peace offering, a sign of respect, and a good idea. I begrudgingly layered myself up, checked the coat's many hidden pockets, and breathed a sigh of relief when I found my key. Part of me had feared Jack might have discovered it while manhandling me to his room.

"You look just like them." Kensey snorted. He and Etienne waited by the night door at the end of a hallway. Beyond the windows, a sunset set fire to the barrens and a tickle of ice traced down my spine. Tonight was a night for saving lives.

The key weighed heavily in my hand. In a few hours, the train would arrive. The little kids in those carriages didn't stand a chance without Kensey and me. I caught my brother's eye and saw the same intense knowing. "I'll meet you at the top of these stairs at zero five hundred hours," I told him.

"Zero five hundred." He gave me a small nod and his classic smile. "I'll be watching the clock." When he wrapped his arm around me, pulling me close, I sighed and returned the affection. His lips brushed my forehead. "Gerome would be proud of us."

He really would have been.

I eased from Kensey's arms, needing the distance from everything I loved now Night was almost upon us. Kensey took Etienne's hand, no longer bothering to hide the touch, and wrapped his arm around him. He said something too quiet and personal for me to hear, and when they parted, Etienne's face was flushed.

Etienne and I ascended the narrow spiral staircase toward night, the weight of my role pushing down with every step. I'd once told Gerome I couldn't do what he did. That I wasn't strong enough to host all this. It was too much, too big. He'd told me a secret, that he'd been afraid too. The station had helped him get through each day, until the days had turned into weeks, months, and then years. Then Kensey and I had arrived, and he'd no longer been alone. That had been the worst of it, he'd told us: the loneliness.

I glanced at the mark on my wrist. I was protected. I was doing good. I was here for a reason, and I had a job to do. This was right.

At the reception desk, Etienne approached first, smoothly stepping back into his role as assistant and guide. Even his body language changed, I realized, marginally impressed. I'd make an excellent staff member of him yet.

A pair of VG watched us arrive. They studied my clothes, and from their lack of reaction, I assumed my wearing their colors was satisfactory. They let me pass, and a quick glance at the desk revealed the guest book was back in its place. Etienne went straight to it. I left him to check it over and set about my early evening rounds. All I had to do was avoid Jack and find the ambassador without alerting the VG.

A few keen-eyed Dark Ones observed my passing. Their whispers circled like a draft. After securing the cargo, I'd have to repair my damaged reputation.

Lilith's room was empty. The place had been turned over, likely by the VG. Lilith wouldn't return to the room she was listed under in the guest book, but she would be somewhere in the station. The station was vast, and even larger when it wanted to be. I didn't have hours to search every corner. I had to force her out in the open… or find someone else who could.

My library office greeted me with its usual warmth, wrapping me in familiarity.

I collected a bundle of candles from my desk drawer, kicked back a rug and placed them on the rune markings scorched in a circle in the wooden floorboards.

Rafe had taught me how to summon demons. Summoning was a crude method of communication, like hooking a fish and yanking it from its pool, that resulted in one very pissed off demon. I'd performed it once, and only then because Rafe had told me I was performing a ritual to the gods that would double the protection over my guests. He'd lied. The thing I'd summoned—a monstrous creature full of rage, like a boulder with claws and fangs and eyes like burning coals—had been a guardian for something bigger that Lilith had wanted distracted. As soon as I'd realized they'd lied to me, I'd sent the guardian away by reversing the summoning. I'd refused to speak to Rafe for six months after that, and I never did learn why Lilith had wanted it out of her way.

That misadventure had burned runes into the library floor. I'd tried to scrub them out, but magical markings always scarred.

And now I was using them again.

After placing a bowl in the center of the markings, I lit each candle, scribbled a name on a piece of paper, used a candle's flame to light the paper, dropped it into the bowl, and stepped out of the circle, muttering the words Rafe had taught me.

"Nocte noctem aperuit suscipe tenebris," I whispered, hearing Gerome telling me not to dabble in their magic. It wasn't meant for me, and I knew that, but just this one time…

My fingers twitched at my sides. I wouldn't have been doing this if there were any other way, but I'd run out of time and options.

What if he didn't appear?

The runes fizzled, burning from within. Embers simmered at their edges, and with a crackle of sparks and an ear-popping flash, a demon burst into being in front of me.

Raphael.

My treacherous heart leaped to know he was alive but quickly stuttered.

He knelt on one knee, his head down, hair covering his face so that only his horns showed. He wore the same waistcoat and pants I'd left him in, but they were now clean. The last time I'd seen him, I'd tried to haul him onto the platform, scratching us both up. His big wings had flopped about. The bent one was fixed now. Their arches rose above him, twitching as sparks dusted from their trailing edges. Gods, had he always looked so… impressive?

He lifted his head. He didn't smile, like he always had before. Whether I'd had a knife at his throat or he'd had his tail up my skirts, he'd always smiled. And his eyes… they'd been a dazzling blue and green, but now two glossy black orbs looked through me, seeking something. He blinked, and their color slowly returned.

He was Rafe but also wasn't. Little things were wrong. He'd always been animated, always moving, gliding from one suggestive glance to another, but now his stillness made him cold.

He straightened and tipped his head, eyeing me as though I were no more interesting than a speck of dust. "What do you want?"

He didn't even sound like himself. Gone was the playful purr and rumbling tease.

I wanted to ask if he was all right, if he was hurt. I wanted to tell him he was a fool, that this was all his fault, that he should never have taken me outside the white line because this was what happened out there… always. I wanted to thank him for saving me. I wanted to see his smile again. But the flat look in his eyes said none of that mattered.

Swallowing, I remembered my cause. I had a job to do, and whatever I did or didn't feel for Rafe didn't matter. "Where is Lilith?"

His brows pinched. "Why would I tell you?"

"She and I have unresolved business."

His eyes narrowed some more, and without his smile, the look was edged and angry. "Then summon *her*."

"I can't… This circle was all you taught me. Remember? You told me it wasn't strong…"

He looked down as though just now realizing where he was, and smiled, but the smile was a wicked slash, shallow and sharp. A predator's smile. His gaze rode me from head to toe. My human instincts squirmed, trying to get away. Tutting, he turned and admired my library, circling his summoning prison. He couldn't escape the circle because his name had been on that piece of paper. Until the candles burned down or I dismissed him, he'd be *between*, neither in this realm nor in the demon one.

He drew closer, stopping right next to the invisible line inches from me. Nerves fluttered low in my belly. He seemed taller and bigger than I remembered, or maybe I was smaller now.

His top lip rippled in a silent snarl. "Such an odd little thing you are, trapped inside these walls. A dark butterfly captured in a glass jar. I remember feeling"—he closed his hand into a fist and placed it over his heart—"*something* for you. But don't worry yourself, that's all gone now. I'm struggling to remember why I cared at all. Really, I should have let you die all those years ago, let you toddle off"—he walked his fingers in the air—"into the barrens and get yourself eaten by some hungry thing. Why, I could have eaten you myself. I hear human babes taste like chicken."

My heart raced, each word cutting like the flick of a blade. I hadn't known he'd *cared,* and that made the loss of his soul harder to bear. I hadn't ever considered demons could care. I'd barely considered him at all in the years I'd known him. He'd been Rafe, another fixture of the station. But to hear him admit he'd cared in one breath and then to hear him tear it all away in the next?

"This isn't you," I said too quietly.

"Isn't it? Do you think you know me?"

"I do know you."

"Are you so naïve?" He stood so close the circle's barrier visibly shimmered between us. "Did you think me your... *friend*?"

"You'd come to me when you were sad. You never said why, but I could tell, so I let you stay, sprawled in that chair by the fireplace, even though Gerome would probably have bargained with an inferni to get rid of you, had he ever found out."

"I came to you out of boredom."

"Fine. The time we read the wizard books together and you laughed at all the wrong details. You wanted to read with me. You got so persistent I had to tell Gerome I was sick so you could finish the series."

"That was not friendship, dear Lynher. It was grooming." His smile curved like a blade.

No, he did not get to ruin those times for me, or his former soul-carrying self. His words hurt in ways they shouldn't, but I couldn't let him see how he wounded me. I shut it down and hid it behind my mask like always. "Rafe, I just… I can fix this—fix you. I just… I need to get through tonight. All right?"

His smile lingered. "There is nothing wrong with me." He lifted a hand and tested the barrier. It rippled and sparked.

"Lilith—I need to speak with Lilith. Find her. Tell her I—"

"No, I don't think I will."

"It's important."

"I can see it is to you." He walked the circle again, tail licking the air. "But what's in it for me?"

"I…" He'd always helped before, as if he'd enjoyed being involved whenever Lilith had called him, but this new, soulless Rafe was so very different. I had nothing to offer, besides… a favor. Favors for favors was how the rest of the Dark Ones did things. They always wanted something, and an incubus's needs were no mystery. "A trade."

"A trade?" His eyebrow arched. He'd circled all the way around and returned to face me. "What kind of trade?" The answer was already in his sly eyes; he just wanted me to say it.

The one thing I'd come close to giving him while weak. The same thing my brother thought I already had. "A kiss."

It sounded simple, but a kiss in his expert hands was a weapon. "From you?"

"Who else?" I snapped, tasting nerves on my tongue. "It's a fair trade for Lilith's whereabouts."

His lips parted, and his gaze wandered, scorching where it skimmed over my body, seeing through the clothes I'd buckled up so tightly. Finally, a spark brightened his soulless eyes. "I want more than a kiss. You owe me that. I lost my soul for you."

"That wasn't my fault. You should never have taken me outside. A kiss is all you get. Nothing more. Or I will find Lilith myself. It will take longer, but I know she's here somewhere…"

"Hm... a kiss..." He tasted the promise, running the tip of his tongue across his bottom lip. "From the darkly sweet Miss Lynher Aris." He snapped his teeth together and hissed in, expanding his chest, breathing me in. His wings pulsed outward an inch and closed again. He wanted more. He always had. It was a part of who and what he was. A kiss after all these years would be a victory in his mind. But in mine, it was just a kiss and a small price to pay to find Lilith for the sake of a cargo of children.

"Very well," he agreed. "But the kiss happens at a time and place of my choosing."

"Fine. Where's Lilith?"

Lilith's room looked the same as when I'd visited at dusk. Upturned furniture, tossed sheets, open dresser drawers, contents strewn across the floor. The VG hadn't left a single item untouched. This time, however, I had an advantage standing beside me.

Rafe wandered ahead, wings clasped behind him and tail lashing, and stopped in the middle of the room to scan the scene, hip cocked. "And vampires think they're the superior race. They never look beyond what their eyes tell them."

Technically, vampires came from the same genetic line as demons—they'd even had wings once. According to legend, the queen had chewed hers off in defiance of their god, and her soldiers had copied her like the good little puppets they were. Vampires needed blood to survive and demons fed on emotion, but the same creation god, Alohim, had birthed the two races, and at their core, they shared similar needs and vices.

Rafe headed to the dresser and righted its large oval mirror. A jagged crack had split the glass in two. He waved his hand over it, wiping the crack away and making the mirror whole again. Then he spread his fingers on the glass, and an almost invisible ripple washed over him, stirring his hair and wings, and then passed over me, righting the room around us and spilling green velvet drapes among lush jungle plants. The switch in surroundings unbalanced me. I reached for a tree that hadn't been there moments before.

Rafe saw me stagger and smiled, his teeth sharp.

"Ah, Lynher Aris," Lilith said. "Raphael and I wondered where you'd gotten to, darling."

I turned to find the source of her voice but found only shiny, rustling plants. The room looked and felt like the outside, only hotter, but we were still in the station. I was still protected, I reminded myself.

"You were already looking for me?" I asked, searching for her outline among the foliage.

"I sent Raphael to find you. We still have the arrival of the train to discuss, do we not?" Her voice bounced back, originating from multiple places.

Then I hadn't needed to bargain with Rafe to find her. Rafe circled me, flashing a knowing grin. I'd bargained away a kiss for no reason. I glowered back. This new Rafe was an asshole.

Lilith melted from the green undergrowth, her demon skin sloughing off its almost invisible camouflage. She stood just a few feet in front of me and looked down from her impressive height, her demon mind working behind sharp eyes.

"Ghost's death has caused some problems," I said.

"Hm." Her lips twisted. "He wasn't Ghost, just another puppet." She lifted her chin. "But you already knew that, didn't you, Lynher dear?"

"I planned to explain but didn't have time before you ate his heart. How did you get past the station's defenses?"

She wasn't impressed, and like Rafe's hungry glare, hers roamed over me, sizing me up as a possible meal. "Do you know where the real Ghost is?" she asked.

I breathed in, tasting dampness and heat. Rafe had taken up residence against a palm tree, pretending to examine his nails while he listened and watched. His tail lay limp on the ground, motionless but for the occasional flick at its point. Between him and Lilith was a dangerous place to be.

"I do."

Lilith noted my wandering gaze and gestured dismissively at Rafe. "Leave us, *habibi*."

Rafe didn't move, he stared at Lilith, his wings and tail still.

"Raphael." Lilith faced him. "This does not concern you. *Engila.*"

His tail lashed, he curtly bowed his head, and then he vanished, leaving Lilith staring at the dissipating sparks. "I thought he'd be easier to control without his soul, but…" She smiled and curled her fingers into her palm. "… he was always a challenge. Let us focus on our mutual problem—Overseer Ghost and those defenses."

"Wait…" She'd wanted to remove Rafe's soul *before* the accident? Everything he did he did for Lilith. He lived and breathed for her. If she'd told him to take me outside the station, he would have done it. She'd known the reception waiting for me beyond the white line. It was a death sentence for any human. Had she tried to kill me? "Did you order Rafe to take me outside the station?"

"It was the safest place for you. The vampires, in their frenzy, might have hurt you, my darling Lynher, and where would we be without our wonderful hostess?"

Where, indeed, because I didn't have a successor. "You do remember I'm human?"

"Oh, I forget sometimes." She laughed her high, tinkling laughter, sounding patronizing and dismissive all at once. "There was no harm done. You're here, aren't you? And with barely a scratch on you."

No harm done *to me*, but Rafe was forever changed. Either she'd planned that, or she'd planned for me not to return. She smiled and blinked, perfectly innocent of any wrongdoing, but she'd also gorged herself on a vampire general's heart less than a day ago. She'd gladly consume mine too if it suited her.

"Tell me all about the real Ghost," she said, her smile hiding the order.

I didn't have to follow anyone's orders, save those of the station, and certainly not those of a demon whose motives were questionable. "You've had your vengeance. You killed the vampire who killed your succubus—"

"Her name was Sonel."

A name. Jack had asked me about the succubus's name, and I still didn't know why. There were too many loose threads, too many missing teeth in these great cogs. Control was slipping through my fingers. If I offered Lilith more power, she'd twist it and make my needs work for her. Kensey had warned me. I shouldn't ask her to help again. I shouldn't even be in her room. I had to figure this out myself. "Ghost leaves tonight, and most of the VG will go with him. The matter is resolved."

"Perhaps, but I rather enjoyed dancing with the vampire general, and now I wonder if I might enjoy dancing with the real Ghost before he leaves. You can help with that."

And tear his heart out of his chest.

She could kill Jack.

His death would be a huge blow to the VG, but the risk was too great. If her actions came back on me or the station… But was the death of a vampire of his standing worth the risk? "If I tell you where he will be… you can't kill him. You can't, Lilith. The vampireguard will not stand for it. This station is too important. Just… distract him."

"Distract him… hm? What naughty thing are you planning? Oh, don't worry, I won't stop you. But I could kill the overseer, just a little bit…" She touched a leathery leaf and drew it between her fingers, collecting the moisture. Then she lifted the glistening drops to her soft, black lips. "It's been so long since anything has dared challenge me. I just… I must see this creature. I must… taste him."

"Fine, but taste him somewhere private. Somewhere away from the station. I'll send him to you, but it can't come back on me." I could maneuver Jack. He wanted something from me, and if all I had to do was point him in the right direction and push, I could do that, and see him away from the high-value cargo.

"That seems… reasonable."

"Are we settled?"

"Agreed."

Good. I turned and headed toward where I assumed the door was behind all this undergrowth. Sweat had soaked down my back and glued my hair to my face. I needed fresh air and space and a moment to catch my breath. This night would be a long one, and it had only just begun.

"Oh, and Miss Aris… About those defenses, did Gerome never mention a loophole?"

My steps slowed, and I paused to glance behind me but saw only leaves and vines. "He did not."

"It's all about intent, dear," her voice sailed out from behind the sweating vegetation. "If the intent is not *lethal*, then the station might… look the other way. Else nobody would have any fun inside these walls."

"But you ate his heart. How is that not lethal?"

"Practice…" she replied, like that settled things, and then added, "regarding my Raphael and his affliction. There are books in your library, books about phantoms…"

"There are…"

"I suggest you check them for a solution. If you desire to help him, that is." Her words hissed into silence, leaving me alone.

She'd possibly ordered Rafe to kill me and now she was helping me restore him? She hadn't planned on him losing his soul; it was me she'd planned on losing. I'd restore Rafe all right, but not for her. I'd do it because I owed Rafe.

I pulled the relevant books from my library shelves and piled them high on my desk, frowning at each one. I knew every book. I'd lived with them, grown up around them. I'd learned to read among their pages. They were personal… and it bothered me that Lilith knew of their existence.

Like Gerome had told me, chasing down answers to impossible questions would drive me insane. Instead of asking why, I skimmed a few pages of the largest tome, looking for references to the taking of souls and any recourses. The more I read, the more I knew I had to restore Rafe to the way he'd been before, even if he didn't want it. He didn't know what he wanted. Without a soul, he didn't know how to care. I had to put that right.

The library door swung open, and in walked Jack. His cane clipped the wooden boards, emphasizing the stiffness in his right leg. He wore a dashing combination of high-waisted black pants, a black velvet patterned vest, black boots, and a black tailcoat. The red thread stitching it all together, proclaimed him as a vampire.

A twinge of disappointment tightened my chest. Somewhere, deep down, I'd hoped he wasn't a blood-sucking leech. As he approached, I recalled the images I'd seen in books about the war. The pyres of burning bodies. The earth painted with human blood. Mounds of discarded jewelry—all that was left of humans. This man was the worst kind of monster.

He stopped at my desk and regarded the chair as though considering sitting, but he must have thought better of it, because he skimmed the books I had open in front of me instead, then finally he looked up, meeting my gaze. I'd already guarded my heart and mastered my mask. He saw only Lynher Aris, hostess extraordinaire.

I hadn't locked the door, so he could technically wander in, but that didn't make it right. His kind believed they could go anywhere, through any door, take anything, steal and kill and feast on the innocent. And he had the balls to stand in my station, in this sanctuary, and look down on me.

He swallowed, throat bobbing. "You were never supposed to discover the truth." He sounded apologetic. Gods, he was good at this act. "It would have been safer that way."

"Safer for who?"

He didn't seem to like my question, because he just stared, trying to make me feel small. At least his charm hadn't kicked in—yet.

"Lynher—"

"Miss Aris."

"There is much you don't understand." Again, he sounded apologetic. It was how he tricked people and lured them into his web. Poor Jack. Just passing through Jack. Nothing to see here Jack. "I would explain, but I don't have much time, and I don't think you'd—

"Let me ask you something, *Jack*," I plowed on, my tone making him straighten, "Are you Ghost?"

His cheek flickered. "Yes."

"And everything that's said about Ghost, is it true?"

"I can't know everything—"

"You know what I'm asking, *Just Jack*, so don't play the fool. It no longer works on me."

His dark eyes narrowed. The look should have been sharp, but his smile softened it. "In all this time, nobody has revealed the real me, but you did in less than forty-eight hours. Some say you know magecraft, Miss Aris. I'm beginning to ag—"

"Answer the question, please."

"Yes. Ghost is everything you've heard… and more." He held my gaze, unblinking. A silver shimmer in his eyes gave away his vampire nature. It had been there all along, but he'd kept it hidden. He didn't bother to hide it now. His stillness was vampire too. His breathing and pulse had thrown me, but he used the human act as camouflage, and it had served him well, until now. Now he had nowhere to hide. Lilith had killed his puppet. He was exposed. Did that bother him? Did he feel vulnerable? I hoped so, because he was in my station, among my people, and I would not allow him to hurt anyone under my protection.

"The situation is delicate." He grasped his cane, placing his hands atop its engraved handle. The act shored him up, straightening his shoulders and lifting his chin.

"For you, perhaps." I closed the book I'd been reading and stood. "Your general, the vampire standing in for you, he mentioned there would be a train stopping to refuel at five hundred hours, just before dawn. He's no longer with us, but I'm assuming the train is still arriving?"

"It is." The pulse in his neck fluttered, so perfect was his act. "Felipe was—"

"And will you be leaving on it, sir?" I didn't care what Felipe was, just that he was dead and there was one less vampire in the world.

"I will be, yes."

"Well then, please do enjoy the station's hospitality in your final hours." My tone was kind, but he saw the ice in my eyes. He didn't move.

"Lynher—"

"Miss Aris." I wanted to yell at him to leave, to get out of my sanctuary, to go far, far away so I wouldn't have to see his charming face again or listen to his soft words, knowing the creature he truly was. Instead, I smiled and waited for his pretend awkwardness to sharpen into intent.

Breathing in, he broke the stare, finding a spot over my shoulder to focus on, then turned away. Even then, some stupid human part of me wanted to call him back, as though I'd done him some disservice by turning him away too soon. Gods, I'd never met a creature so adept at hiding its nature.

"Sir?"

"Yes." He turned, obscenely hopeful, like I might call him back.

"Why did you ask if your general had gotten the demon's name before he killed her?"

"Because he didn't care enough to know it… and now I suppose he never will." He limped out the door, leaving his cryptic words hanging in the silence, as though I could pick them apart and fathom their meaning. The sooner five a.m. came around, the better. I was ready to be forever done with *Just Jack.*

11

NIGHT

The clock over the Grand Hall struck midnight. The train of guests came and went. I went through the motions, doing all the things expected of me with one eye on the clock's moving hands. At 04:50, I snuck away from the fray and onto the platform. Dawn approached. It made the air tight and the sky warmer.

The sun would rise around 5:40 a.m., signaling day. The high-value cargo was due at 5:00 a.m. I had to secure the cargo and get to Kensey, unseen, before the sun rose behind the surrounding abandoned buildings.

I watched the sky from the platform, breathing in and tasting the same dust that always spiced the shifting air. The tracks snaked into the dark, beyond the reach of the station's lamps. Somewhere down those tracks, children clung to each other, rocking with the carriages as the train's wheels screamed. Taken from their homes or picked wild from the streets, they'd be afraid, in shock, cold, and tired. My face would likely be the first they'd seen since being shut in the carriages like cattle. Gods, it was cruel, but that was vampires. Perhaps the resistance might one day stop it, but I doubted it. Dreaming such fancies was where Kensey excelled.

"Ma'am…" Etienne approached, bringing with him a breath of warmth and station-scented air, like cinnamon and citrus. He'd let his hair flop loose instead of slicking it back. It suited him better, although now he constantly had to sweep it back.

He looked down the long platform. "Is there anything I can do?"

"No, Etienne. Just your job. Keep everything running smoothly while I… until dawn."

"Yes, ma'am. I… I wanted to thank you… for everything."

I nodded and glanced over his head and through the glass doors at the huge clock on the distant wall. The large hand clunked closer to twelve. "All right…" Quickly, I unbuttoned my coat and started the long walk toward the end of the platform. "Good night, Etienne."

"Good night, Miss Aris." His voice followed me until the wind stole it away. My heeled boots clopped on the platform. The white line ran by my side. Beyond it, darkness loomed, so thick it was as though the entire world was dark.

A metallic *ting* rang in the tracks, signaling the weight of the train rumbling over them. My heart thumped harder. I pulled my coat off and turned its arms inside out, revealing the bright red silk lining.

Faster. It was almost time. The tracks groaned, and far ahead, a beam of light pierced the night. It started small and quiet, like all important things, but grew bigger with every breath, every footfall, every heartbeat. The wind gathered, whipping dust around me and lashing my hair free of its pins and curls. It was no ordinary wind, like this was no ordinary train. There was magic in it that made the blood pump quicker and set my teeth on edge. My wrist warmed, the station's mark reacting either to the presence bearing down on us or the fear and anticipation spilling into my veins.

Ahead, the platform sloped off into the night. I stopped and lifted my coat, stretching its splash of red between my hands like a flag. The train's single beam flew over me and flooded the world in white. *Brake*. The train was huge and hungry, like a primordial creature made of iron. *Brake now*. Wheels squealed, metal on metal. The train wailed its horrible sound, but it was slowing.

The train heaved to a halt, huge and black, all iron and engineering, with wheels twice my size. Steam blasted over me and through my clothes. I did not greet this beast like I did the guests' train. Two black carriages clunked to a halt behind the engine. No windows. Windows weren't needed for cattle.

"Lynher!"

Jack's shout bounced around the train's boiling groans and ticking metal, but the steam had swallowed me. He couldn't see me inside the boiling white clouds, not even with his vampire eyes.

I grasped the carriage door's cold iron handle, planted a boot on the carriage step, and heaved the huge rolling door aside, holding my breath, waiting to see their faces and tell them they were safe, that we just had to do one more thing but they needed to *hurry*.

The steam cleared.

I blinked at the sight inside the carriage.

"No..."

My heart fell.

The carriage was... empty.

No, no, no... this couldn't be.

I leaned in and scanned the dark corners. Nothing. Not even a scrap of clothing. The carriage was pristine. That was... impossible.

I dropped from the step, raced to the second carriage, and threw open its door, finding it as empty as its twin.

The clouds of steam fell away. Time had slipped through my fingers. I should have ushered them through the secret door. They should have been on their way to Kensey, who would have greeted them with a smile. They should have been safe.

"Lynher!" Jack strode through the fading steam and slowed as I swung a vicious glare on him.

"This is you!" I snapped, raising my voice over the engine's hissing and huffing. "It's your doing!"

He slowed, his limp making his stupid steps wooden. He grabbed the carriage handle and peered inside. "I don't understand. Where are—"

"—*the children*!"

"Where are they?" He set his cane down against the carriage side, grabbed both handles, and climbed inside.

I couldn't breathe. This wasn't right. Why have empty carriages stop here? The children had to be here somewhere. They had to be. I entered behind Jack and watched him limp into the darkness where the lantern light didn't reach.

"This isn't right," he said.

"Where are they!" I plucked my knives from their hidden places. "Where are the children? What have you done with them?"

He scowled back at me, only marginally surprised to see the knives in my hands. I knew how I looked, how I sounded. Certainly nothing like the Lynher Aris I'd shown him. "Oh, we both have double lives, *Ghost*. Did you think I was just a pretty human put here for your *enjoyment*?"

"Lynher… wait…" He stepped closer, hand outstretched.

"Stay back, and stop calling me Lynher. You don't know me."

The sliding door rattled on its running wheels. I glimpsed a figure, heard Jack shout, then the door slammed shut, plunging Jack and me into darkness.

No, no, no…

I rammed a shoulder against the wooden door, got my knives in the gap, and twisted, trying to lever the panels open. The door didn't budge.

Jack's icy presence prickled my skin. It was too dark to see him, but he was close.

"Lynher, step aside… let me." His hand landed on my shoulder.

"Don't touch me!" I slashed blindly, missing.

The carriage jerked, pulling on its couplings, and shunted back again, rocking my balance. The figure outside, the one who had locked us in. I knew him, but he couldn't have done this. "Etienne, open the door!"

Metal wheels slipped on the tracks, screaming until they hooked up and pulled forward, jerking the carriages again. This time, they kept on shunting and grinding. The train huffed and grumbled and growled, moving off.

"*Etienne*!"

I couldn't find any handle or seal. There was nothing to grab a hold of—no lock, no hinge.

Metal wheels galloped along the tracks in a rhythmic *clatter-clatter* that sounded like a huge metal heartbeat, and I knew from the ice in my veins that I'd left the station grounds.

Oh gods.

I couldn't be away from the station, away from Kensey. This couldn't be happening.

I pressed my hands against the carriage side, feeling gouges and missing pieces beneath my soft fingertips. I wasn't supposed to be here. This wasn't meant for me. The children… where were the children?

And then the truth fell like an axe.

I was the high-value cargo.

12

DAY

Light poured through all the tiny holes in the carriage sides, thrusting through the air like spears. The light moved and shifted, and when the shafts stroked across Jack's clothes, he fidgeted, trying to move away. Sunlight made vampires uncomfortable. Too much would slowly kill him. He deserved it.

After pacing like an animal stuck in a cage, I'd tucked myself in the corner farthest from the overseer, keeping my knives close at hand. If he closed his eyes, if he slept, I considered it my duty to drive the blades into vulnerable parts of him. I'd imagined little else over the last few hours. Where best to strike on his body? Would cutting his throat work? I'd have to be quick or he'd overpower me. Then it occurred to me that wherever we were going, if we arrived and Ghost was dead at my feet, my reception would be worse—if it could get any worse. So I watched him stare at the carriage wall instead, flinching away from the light.

The carriage rocked and rumbled, not slowing. We had to be miles from the station. Kensey would be worried. And Etienne…

Etienne had done this. How or why? It made no sense.

Jack dropped his head back, eyes closing. "You need a better assistant." He still had a lofty, untouchable tone, as if being trapped in a carriage were a mild inconvenience. Considering how old he had to be, maybe it was. Maybe this was dull to him?

"Don't you usually sleep in the day?" I rolled one of the knives in my hand, watching the light play on the smooth blade.

"Usually."

"Then why aren't you?"

He looked over. "Because you're caressing those knives like you have a plan for them."

Was the formidable Ghost afraid of me? I smiled, but he merely sighed. His forehead was creased enough to convey his annoyance, but he certainly wasn't afraid.

I looked at the knife in my left hand, testing its weight. I could throw it. It might even hit him in the heart. "Would it kill you?" I asked.

"What do you think?"

It wouldn't. He wouldn't have survived this long if a little throwing knife could take him down.

I looked away, preferring to admire the pinprick holes letting the light in. Maybe Etienne shutting me in here had been a mistake. Maybe he'd meant to shut Jack inside. But Etienne had known I was here. He'd done this on purpose.

And now Etienne was at the station, pretending everything was fine, knowing what he'd done. Someone must have gotten to him. One of the Dark Ones. Was it Lilith? But if he'd been coerced, why not tell me?

He'd fooled me, that was why, like Ghost had fooled me.

I should have seen it in Etienne. He'd been so… nice. And Kensey had vouched for him, loved him even.

I really wasn't a very good host. If Gerome were here, he'd tell me what to do, but he was dead, and soon, I probably would be too.

Climbing to my feet, I examined the door, its seals now visible. It didn't look like it should hold together so well. There was no lock, no keyhole, and no handle. I'd tried digging my blades in and levering the door open, but it hadn't budged an inch. The internal scratches were more visible in the light too, like this carriage had once held animals and they'd clawed at the walls to escape. I tried not to think too hard on what that meant.

"Where is the train taking us?" I asked, glancing behind me to see Jack still tucked in his corner, watching me.

The ordeal had dislodged a few bangs over his hazel eyes. In the dappled daylight, he could still pass as human, perhaps more so now that he wore a weary look in the lines around his mouth and eyes.

"One of two places. Camp Altoona is the closest, but we're likely heading to Maryland."

"Shouldn't you know where it's going? Weren't you supposed to be on this train?"

He spread his hands. "Things have changed."

He'd been as surprised as me to find the carriages empty. "You were expecting children in the carriages?"

"I was." No hesitation. No sign of guilt. *Soulless drone.*

Unable to look at him anymore, I returned to examining the door for a weakness. "Wherever the kids are, I hope they're safe from the likes of you."

His laughter crawled over me. "You don't see it. Trapped in the station your entire life, things must have been very simple for you."

"I'm not *trapped*. The station is my home."

"You don't think it controls you?"

"What?" When I looked at him again, the bastard smiled. "You don't know me, and you don't know how my life works."

"Have you ever left its grounds? Set foot beyond the white line?"

"Yes." I planted a hand on my hip.

He hesitated a beat. "For more than a few minutes?"

"Yes." Maybe. When I was small. I didn't remember, but I must have. There had been times when Kensey had found me, and the time Rafe had found me. I had been beyond the white line enough to know I never wanted to go beyond it again.

Yet here I was, miles from it, trapped in a box with a real monster, my only weapons two throwing knives. My clothing didn't have secret pockets out here, and I'd left my coat on the platform. If Jack decided he wanted me gone, I had little to defend myself with.

So why hadn't he attacked me? He surely knew I wasn't the Lynher Aris he'd been expecting. I'd said too much on the platform and revealed too much while dosed up on Caine's venom. If he was so inclined, he could put all my puzzle pieces together. He'd have to be a fool not to know I worked for the resistance in a roundabout way. The vampires' missing cargo after their trains had passed through the station. A brother who didn't exist. The death of his puppet, albeit by Lilith's hand.

Jack knew too much.

I couldn't let him return to his kind.

Somehow, I had to kill him. To protect the station and Kensey.

Gods, Kensey had fallen for Etienne.

I had to get back.

Kensey had to know before Etienne hurt him.

I pressed my free hand flat against the carriage door and bumped my forehead against the wood. Outside the station, I really was just human, just food and sport to the Dark Ones. I wasn't *killing* anyone. My illusion of strength had fallen the second the train had left the station. I was prey now.

Jack continued to watch, his eyebrow raised in silent question. Hate churned my empty stomach. Maybe hate was all I needed. I hoped so, because I had nothing else.

Stabbing the knife into the door seal, I wiggled it some more. Just a crack. If I could make some progress and get both blades in, I might be able to pop the door open—

"The carriages are spelled. They only open at designated locations."

The hate churned some more. Why hadn't he told me that before? "So, you've watched me try for hours to what… entertain you?"

"Isn't that your job?" His mouth twitched.

I'd never wanted to throw my knives more. He appeared relaxed, tucked in his corner, but like Caine, he could spring from that spot and tear open my throat in a blink, and there was no station magic here to save me at the last second. I'd bleed out across these boards, drunk on venom, and he'd laugh while I died.

I returned to my corner and paced that end of the carriage, listening to my boots strike the boards. "What happens when we reach our destination?"

His gaze tracked me. "You're too old for the farms—"

I flung a knife. It was in my hand and flying free without a second's thought behind it. I just needed him to bleed, to hurt. But the carriage rocked, and the knife twanged off the side—and he was gone.

My back slammed into the carriage panel. My head smacked against the side too. His iron-cold arm lodged under my chin, pinning me. Jack was all I could see. His handsome face had hollowed. The shadows had sucked all warmth out of him. His eyes pulled me in, my head spinning from their charm, but it was the vicious fangs that snagged my glare. Two primacy fangs curved to latch on and not let go. Next to those, two smaller teeth, just as sharp—those delivered the venom. One bite and I'd be his, and there was nothing I could do to stop him.

"Attack me," he breathed, his mouth close to mine, our breaths shared, "and I will return the favor, *Miss Aris.*"

Most vampires were beyond speech by this point. Feral and blood-driven, as soon as they dropped their civilized act, they turned into mindless beasts driven by desire. But this bastard had full control. It showed in his eyes, still startlingly *normal.*

I spat in his face.

He blinked, and his features performed a strange combination of a frown and grimace. He eased back, studiously plucked a handkerchief from inside his jacket, wiped the spittle from his cheek, then tucked the handkerchief away, every move precise. Then he limped back toward his corner. I swallowed, wedged against the side, trembling with fear and rage and the knowledge that I was somehow alive. This wasn't how vampires behaved. What was *wrong* with him? A game? Maybe I *was* his entertainment, something to pass the time before we arrived at my final destination.

"You sicken me." I spoke with venom of my own, letting him hear the rage and injustice. When he simply slid back down the carriage side and wedged himself into the corner again, the rage grew hotter. "Your kind is a scourge on this world. You had no right to it. You came and you took and you killed and now look at it. You destroyed it."

He drew his good leg up and balanced his wrist on his knee. "Get it all out. Say what you've always wanted to say, because after we arrive, you'll have no tongue to speak."

I was going to die, but it wouldn't be in vain. I'd tell him what nobody dared. "The vampires' reign cannot last." I pulled on my sleeves, straightening my clothes, and braved a few steps closer.

"It has held well enough for the last five decades."

"You feed and you consume and you'll do that until there's nothing left! The Dark Ones won't stand for it. Someone will rise up against your queen."

"And that will be better how? The fae, do you think they'd be kinder? Or the chaos-loving jinn perhaps? They'd likely set the whole world ablaze. Maybe you'd prefer a demon overlord. You seemed quite attached to that incubus—"

"Anything is better than *you*."

He chuckled. "For someone who has seen nothing of the world, your worldly knowledge is astounding."

"And I suppose you know everything?"

He picked at fluff or dust on his sleeve. "Far from it. I don't know what will happen to me when this train stops, for example."

He didn't? "Why not?"

He smiled. Apparently, that smile was all the answer I was getting.

Folding my arms, I slid down the carriage side and propped myself against the corner. I couldn't die here, with *him*. I wasn't finished. I had too much to do, too much to fix. My staff weren't ready for my absence. They didn't know what to do. Would they leave? Without them, the station couldn't host any guests. Nobody would stop there. It would fall apart. And Kensey... Oh, Kensey. He'd be okay. He'd have to be. Would he stay? Would he become the host? He wouldn't survive the Dark Ones. He'd say something that would get him killed. No, he had connections *outside*. He'd leave too.

"Why were you reading about phantoms?" Jack asked.

We'd been silent for some time, the rhythmic beat of the train's wheels lulling my mind far from the hell I was trapped in. But his question rudely yanked me back into the present. "I don't have to speak to you."

"True." He shifted so his back rested against the front of the carriage, angling himself toward me. "We could spend the rest of this journey in silence, but it would surely feel longer." He waited to see if I'd answer, and then continued. "The incubus you seem attached to. Did he lose his soul to a phantom?"

"No."

"You're a good liar, but right now, you're exposed and hurting, and your lies are easily unraveled. Gerome taught you well."

"*You don't get to say his name,*" I hissed.

"He was always so charming while sharpening his knives behind his back. You're so much like him. He taught you to believe the lies the station shovels you, the lies he reinforced."

"Shut up or I'll throw my second knife, and maybe it'll hit somewhere more"—I dropped my gaze to his crotch—"painful."

Rumors were, male vampires had their genitalia severed as soon as they matured enough to serve their queen—those that weren't breeding partners, anyway. But I'd seen him naked. Briefly. Maybe he'd gotten to keep his dick because of his *service to his queen*. I flicked my gaze up, found him half smiling, and sneered away, hating the heat warming my cheeks. *Hating him.*

"You trust too easily, Lynher. Gerome, Etienne… your brother."

"I don't have a brother."

"Right. What was I thinking?"

At our destination, he'd tell his vampireguard all about Lynher and Kensey Aris working to undermine their order. As I would die anyway, I might as well die trying to take him with me. I needed to strike his heart, like Lilith had done with the imposter. Cut it out. But he wouldn't hold still while I carved him up with a throwing knife. I needed a way to disable him. The problem was, Jack didn't have weaknesses. Even with a limp, he would not go down easy.

"I see the ways you want to kill me in your eyes, Miss Aris. It's… stimulating," he purred, the words sounding suggestive and wrong.

"Lilith was supposed to kill you in the Grand Hall."

"Which is exactly why I employed someone like Felipe to play at being me, but you saw through the deception. I still don't know how you did that…"

"You never will."

"My act was flawless. I can count on one hand those alive who know the truth."

"I was on to you the first time I saw you."

"On the platform? Surely not."

"No, not then." I'd forgotten about that meeting. "In my library. You were waiting for me. I knew there was something wrong with you then."

"No, I saw the way you looked at me. You didn't know me then. Sometime in between, you figured it out. For what it's worth, I'm impressed."

"I don't care if you're impressed."

"But you do care, very much. It's a weakness in all humans."

"Caring is not a weakness, but I understand why a vampire would think so. You can't help it. You're just the queen's puppet. You don't feel anything outside of her control, do you?"

The glittering spark of humor that had been there since daybreak snuffed out of his eyes. He tried to hold his smile, but a fracture tilted his expression, turning it wooden instead of real. I'd found something to needle him with.

"Most vampires can't even think for themselves. You're like toys… She winds you up and lets you go, until you rush back to her, needing her like the good little puppets you are."

He tilted his head back and closed his eyes, his face falling blank. So, he didn't want to talk anymore. Screw that. It was his turn to entertain me. I got to my feet, crossed the carriage, then knelt next to him, folding my legs beneath me. His eyes were still closed, but he'd have heard me settle. "I always wondered how that works. Is she in your head? Or is it something inside that pulls you? Something you can't deny?"

"You wouldn't understand," he said grimly, eyes still closed.

I eyed his chest and watched the unnecessary rise and fall of each breath. Their hearts were in the same place as mine. Lilith had proven that. "No, because I'm human, and I have free will."

He opened his eyes but didn't start at finding me so close. His scrutiny of my face warmed my skin, but I stayed firm, eyeing him back. I couldn't kill him, not with my tiny knife, so I had to play this smarter. He was likely my only chance at surviving what came after this rattling box.

The carriage clattered around us, its rocking shifting us in the same monotonous rhythm. I'd seen how dangerous he could be, yet he didn't look it now. He looked… tired. My stupid, caring heart wanted to believe that look. Perhaps it was part of his charm, but so subtle I couldn't feel it undermining me.

He lifted his hand to tuck a loose lock of hair behind my ear. Moments ago, I'd have whacked that hand away. I wanted to. He'd sought me out at the station, perhaps to tease me, but even so… he'd wanted my company, putting himself in my path time and time again. To get back to Kensey and survive, I had to *use* him, not fight him.

Mentioning his queen had sliced off some of his snark, perhaps leaving him exposed. "Is she in your head right now?"

"Always."

"Always?"

"It's…" He dropped his gaze and wet his lips. "Never mind."

"When did you meet Gerome?"

"A lifetime ago." He brightened, the subject more appealing.

"At the station?"

He nodded and rested his head back again, watching the dancing shafts of light. His face in profile was a marvel. It wasn't right that the queen made her spawn so… perfect. And when she'd made this one, she hadn't skimped on the details. Besides his body, which I'd seen more of than was proper, his face had a stunning symmetry that tricked my brain into thinking he was beautiful. Defined jaw, pronounced cheekbones, and tapered eyes, the dark kind with a touch of green that made them hazel and unerringly human. I could spot a vampire in a crowd in seconds, but he continued to fool my better judgment.

"He was recently killed?" he asked, and it took me a moment to realize we'd been speaking of Gerome.

"The VG got him."

"Do you know why?"

I sighed and picked at my boots. It was too easy to remember when the VG had come to me, and when I'd seen them carry in his body, so limp and gray and lifeless. "Do you know why they killed him?"

Jack looked up from watching me play with my bootlaces. "Gerome had secrets."

Secrets. Like the resistance? "Do you have secrets?"

"Many." His smile returned, but small, like he'd hung it there because he was supposed to. He'd said I'd seen the truth in him, but that was likely a lie too. Did anyone know him? Would anyone want to?

"I guess I won't be around much longer to find them out." Leaning back, I rocked with the carriage. His presence, so close beside me, either flushed me with heat or drenched me in cold. I didn't understand him, didn't know him, and didn't want to, but if it meant surviving, I'd act like his friend.

He shrugged off his coat, and held it out. "Take it."

I *was* cold. I wasn't dressed for the outdoors. "Thank you." I folded the coat around my shoulders and pulled it closed under my chin. Spicy warmth enveloped me, tinged with an exotic scent, not dissimilar to the station's spicy warmth. I hugged it closer, feeling safer now wrapped in the smell of home.

We fell quiet again. He watched me from the corner of his eye, pretending not to.

"I don't want to die," I whispered.

"Nobody does."

"Have you ever…" I dry-laughed at my own foolishness. "Never mind."

"Now I simply must know. Ask your question. You may not get another chance."

"Have you ever saved people instead of kill them?"

He breathed in and sighed out slowly, thinking over his answer. It didn't seem like a difficult question. Not to me. He'd lived longer than me, decades, centuries even. He must have saved someone in all that time. Just once?

"No," he said flatly, reminding me why we were on opposite sides of a war and why my time was fast running out.

13

NIGHT

The carriage jolted and its brakes squealed, startling me awake. Jack had moved to the far side of our box while I'd dozed and shivered and dreamed of Kensey coming after me. The Dark Ones had hunted him because he was made of hope and light and everything *day*, and he hadn't known how to hurt them. The dream had ended with him surrounded, his hand outstretched.

I pulled my blanket closer, breathed in the smell of home, and then remembered the blanket was Jack's coat, destroying the comfort I'd found wrapped in it.

"Get up," Jack ordered, his glare pinned to the door.

The carriage screamed to a jolting halt.

Stiff and aching, I got to my feet and discreetly tucked my remaining knife up my sleeve and against my wrist.

"Don't say anything." He came forward and stopped in front of the door, his chin up and shoulders square. Every inch an overseer, like he proudly stood atop a pile of bones.

I stood behind him, off to his right, his coat over my shoulders and buttoned at my neck. Maybe I could take a few down before they killed me?

Boots marched closer outside. Orders were barked. There were many of them out there… I was about to die. At least I'd do so standing and proud. I would not die kneeling to a vampire.

My pulse thudded hot and alive in my throat.

Jack turned his head. His gaze was hard, his mouth a thin line. This was where we parted ways. Someday, someone would kill him, someone good, and end all this madness.

The door rumbled open.

Floodlights poured in, blinding me of everything beyond Jack's silhouette.

I dropped a dagger into my fingers, flung an arm around Jack's narrow waist, then pressed the edge of my blade to his neck.

"*Stop*," he hissed, stilling.

Too late. This was happening.

I blinked into the light. Shapes appeared, white on white. "Stay back! I have him. I have your Ghost!"

As my eyes adjusted from the dark to the light, countless faces took shape. So many vampires, all waiting on a platform, all dressed the same, all bloodthirsty drones. The more I looked, the more of their number I counted. Thirty, forty, so many. They filled the platform and went on through huge open gates, the tops bristling with razor wire. Floodlights bleached the world of color. Beyond all that, horrible blocks of gray stone buildings waited, iron bars over the windows.

"*Stop, Lynher…*" Jack's charm rolled over me, much stronger than before. It poured over my tongue and into my ears, filling me up with warm amber and honey, charming me into believing I could listen to him, that he'd keep me safe. I fought it, felt it stutter, but then it plunged harder inside, deeper, faster, hungrier. I couldn't stop it. Jack wasn't like the others. I'd seen it in his eyes, but now I felt the difference in him infecting my veins, turning my body against me.

I lowered the knife even as I silently screamed for him to get out of my head.

My human heart beat his will through my veins in waves.

The knife fell from my hand and clattered on the carriage boards, and I watched my one chance at survival shatter under the too-bright lights.

A few vampires moved in, but Jack lifted a hand, stopping them—puppets on his strings. He covered my hand on his hip, unfolding my embrace as easily as swinging open a gate. He turned, lowered my arm to my side, and met my eyes.

I made sure he saw how hate blazed through me and made him feel it too. It lit me up and burned inside. Hate for him, hate for them all. They could kill me, but I wasn't alone in hating him. One day, their reign would end. I might not see it, but I knew it would happen.

"Foolish girl." His cheek fluttered, and his eyes had turned cold. He stepped back, withdrawing some of his charm and leaving me gasping.

"Get her out of my sight."

Vampires plowed in, swallowing him from my view. Cold, iron hands grabbed my arms. Someone tore Jack's coat from around my shoulders, yanking it so hard a button cut into my neck and popped free. There was no use fighting. Better to conserve my strength for a later opportunity.

They dragged me through their numbers. Over a hundred soulless pairs of eyes watched me pass. These were true drones—the queen's workers, her army. They didn't think. They *acted*. They didn't even look alive behind those cold, dead eyes.

I glimpsed Jack in the crowd, his brow pinched as he talked rapidly with another male vampire. He didn't seem pleased. But the sight of him was soon lost among the drones.

Metal tainted the air; I tasted it on my tongue. Or was it blood?

Mud pulled at my boots. They marched me through the slop to the sound of the gates slamming closed behind me. I let my chin drop and thought of Kensey reaching out to me in the dream. I'd thought I'd dreamed it up to save him, but now I wondered if he'd been reaching out to save me.

They took my knife first.

They stole my clothes next.

After the time I'd wandered into Lilith's room and emerged days later with no memory or sense of time, I'd felt empty and exposed, like I'd been turned inside out. I felt the same way now, wrapped in a threadbare cotton gown, my skin burning from the high-pressure hose they'd turned on me. I wasn't myself. This wasn't real. They'd stripped me of every single layer that made me me. The drones had watched me come undone. I was strong. I'd always been strong. But this… I wasn't sure who or what I was in this hard, horrible place. Was I even human anymore? I didn't feel it.

As they dragged me from one windowless room to another, I couldn't fight, and so I went, one foot in front of the other. When they demanded that I show them my wrist, I lifted my arm and pulled back the sleeve.

"What is that?" The station's mark on my arm had caught the guard's eye. It had dulled to a washed-out gray. Out here, it wasn't much more than an ugly tattoo. But seeing that symbol of home summoned a knot in my throat. Already it seemed that woman in her pretty dresses and daggers up her sleeves was someone else entirely.

A second vampire joined the first. He had darker, longer hair and wore it tucked behind his ears, his mean face narrow and angular. "It's nothing," he grunted. "Get it done." He went back to checking the papers strewn across a table.

The first, his hair sandy and his face rounder, picked up some kind of gun and slotted a cartridge inside. "I've seen a cross marking like that before."

"When?" the mean one asked, not looking up.

"I don't know." He shrugged. "But it's familiar, isn't it?"

The mean one frowned at me and came over. He grabbed my arm and lifted it to get a good look. "Then do the other wrist." He roughly tossed my arm down like a piece of meat. "She's due at processing before dawn."

Sandy-hair grabbed my unmarked wrist, pressed the gun to my skin, and fired. Pain blasted hot and heavy up my arm. I tried to pull away, only for the vampire to tighten his grip. He yanked me off balance and admired the puckered burn mark. A quick swipe of his thumb while his partner wasn't looking, and he swept up a dribble of blood and burned skin, bringing both to his pink tongue for a taste.

I stared back flatly. Like with any Dark One, if I reacted, they'd only poke at me some more.

His grin wilted. "Ah, damn…" He spat to the side. "She's claimed."

"By who?" the leader barked.

"Don't know, but her blood's spoiled."

"Shit." Mean Face grabbed my gown in his fist and pulled me onto my toes. "Who owns you, bitch?"

"Nobody."

He threw me down. "Hours wasted! Take it to the dens. The overseer can decide what to do with it. Spoiled goods, for fuck's sake… like we don't have enough to do."

The overseer? Was that Jack? Sandy hauled me to my feet and marched me from the room.

It was raining between buildings, and with no protection, I was drenched through and shivering by the time I reached what I assumed were the dens. Steps descended into a basement level. Doors lined a long hallway. No windows. And the doors, made of thick steel, only had small letterbox slits at eye level. The air was wrong here, sweet and thick and hot.

Sandy opened a door using a heavy double-levered handle and shoved me inside. He slammed the door closed so hard it rang like a bell. And then there was just a strange heavy quiet, broken by the sounds of breathing and shuffling.

I blinked into the gloom. Others were huddled in the dark, eyes wide, silent but for the rustle of their filthy rags. The sewer-like stench pulled water from my eyes and burned my throat.

I was in hell.

14

NIGHT

I tried to speak with them but it quickly became clear they couldn't reply, even if they'd wanted to. Some were older than me, but most were younger, all jutting bones and rounded faces, big eyes blinking from behind layers of filth.

Minutes felt like hours. Doors slammed. Boots clomped. There were no screams, no howls, no moans. Just silence, and that was worse, because the silence was full. With no light, no hope, these people were waiting for death to claim them.

When the door opened and a guard dragged me free, I sucked in lungfuls of cleaner air, quiet tears of relief falling. I was free of that room, if just for a moment. Free of the looks on their little faces that would haunt my dreams.

The guard marched me up a tower of never-ending stairs. My legs wobbled, my belly empty and aching. Then finally, he knocked at a door.

"Come."

The décor inside was austere, like the unfamiliar overseer behind his desk. The desk looked familiar, more than familiar. It had the same clawed feet and ornate carvings as mine in my library. No, not *like* it; they were *identical.* No, no, it couldn't be. My mind, having never been outside the Station, was grasping for familiarities.

I stumbled in, dragged along like a broken pet, waiting to be shot.

"Leave it," the overseer said.

The guard deposited me on a rug. Its pile was deep and warm and soft enough to swallow my toes. I'd never felt anything finer. I reflexively wiggled my toes, wondering if, when I moved from this spot, I'd leave dirty footprints behind. I hoped so.

The overseer was not Jack. Disappointment sat in my empty gut. This male vampire was rounder, shorter, and with a long face full of hard snarls and small, flinty eyes. He heaved himself from his chair and rounded the desk, walking right up to me. We were the same height, but his bulk and presence filled the room, trying to crush me. His charm rolled over me, hot and wet and slippery, but like most others, it didn't stick. Maybe he wasn't trying.

He grabbed my marked wrist first, examined it, and then stepped back. "What do you think?"

What did I think about what? I scrabbled around my head for an answer.

"Caine claimed her—erroneously," a familiarly accented voice said from behind me. "His intention was to kill."

I stiffened, caught between wanting to look and not wanting him to *see* what I'd become, trembling in rags, legs caked in mud. I'd see myself in his eyes, and I couldn't have that, because it would break me. It was worse, somehow, knowing Jack had seen me *before* as Lynher Aris and now *as food.*

"Caine needs more discipline," the heavy one said, returning to his desk to park his plump rear against its edge.

Jack emerged to my left, gracefully cruising into my peripheral vision. He approached the desk and stopped partway between it and me. Every tailored stitch and every strand of hair were all perfectly in place. He didn't seem real. Nothing about this felt real. This room, them, the desk… was I still in the dark somewhere beneath this building, listening to the dead shiver?

"Have you seen the mark before?" Bulky asked.

"Not that I recall," Jack lied.

I blinked. He'd told me he'd been to the station before. He'd seen the mark on me. He knew what it did and what it represented. Why not tell his overseer companion the truth? I could tell Bulky how his overseer pal had lied, but he'd probably laugh.

Bulky's expression pinched. "Didn't this one threaten you?"

"Yes." Jack stiffened. I only noticed because I was determined to stare him down.

Bulky waited for more, but Jack showed no signs of elaborating, so he gave in with a resigned sigh. "I don't have time for all this nonsense. I'll have it drained and sent to the burn house."

"Of course." A piece broke off Jack's wooden smile.

"I'll tell you," I blurted, pointing at Jack. "Only you. And then… do whatever you want."

"My apologies, Ghost," Bulky blustered, bulbous face blotching. "Her tongue hasn't been removed. An oversight. *Guard*!"

"It's quite all right." He casually waved away his partner's groveling. "There's some merit in its words. I'll take it off your hands."

"Aren't you due to leave for the capital at dawn?"

Jack dipped his head respectfully. "More than enough time to get what I want out of it."

The guard reappeared, and I was marched behind Jack's tall frame, through labyrinth-like hallways and into another room, this one more plain than Bulky's suite. A daybed, a dresser, a cupboard. All dull brown. All unremarkable. How typically Jack-like.

The guard pulled a length of rope from his pocket to bind my hands together.

"That won't be necessary." Jack waved him away and stared at me until the door had clicked closed. "Lynher Aris." His lips pulled on a sideways grin.

Part of me wanted to burst into tears. Another part wanted to spit at him again. And more wanted to yell and ask him if he knew what they were keeping in the basement here. "You fucking bastard."

"Such a sweet tongue. I'm pleased you still have it." He went to a table, poured ice water from a pitcher and then handed it over. I considered throwing it in his face. Maybe I would with the second glass, but my dry throat demanded I drink. I gulped it down without stopping to breathe, acutely aware of his gaze on my neck, and then handed the glass back.

Dirty fingerprints marked its shiny surface. I looked at my hands, trembling fingers dried with filth.

He set the glass down, not refilling it, so I took myself across his shiny floor, leaving dirt flakes in my wake, and poured my own damn glass of water. When I was done with that one, I pitched the glass against the far wall and watched it shatter, delighting in the bright, tinkling sound of raining glass.

"Did that help?" he asked.

"No." Now I was breathless and shaking and felt like I might fall, but I couldn't. If I fell, I might not get back up. My skin itched, and my blood was cold. I scratched at the thing they'd shot into my arm. "There are people… underground. *Children*! Why are they there?"

His cheek flickered. He turned his head, looking away in shame, I hoped. "They only light the burn houses when they have enough—"

I groaned and leaned too hard against the table. I couldn't do anything for those poor people or for myself, but I could take Jack back to hell with me. I lunged at him, got my filthy fingers around his smooth lapels, and pulled. We stumbled against the table, and the pitcher toppled. Water spilled. I grabbed the pitcher's handle, funneling all my rage and hate and fear into it and swung.

He caught my wrist, twisted it, yanked me forward, and slammed me facedown against the tabletop. His fangs would be in my neck next, and I'd die drunk on his venom while thanking him for being so terribly *nice* as he killed me. *"Get off!"*

"Silence!" The word burned the back of my neck.

"Get off me, you son of a bitch, or I will scream this place down, and when they come running, I'll tell them how I saw you out cold, naked and vulnerable, in one of my beds, with all your markings on display."

His growl rumbled through him and down my back, but he let go. When I turned, he was all the way across the room, straightening his hair and cuffs, putting all the pieces back together again.

"Why are you lying to them?"

"Lower your voice."

"Why?"

He tore open a closet and rummaged through the interior, swearing when he didn't find what he wanted.

"Tell me." I approached on wobbly legs.

He slammed the closet door closed and marched to the main door, his limp more pronounced. "Stay here."

The second he was out the door, I gave it a tug. When that didn't work, I tried the windows, but they were all sealed, with no means of opening them. There had to be something I could use to escape or as a weapon against him. I tried the drawers in another desk, smaller and more basic than mine, and came up empty. Then I searched the closets, leaving the doors hanging open. There was *nothing*.

The door lock rattled, and he strode in, spare clothes draped over his left arm, boots held in his left hand, and a covered food tray in his right. He dropped the boots and locked the door again, his eye catching mine to confirm I'd seen, and then he tossed the clothes onto the bed and set the tray down on the desk.

He eyed his open closets and ransacked dresser. "Did you find whatever you were searching for?"

"No." I poked at the red lump in my wrist. "What did they put in me?"

"A tracker. Stop scratching it."

"It hurts."

"It will hurt more if you dislodge it."

"I hate you, and this place, and your wretched species."

"Good, because we're leaving. But before that, change your clothes and eat." He lifted the lid off the tray, revealing a medley of fruit and bread. I lasted all of a few seconds before descending on the food, taking bites out of everything. Apples had never tasted so divine. I ate until the plate was clear, and only then did I realize he'd been watching the entire time, propped against a far wall like a proud, elegant statue that had murdered generations for fun.

"Hurry," he said. "My train leaves at dawn. I do not intend to be on it."

Was this a game? I'd play it if it meant escaping this hell, so long as I didn't end up in a worse one. But nothing could be worse, could it? "Why are you helping me?"

"I'm helping myself." He glanced out the sealed windows. The iron bars painted the same shadow bars across his face. "Now hurry."

I picked up the dark cotton pants and blouse. All black with red threading. Vampire clothes. They'd fit—he'd been paying attention. Plus, they were better than the thin gown the drones had thrown over me.

I stripped off my damp gown and tugged on the clothes, not caring about modesty. The drones had already stripped that away too. My fingers trembled as I buttoned up the blouse. Simple as they were, the soft fabric felt like a gift against my cold, mottled skin. I wanted to hate him, but I couldn't right now, not with my body warm and belly full. I'd hate him again later.

"It's all I could find," he said, as though he had genuinely sought out clothing I'd find more comfortable.

"It's fine." I rolled up the sleeves. Were we really leaving? Was that what was happening here? But there were people inside the chambers and other buildings like this one. How could I leave them? I knew how *he* could. He cared only about himself.

"Why are you afraid of the dawn train?"

"Ask your questions once we're outside the farm." He pulled a coat from the closet and handed it out.

I looked at the coat and then up into his pleading eyes. "Those people… I can't leave them."

"They're already dead." He shook the coat, urging me to take it.

"No, they aren't. I can't just leave. I can't." I picked at the tracker in my arm, trying to pry it free. "There are kids down there, Jack. They're alive."

Lowering the coat, he sighed through his nose. "And what would you have me do?"

"Something. Anything. You don't even have to do it. I'll do something. Just… help?"

He laughed. "You don't know what you're asking. Even if we freed them, there is nowhere for them to go. That's what I meant. They're dead. Today… tomorrow, it's all the same."

I searched his eyes, hoping to see a spark of emotion, something other than self-preservation. "I'm not going with you."

"Lynher—"

"Miss fucking Aris."

"*Fuck*," he snapped back. "Why do you have to be difficult?"

The way his clipped accent made *fuck* sound so utterly obscene had me half smiling. "Because… because it's working?" And it was. My stubbornness had him rattled. He really, really wanted to be gone before his train arrived. "Because, unlike you, I have my own mind and I know what is wrong and leaving them down there to die is wrong."

He rolled his eyes, backed up, and then came forward again as an idea occurred to him. "I could bite you and have you follow me about like a pet. I'd like to see you smile then."

"Do it." I lifted my chin and swallowed. *Stupid, stupid, stupid.* My fingers curled into fists.

His gaze flicked to my throat, but his mouth twisted. "You're claimed. Your blood, *should* I taste it, would be unpleasant… somewhat like its owner."

He'd called me unpleasant. The mass-murdering, blood-sucking bitch-queen's slave hadn't looked in a mirror lately. "I'm not going anywhere until we've at least tried to help them."

"Only Lynher fucking Aris would dare issue orders to *me* in a bloodfarm." He growled low in his throat and threw the coat at my chest. "Fine, but only because it will stop your arguing. I do not have the luxury of time."

Jack made for the door. Throwing the coat on, I hurried behind.

"Keep your eyes down. Don't say or do anything," he murmured. "And stay behind me."

We came upon the first drone standing outside a stairwell door. She observed our approach, but with my head down, I missed her reaction, if she'd even had one. Most drones didn't speak; they were empty vessels, but they were also the eyes and ears of the queen. Did the queen see us through her, I wondered, shivering as I passed under the drone's glare.

Jack hurried down a stairwell. Down and down we went, until the air changed and I tasted death on my lips. The low ceiling and long corridor flanked by steel doors made the air feel heavy. I dragged it over my lips, breathing too hard.

"Which room?" he whispered.

"Third on the right."

"Open the door," Jack said, speaking calmly to the drone between us and our target, his tone leaving no room for argument. The drone flicked over the door's locks. As he was about to turn back around, Jack grabbed him by the back of the head and slammed him face-first into the wall. The sickening sound of bone cracking was followed by the tumble of dead weight as Jack tossed the unconscious vampire aside like trash. I swallowed and stepped around the motionless body, avoiding looking too long.

Jack yanked the door open. "Everyone out!"

They shuffled from the dank air, adults and kids alike, all wrapped in filthy rags, eyes wide and streaming. They all shied away from Jack, although he was too busy staring at me to notice. They didn't seem all that pleased to see me either. Their flighty glances flicked over my vampire clothing, assessing me as the enemy.

"It's okay…" I held out a hand to a little one. "We're getting you out of here."

Jack's jaw hardened. His cheek jumped. "This way." He turned on his heel and strode farther into the facility.

"It's all right." I beckoned them on, hoping Jack had a plan, because mine had ended at getting the door open.

The line was slow to move, but they stayed quiet and obedient, likely because they'd already had their tongues removed. If we could get them outside the farm, maybe we could find them shelter. After that, well… I had no idea. But this had to be better than being locked in that room, waiting to die.

We climbed a set of stairs. Jack opened the door at the top and waved everyone outside. They all huddled in a corner, tucked in the shadows, out of reach of the floodlights.

"All right, here's what you need to do. You stay here. You do not run. You do not break cover. I will lead the guards away. Lynher"—his vampire eyes flashed in the dark—"you're with me."

I told them again to stay, that they were safe, that this would all be over soon, and I followed Jack's tracks through the mud.

"Your soft heart will be your undoing," he said, his gaze on the floodlit guard post ahead.

I didn't reply. It wasn't a soft heart driving me to help; it was my humanity. I cared, and I couldn't change that. No human could. When it came down to the wire, we all cared.

"Overseer." The three guards straightened under Jack's scrutiny, but the one on the left examined me, a human in vampire clothes. He'd hear my blood and sense my warmth.

"There's been an incident," Jack explained. "By the main entrance..."

The leftmost vampire's eyes narrowed.

This wouldn't work.

Lefty glanced behind me, his face tightening. "What the...?"

I glanced back.

One of the kids had bolted.

She was a tiny thing, no taller than my hip, but she could run. Wherever she thought she was going, she'd never make it. Her skinny legs pumped. She slipped on the mud, went down, but got her feet under her again.

The drones moved in as one. At first, I thought the shadows were converging on her, but the shadows merged, becoming an eerier silent flow of blood-hungry puppets.

Our guards started forward from their post, leaving Jack and me alone.

They'd find the others.

"Do something!" I hissed.

Jack's top lip twitched. He looked down, his glare cool and knowing. I heard his words again, about how they were already dead, and moved forward. He flung his arm out, blocking my path. "You can't help them."

The others burst from their hiding place like a startled flock of birds, and the drones swarmed. It happened in near silence. They had no tongues with which to scream. The vampires rushed in and lunged, tearing into the prisoners, bringing them down. Some thrashed in the mud. Some didn't even survive that long. And the girl... she ran like the wind, one little arrow of hope… until a drone tackled her, cutting her legs out from under her. Then he was on her, tearing her throat open.

I pulled my gaze away. Jack placed a hand against my back and shoved, and I let him guide me away from the massacre.

Rain hammered down, soaking through my coat, weighing it down so it felt as though I carried bricks in my pockets. In the dark, the guards all looked like the same hulking lumps of coal, positioned at the corners of each building and along the fence. Jack somehow walked like he owned the world, even ankle-deep in mud. I did my best to trudge along behind him, trying to go unnoticed, trying to be less human, trying not to replay the sight of the girl running over and over in my mind, each time knowing how it had ended and blaming myself.

Should I have left them in that room?

Was Jack right?

We rounded a corner and walked into a yard packed with wheeled machines. Jack opened a door to one of the machines. "Get in the car, Lynher."

Cars. That's what these machines were. I'd seen them in the station's library books. At least I was out of the rain. The windows fogged up. Jack wiped angrily at the condensation.

"If you could breathe less…" he muttered.

The engine burbled to life. He fiddled with the stick, and then we were moving, the heater blasting at the windshield to clear it. Gates loomed ahead, and as soon as I saw them, floodlights swung our way, filling the car, turning everything gray, even Jack.

He pulled up to the guardhouse. The driver's window hummed down, and a guard poked his head in. Water dripped from his cap onto Jack's thigh, leaving a dark stain.

"Papers?"

Jack withdrew a wad of rolled-up papers and handed them over. The guard ducked out again and returned to his little box to check the documents.

"What do they say?"

"I told you not to *speak*," he hissed under his breath.

"Maybe you should have cut out my tongue," I hissed back.

"Maybe I will." His eyes flashed, catching the bright light.

The guard returned and handed the papers back. "All in order. Proceed, Overseer."

The gates rumbled open, Jack worked the gears, and then we were rolling right out of hell. I twisted in the seat to look out the misty back window. The floodlights had swung back to the gate, and I could pretend, in the dark, that we'd made it, but the truth was I now faced hundreds of miles of barrens full of human-eating Dark Ones, with one such monster right beside me. I could run from him, but he was my only means of surviving whatever came next.

I faced the front and watched the headlights fight off the dark.

"I told you," Jack said, referring to how my attempt to do some good had backfired. "But it wasn't a complete failure. The commotion created a fine distraction."

"People died."

"People die every night."

Was that why he'd freed them? As a distraction? I stared at his face, all his angles illuminated by the green light of the car's instrument panels. Just when I'd thought he might have some compassion in him, he snuffed that thought out. He didn't care about a single one of those people. He'd just wanted something to keep the guards preoccupied while we slipped away.

A siren sounded, loud and long, trembling the car's windows.

Light flooded in from behind.

"Hold on!" Jack stamped his foot to the floor and yanked on the car's stick, lurching the vehicle sideways. It fishtailed in the mud, hooked up, and launched us forward.

Wipers thrashed across the windshield, sloshing rain back and forth. Headlights speared into skeletal trees. If there was a road, I couldn't make it out. A tree sprang into the headlights. Jack yanked on the wheel, jerking the car around it.

Screaming rolled through the air, the sound like metal tearing against metal and worse than the siren. It came from outside.

"What is that!"

"Wyvern."

"What?" I clutched at my seat as he threw the car around more brush.

"Don't worry, they keep it on a tight chain. It can't go far from the—"

Jack's sentence disappeared as the world flipped over. There was pain, and heat, and noise—so much screaming. Much of it mine. Then the chaos abruptly ended, leaving just the sounds of tinkling glass and my labored breathing.

I was on my hands in a pool of mud *inside* the car.

Mud dribbled in around my fingers and pooled at my knees. I looked at it, wondering how it had gotten inside the car, and then saw how it crawled around Jack's perfect face, over one closed eyelid, and into his ear. He lay on his side, lips parted. Mud tried to creep into his mouth too. Was he dead? A deep gash on his forehead suggested he wasn't going anywhere anytime soon.

Panic demanded I *move*. Scrambling through the narrow window, I crawled through the mud and out into sheets of rain. Light blinked and flickered in the distance. A howl lifted. A dog, maybe, or a wolf. Vampires often captured the bad kind of lycanthrope, which killed anything when enraged. But those howls were distant, for now.

I was on my feet, stumbling, head still fuzzy and body numb. I had to run, didn't I? Falling into a run, I fought through sharp branches and jagged thorns. Lycans howled, but they sounded farther away. Maybe they were after Jack? An overseer gone rogue had to be more valuable than another bloodbag.

I ran until my thighs were numb and my lungs ached, the air too thin. The rain was so cold it burned. A root tripped me, and I went down, cutting my knees on rocks, even through the trousers. Back on my feet, I stumbled on, gasping, body throbbing. The ground sloped away. I grabbed a sapling to lean on and listened. Beneath the hissing rain, the sound of gushing water reached me. A river.

A few steps deeper into the undergrowth and a gorge opened up, almost swallowing me before I could grab a tree and steady myself.

Glimpses at the bottom revealed frothy white water. There would be no surviving that. I needed a way around—

Thrashing sounded behind me.

The unmistakable sound of snarling beasts bubbled nearby, closing in.

Oh gods, there was no escape. I had to jump.

Thundering paws and snapping branches.

Backing toward the edge, I wiped rainwater from my eyes. The wind coiled and teased at my clothing and hair, crooning at me to jump.

Kensey would never know how I died. Would he look for me forever?

A vampire burst from the brush, teeth gritted and eyes blazing. Jack! He reached out, circled an arm around my waist, and yanked me with him, right over the edge.

Wind, and cold, and rain rushed by. My gut whooshed. Jack somehow twisted, getting *beneath* me and curling me in close.

He caught my gaze, and in those moments, I felt his fear as if it were my own and saw something else too, something real and true and bright behind his eyes.

Water slammed in, thumped against my chest, and tore at my legs—sucking me out of Jack's arms. I gasped, and water poured down my throat. My body heaved as I choked, and more water poured in. Water tumbled me over, turning me around. I reached for something, anything, even Jack, but my fingers sailed through blackness, finding nothing to grasp.

Pain exploded across my head, and finally, the noise, the cold, and the terror ended.

15

DAY

Jack's face was gray, apart from the cut-up bits on his cheek and forehead, which were pink and gaping like hungry mouths.

He lay unmoving, sprawled on the pebbly bank. Shingle and twigs knotted his hair. His clothes hung askew.

Was he dead? His eyes were closed, like they'd been in the overturned car. No pulse that I could see. I could touch his neck, but he'd be cold and wet and feel dead anyway.

I'd found him while staggering down the riverbank. The river was calm now, burbling over tiny rocks beneath dappled sunlight. Jack must have dragged himself out of the water and collapsed where he lay.

"Well, this is typical..." I told the unconscious-maybe-dead Jack. "Was this your plan? They're probably still hunting us, and you're *finally* dead, and I don't have a weapon."

Searching the riverbank revealed little of use, just driftwood. An old water-worn wooden plank had washed up on the shore. I picked it up. The waterlogged wood made it heavy, but I didn't need the whole plank. A few strikes against a nearby boulder split the board apart. A splinter jabbed my thumb, but the pain was worth it. Now I had a strip of wood with a point on the end. Returning to my spot on the bank, I worked the spike some more, peeling bits off, crafting into a shape less splintery and more comfortable to wield. A pointy stick was better than nothing.

The sun had risen, warming the air and dust-sprites danced above the river's shining surface. My clothes were soaked and heavy, but the sun worked to dry them off.

I hadn't died, but now I was in the wilderness, and there were plenty of other ways for the wild things to finish me off.

Jack's hand twitched.

Sunlight fell across his arm and face, turning his skin a warmer pink.

That had to be painful.

His eyelids flickered but stayed closed.

Not dead, then. I was only half disappointed. I needed him, but if he'd died, it would have been a good day for humanity.

He pulled his hand to his chest and hissed, drawing his top lip back like he could growl at the sun and have it obey. Only then did his eyes flutter open, signaling his slow return to the living. The gash on his head began to reseal itself, and within a minute, he was back to his stern-faced prettiness, albeit colorless, apart from the blue lips. How had I thought him human?

Drawing a knee up, he looked over. "Are you carving a stake?" he groused. His hair flopped over his eye. He swept it back with a trembling hand. "Do you think that will work?" He clearly assumed I planned to stab him in the heart. I'd certainly been thinking it.

"It's worth a try."

"How far did we travel?" He eyed upriver, full of ludicrously bright sunshine, prancing butterflies, and shimmering sprites.

"No idea. I don't even know where we are."

He brushed sand off his creased pants and frowned at their state. "I need to get out of this sun," he grumbled, rising to his feet. He stumbled up the bank and took to the shadows beneath the trees. His limp made his progress awkward. It was worse than I'd ever seen it, but then, we had just survived the VG, a wyvern, a car crash, lycans, and a vicious river. All we had to do was survive each other.

"Are you coming?"

I tucked my stake into my waistband and trudged after him.

He limped ahead, maneuvering around the undergrowth and river's edge. "The river should take us to old Wilmington. Once there, we'll find the rail tracks and follow those back to your station."

"How far is it?"

He didn't answer immediately, and the longer he thought about his reply, the more my heart sank.

"It will be difficult," he said.

Great. "Roughly?"

"There are many obstacles to overcome, not to mention the Dark Ones who'll track your scent like you're the North Star."

"How far, *Jack*?"

"Jack is not my name."

"I really don't care anymore. It's what I'm calling you."

He huffed something like a chuckle or a growl. I gritted my teeth and imagined sticking the stake in his back.

"Six days and nights. Maybe seven. That's assuming we're not delayed."

Oh gods, that was a long time for the station to be without me. For Kensey to think me dead. For Etienne to carry out whatever his plan was … Kensey would see through him. Eventually. My brother wasn't as stupid as he sometimes appeared, even around people he trusted. Although… he'd never trusted anyone outside of Gerome and me before. Etienne was a first.

The sound of the carriage door slamming closed haunted me most, knowing it had been Etienne on the other side. Etienne was all stammer and politeness. He could be rigid, that's what had made him a good assistant, but he shouldn't have been able to do this…

What if it had all been a lie? But the station had marked him. It wouldn't have done that unless Etienne's intentions were good. But good people did not shut their lover's sister inside a cage with a mass murderer. Nothing about how I'd come to be trudging through the woods behind Jack made sense.

"I can feel you thinking up all the ways to kill me."

"You'll find this hard to believe, but you're wrong. The world doesn't revolve around you."

"Then you haven't considered my weaknesses?"

I had.

Jack chuckled again, his dry laughter like something made of sugar and spice, with a heart of poison. "You wear the hostess act well, Miss Aris," he went on, "but it's easy to be the queen inside her castle. Out here, you're nothing but bait." He stopped and I nearly plowed into him. When he spoke next, he held my stare. "I'm not trying to insult you. It's the truth. During the day, we can make good time, but at night, things will change. Shelter will help, I think, but I've never escorted a human in the wild before. You're a liability."

"I've never been a liability, and I won't be one now."

I saw a blur of movement and then pain sparked up my arm. In the space of a blink, he'd snatched my wrist and brought it to his lips. Fangs flashed. I tried to yank free, filling my lungs to scream, but his other hand slammed over my mouth. I shoved, but he stood immobile, as hard and cold as stone.

"Don't fight or this will get a lot more *interesting*—" He cut off his own warning and bit down. Pain bloomed, hot and heavy. Horror tried to pull me from the moment and hide me somewhere in my own head—because this was how I died. Then he turned his face away and spat, dropped my wrist, and marched through the brush. "Keep up..." The words came out gruff, like he'd dragged them through hell to speak them.

I looked at my wrist, at the ragged tear weeping blood. The cut wasn't deep, barely a surface wound and not deep enough to inject venom. The tracker. A quick glance around and I found the small piece of metal shining and bloody on the ground.

He could have killed me and had chosen not to. Why? What did he want from me?

By dusk, Jack winced with every step.

He veered us away from the river, deeper into what had once been a bustling town but now resembled mounds of bricks the forest had regurgitated. Daytime noises faded into an eerie quiet, the same kind I'd heard when Rafe had translocated me outside the station. Night was coming. Jack must have sensed it too, because he found a nook made of bricks among the trees. He gestured for me to go inside first, said not to light a fire, and when I turned around to question what the shelter was for, he'd vanished. I assumed he'd return at some point and hadn't just abandoned me in a damp hole.

At least he wasn't feeding on me, though I didn't understand why he hadn't taken advantage when he considered me bait. Why was he even *escorting* me anywhere? Why not kill me and go back to the station alone?

I tucked myself into the damp, dark corner and shivered the minutes away. The day hadn't been too bad. Nothing had stalked us, as far as I knew. The walk might have been pleasant if my damp clothes hadn't chafed. And the company. We hadn't spoken much. I'd said all I needed to in the carriage.

The darkness outside the den had turned thick and clammy when Jack returned, a silvery shimmer in his hazel eyes. His limp had settled too. He'd killed a poor innocent creature to get his blood fix. Better them than me, I figured.

As he rearranged a few rocks like a mother hen building a nest, I recalled the small army of drones that had waited for us the moment the carriage doors had opened. Soulless machines. The drones would be tracking us. They didn't tire, not like I did. They'd hunt, and replenish their strength, and continue their relentless pursuit. Drones like those had devastated humanity.

"Maybe we should keep moving." My teeth rattled as I shivered.

"And have you stumble in front of a phantom or worse?" He propped himself into a corner, wrapped his arms around his torso, then stared at the entrance, seeing far into the dark. "No."

"Why do you care what happens to me?"

Predictably, he didn't answer, saying instead, "You may rest. I'll listen for threats."

He said it like I was his pet, someone to be told what to do and when. I wasn't bait, and I wasn't his pet. I might have been stripped of everything that made me a hostess, but I wasn't useless. I didn't have the energy to argue and knew he'd just glare me into silence, so I folded my arms and pulled myself into a tight ball, ready for the long night ahead.

At least I was out of the hellhole they called a *farm*. The slaughtered peoples' faces haunted me every time I closed my eyes. There were others back there, living a nightmare every second of every day. My gut rolled. I hadn't eaten, but if I had, I might not have kept it down anyway.

Once I was back at the station, I'd tell Kensey about the farm. He could do something. Maybe tell his contacts… But to do that, I had to survive the next few nights.

Sleep was elusive, my mind turning over too many things and the night too cold. My thoughts wandered along with my gaze, back to the enigma of Jack, still staring into the night. The now-dead Felipe was exactly how I'd expected Ghost to behave. Jack's behavior threw me. On one hand, he could be a Felipe, but on the other, he had reflective moments I hadn't known vampires were capable of. And his markings… what were they for? And why had he run from his duties? He might answer me, if I approached the questions from a different angle.

"How did you get the limp?" I asked.

"A fight."

"Did you kill the other party?"

He snorted a laugh.

"Why is that amusing?"

"No, I did not kill them," he drawled.

"Them? So there was more than one?"

"No." He blinked slowly and slid his predatory gaze to me. "I just don't want to give you any more information than you already have."

Now I laughed. "What am I going to do? Tell the squirrels?"

He leveled me with his stare. "You're with the resistance."

I looked away and chewed on the inside of my cheek. Denying it was pointless. We were way beyond pretending I was just the station's hostess. "You think that, yet you're helping me." Our gazes met in the dark. "We're enemies. What's in it for you if we make it back to the station?"

"You're smart, Lynher. Figure it out."

There was nothing for him at the station. Just… "Sanctuary?"

He bowed his head, admitting it without saying the words. He *was* running, but what from? He *oversaw* the VG, at least the East Coast nest. They all worshipped the infamous and terrifying Ghost. Perhaps whoever or whatever it was had been the source of his broken leg.

He wanted sanctuary, but it wasn't that simple. "Are you hoping the station will mark you because I'm with you? Save me and you get a free pass, is that it?"

"No, Lynher." He returned to staring into the night. "In all honesty, I don't need you at all."

Liar. I knew something he didn't. The station wouldn't take him in. It only took in those worthy of its protection. Lilith was an exception, but everyone else who lived there was good. Mostly. Jack was not the kind of creature the station saved. It would sooner devour him than grant him asylum. He was doing all this for nothing. And I'd use him every step of the way.

16

NIGHT

"Wake up."

Jack's silvery eyes brought me out of a cold dream. I gasped. A rough hand smothered my mouth, holding me down. This was it. He was going to tear out my throat and drink me down.

"Be still. It's me," he whispered. "Take this."

My panic waned, but the intensity in those eyes made sure it didn't completely disappear.

He peeled open my fingers and placed my throwing knife inside—the one I'd lost to him in the carriage. "Follow me." Urgency made his words sharp. "Quietly."

He'd had my knife this whole time? I tightened my hold on the familiar weapon, checked that my stake was safely stowed, and followed Jack out of the den.

The night was thick and quiet too. Every breath coated my lungs. As light-footed as I was, my boots still stirred the leaf litter. Jack moved through the dark like a shadow, black on black. If he got more than a few strides ahead, he'd vanish. I tried to stay quiet, to control my breathing, to step lightly, but as Jack moved farther ahead, his image flickering in and out of my vision, he finally did disappear, and panic started rattling my bones again. The woods felt too thick, like they breathed with me and around me, eager to bury me among the worms so Kensey would never find me. I knew how to entertain a hall full of monsters, surrounded by light and laughter, but this wasn't that. This was the world outside, and Jack was right—I hadn't lived it, hadn't really seen it. I wasn't prepared.

A child's laughter bubbled out of the dark, bright and careless and thoroughly *wrong*. Goosebumps spritzed across my skin. Something hunted me. My heart thumped, urging me to run, but running out here was always bad. I'd learned that with the phantom. The monsters didn't stop until their prey was dead, or they'd gotten whatever they wanted.

Damn Jack. Damn him to whatever hell vampires feared. He'd left me in the dark alone.

I kept moving forward over gnarled ankle-breaking roots. Fog seeped between ghostly trees, its wetness on my lips. Maybe it would hide me? I kept on moving. More steps, more clambering over uneven ground, trying not to make a sound, *not* to run.

Laughter to my left, far away. Farther away was good.

Then it sprang up close to my right, and the fog swirled, something moving inside it. Something close. Something hungry. Sweat slickened my grip on the knife.

"Hello." A girl appeared in front of me, dressed like the dolls my brother and I had found in one of the Night Station's many secret rooms. Tiny wooden things with overly large smiles and too many painted-on teeth. Kensey had sworn their glass-eyed stares had followed him. Then, when they'd started showing up around the station, we'd rammed them in a chest, padlocked it, and stuffed it down a laundry chute. We hadn't seen them again, but they were still down there… wherever that chute went. This girl had the same little blue dress, flared at the hips, and white pop socks. She did not belong here.

"It's polite to say hello back," she suggested, her voice as sweet and sickly as too much candy.

"Hello," I croaked. I had my knife out. The little-girl act wasn't fooling me. She was wrong on *every* level, and whatever she was, she probably wanted to devour me in some hideous way.

"Will you play with me?

Her image spluttered, like a lamp about to snuff out, and then she was closer, her outline swelling until she stood as tall as a man. Her mouth yawned. Her pink tongue lashed. Her pretty blue dress shimmered, turning to scales. And I knew what she was: a rakshasi, a shape-shifting flesh-eater.

She reached for me. I slashed wide, hoping to zip open something of her form enough to slow her down, but her claws grabbed my arms. Gnarled roots conspired around my boots, sending me sprawling. The rakshasi snapped at my neck. I shoved, writhed, and got a kick in, launching her backward.

I was on my feet and running, knowing I shouldn't. There were worse things than her here and they'd hear my retreat, but prey ran, and I was prey.

A snake the size of me slithered into my path and reared up, its jaws wide, fangs extended. The rakshasi. Its hiss surrounded me like a storm. My heart slowed, or time did. I skidded, trying to slow, but leaves and twigs upset my footing. I was on the ground again, scrabbling backward, with the enormous snake slithering toward me.

It reared up, my death in its serpentine eyes, and struck.

Heat sizzled up my arm, through my veins, and drove rods through my heart, delivering a shock of something *not me.* The knife flew from my hand and plunged into the creature's right eye. Its scream lit up the night, shattering the silence and sending out a beacon to every Dark One nearby to come and feast on the human who had dared hurt one of them.

I had the stake in my hand next. There were no thoughts, just movement, and fear, and strength. *So much strength.* I stood, distantly aware that this wasn't entirely under my control.

The rakshasi thrashed its head from side to side and then saw me. My knife was still lodged in its bleeding eye. Its hiss filled my ears and buzzed through my bones, and then it struck again. I thrust a hand up, jolting its jaw high, and thrust the stake into its scales.

The beast slumped forward, slamming into me, and for a terrible moment, as I lay beneath its weight, I thought it had pinned me down, and now it would eat me; every single inch of Lynher Aris would dissolve in its belly.

But it wasn't moving. And I was still breathing. Not dead. Not yet.

I shoved and heaved its mass of warm scales off me, rolled aside, then turned back to see if it might rise up and slither after me again. But it stayed still.

Had I killed it? Had I done that?

The station's mark on my arm sizzled, and as I pulled my sleeve back, its glowing edges settled back to their dormant state. It shouldn't have come alive out here—it only worked close to the station—but this had been different. I wasn't sure what it had done, but its remnants buzzed through my veins. I'd been so much stronger, brighter, fearless.

"Let's keep moving."

I jumped and twisted to find Jack watching, one hand casually braced against a tree.

He'd left me.

He'd gone.

Now he was back.

Bastard.

I snatched the knife from the rakshasi's eye and whirled, ready to fling it at his heart.

"Do that and you'll never find your way home."

He'd been watching the entire time. He could have killed the rakshasi with a flick of his wrist.

"Why didn't you help?" I pulled the stake free, wiped the congealing blood on the forest floor, and warily eyed the overseer.

"You had it in hand."

I'd been fighting *for my life.* At no point did I *have it in hand.* Tucking the stake home against my back and the knife in my pocket, I straightened up to him. He straightened too, and there we stood, eyeing each other. He was right—I couldn't get home without him—but if he would conveniently disappear every time something tried to eat me, I wouldn't get home at all. *"Why didn't you help?"*

His jaw worked, as though he were chewing over an answer, but instead of voicing it, he turned and started through the brush. "The railroad tracks are this way..."

I wanted to repeatedly stab my knife into his back until answers fell out. Throwing one last look back at the dead rakshasi, not quite believing I'd brought it down, I started after Jack.

"Keep up, Miss Aris," he called. "The road is long and the journey has just begun."

17

DAY

The tracks pierced the heart of the ruined buildings and swept out the other side, toward toothy mountains. The station was beyond those. And as we walked alongside the iron rails, the distance between us and home seemed too big to think on.

Once again, we talked little and Jack's limp became more pronounced as the sun arced through the sky. He wilted beneath its rays but stayed on the tracks with me instead of veering off into the never-ending forest. It cost him physically.

At dusk, he grunted something about going to feed and told me to continue walking on the tracks; apparently, the iron deterred most minor beasties, and the sky was still too light for anything bigger to come hunting.

He returned later with two dead rabbits, told me to sit on a fallen tree, and set about creating a campfire. I kicked off my boots and rubbed my feet while he worked. He cleared the ground, gathered kindling and moss, and lit the fire with a click of his fingers. I hadn't known vampires could do that kind of magic—or that anyone could spark a flame like that. I'd only managed it in the station because it listened to me and knew the click meant light. Out here, only darkness listened.

"Can all vampires do that?"

"No." He crafted a brace out of sticks and held his hand out. "The knife?" At my hesitance, he sighed. "Your rumbling stomach is driving me to distraction. You'll get the knife back once you've eaten."

I handed it over and again watched as he prepared the rabbits, stripping them of their fur and guts for roasting. For someone who only needed blood, he knew how to prepare his meat in other ways too.

Overseers were always different than most in the VG. Although obviously the queen's slaves, they could think for themselves. The queen wasn't omnipotent. She needed a hierarchy to control her vast army, and so she'd created vampires who thought and behaved more like individuals. Overseers. The only other overseer I'd met was the one from the farm, and while he too had seemed autonomous, Jack was on another level, one perhaps unique to him. Maybe it had something to do with all those tattoos?

The rabbit was delicious, and I was so ravenous I didn't care how Jack openly watched me eat.

"How well do you know your Etienne friend?" Jack asked when I was done with the meal. He'd propped himself on his side. The firelight stroked over his long limbs, warming all that darkness. He almost looked harmless again.

"I thought I knew him better than most." I sat across the fire from him, watching the vampire through flame and smoke.

Darkness and cold crept in. We were close enough to the tracks that Jack seemed content to stay the night, but I felt exposed. The trees alongside the tracks were thin, kept small by the trains thundering past. We hadn't seen any of the engines and carriages yet, but we would eventually.

"Was his locking you in the carriage with me out of character?" he asked.

I chuckled dryly. "Etienne would never... Well, I thought he wouldn't. He only recently began working with me, but I've known him for years." My brother had. I'd known of Etienne, but it was

Kensey who really knew him. Or we'd thought we'd known him. How had we both gotten it so wrong?

"You saw him close the door?"

I nodded.

"It was no mistake."

"He had a reason to do what he did. I just need to speak with him. As soon as we get back, I'll—"

"He knew the train's cargo and destination, yes?"

I nodded. "He overheard enough to put the pieces together."

Jack's fine eyes narrowed. "Then he believes you're dead."

And so would my brother. Oh Kensey… *Hold on. I'm coming home.* Without me, he might leave, or he might come looking for me, like he always had when I'd wandered off. But he had to know he'd never survive outside the station. He *had* to know that.

Jack watched my face, trying to decipher all the thoughts in my head.

"Did you tell him about the high-value cargo?"

I dropped my gaze to the fire. "He knew." Someone had gotten to him. It could only be the VG. What if Jack—the infamous *Ghost,* known for his cruelty and cunning—had convinced Etienne to lock me in? "Why was the train empty, Jack?"

"I don't know."

"Are you lying?"

"Why would I?"

"Maybe because you wanted me on that train. Maybe because I was your high-value cargo?"

Firelight warmed his smile. "You belong in that station. I wouldn't be so foolish as to remove you."

I didn't pretend to know what he meant. "How do I know you didn't orchestrate everything?"

"You witnessed our reception at the farm. They were not expecting us."

"They were not expecting me to hold a knife to your throat, no."

He laughed softly and touched his neck where my blade had kissed him. No mark remained, but the blade had cut. Did he remember how that had felt, to be cut by a bloodbag? "I was not due to be on that train," he admitted, and the laughter fell from his eyes, turning them dark again. "I wasn't due to be at your Night Station either, although I hear the resident VG learned of my arrival at the last moment."

"So why did you grace us with your presence?" I chanced, not expecting an answer.

"The same reason I'm returning."

"Sanctuary?"

He breathed in and sighed heavily. "Indeed."

"I know why most people need sanctuary, and it usually has something to do with the VG. So why does an overseer need sanctuary from his own people?"

He looked up, but there were no stars tonight, so what did he see in the darkness high above? "There's a big world outside your station, Miss Aris. A great many monsters, some worse than me." His smile had lost some of its luster, like he was trying to convince himself of his lies as well.

Monsters worse than him? If he was trying to make me feel sorry for him, it would never happen. "So if you weren't meant to be at my station, you weren't involved with the high-value cargo?"

"I knew of it. Such things are under my remit. I chose to use its arrival as cover for my travel arrangements. Felipe was—" He cut himself off, his gaze flicking to me.

"An asshole?"

He laughed, and a traitorous smile found its way onto my lips. Gods, he had a lovely laugh, the deep kind, too honest and true to be his. He must have stolen it from someone.

"He really was an arsehole," he said, his accent adding an *r*. "I'll not be mourning his loss."

While he'd played his games, I had bowed to that asshole, and would have done worse had it come to it. My next question came out hard too. "Do you care, Jack? About anything besides yourself?"

He kept smiling, his gaze on me, but both had sharpened. "What does my answer matter? You already believe you know everything about me. I am your villain, am I not? Your convenient source of all vampire crimes?"

"I know the truth, yes."

"Do you?" Light caught the silver in his eyes and highlighted his wooden smile.

"What is there to know? You're an overseer. You hunt and kill my kind. It's what you were made to do. You already admitted it. I don't need to know anything else about *Just Jack*."

"Such an enlightened life you live." Leaning back, he tucked a hand under his head and stared at the sky. "Gerome was quite the teacher. Did he bounce you on his knee while he told you all about the vampire scourge that tore through human lands?" He turned his head, and I saw how his smile had gained a new edge.

"You are not fit to speak his name."

"Gerome wasn't a saint, Lynher."

"Stop calling me Lynher. My name to the likes of you is Miss Aris. You didn't know Gerome. He was worth a thousand of *you*. You're little more than a grunt. Dress you up, make you walk and talk, but you're still a mindless drone like all the others."

"If I were a mindless drone, I'd have killed you in that carriage or a hundred times since then, as I suspect your friend Etienne planned when trapping us together—"

"So, you have some free will? Just enough to make you think you're in control. When you die, and you will die, *Jack*, a hundred others will be waiting to take your place. You really are a ghost, because nothing and nobody cares about you. You don't even have a proper name—"

He leaped to his feet, and I had my knife out in the next breath, but he wasn't focused on me. Head tipped skyward, he asked, "Did you hear that?"

I couldn't hear a damn thing over my racing heart.

Jack kicked leaf litter and dirt over the fire, grabbed my free hand, and pulled me into a run, down the bank and into the spindly tree cover.

I heard it then, a sound like a heartbeat but a thousand times bigger, coming from *above*.

Trees sprang up all around, looming out of the dark. We tore through them and burst out onto an area of flat land. Dry ground crunched and cracked under my boots. Jack yanked, almost pulling me off my feet, and whirled, snatching the knife from my hand so fast my fingers burned. He shoved me back, yelling, "Run!" and dashed toward the noise.

I saw something then, but struggled to understand *what*. Its size, hanging in the dark sky, was almost too big to comprehend, with two enormous sheets stirring the night either side of its bulk. *Wings*. So big, with trailing, tattered edges and hooked hinges.

The creature opened its maw and *roared*.

The wyvern.

The VG had let it off its leash.

And Jack was running *toward* it, seeming ridiculously small in its shadow.

The wyvern wasn't watching him. Its red-eyed glare had fixed on me.

My carved stake wouldn't cut it.

I twisted on my heels and bolted, head down, legs pumping. There was no cover, just shadow upon shadow in every direction. Jack had pulled me into a killing field.

That bastard.

Every damn time… He really was using me as bait.

The wyvern roared so close and so loud overhead that I stumbled and clutched my hands over my ears to keep my skull in one piece. It sailed past, whipping up a storm of dust beneath its wings, and then banked ahead, coming around for a second go.

Oh gods, there was nowhere to hide, and I couldn't outrun it.

I slowed to a jog and then a complete stop and looked the wyvern in its mean eyes, *recognizing* it. It didn't think or reason; it had been created to end old towns, and it wasn't even of this world. The mark on my arm sizzled to life, but what good would that do me? I'd burn its tongue while it swallowed me whole?

Lower, it sailed.

Faster.

Its jaws opened.

Its eyes burned.

Then my knife flashed overhead. So tiny a thing, but it struck true, popping the creature's right eye. But instead of pulling up, the wyvern's head dropped. Its chin snagged the ground, pulling it out of the air, and then it was rolling, wings flailing, coming in like a mountain about to tumble right over me.

A wrecking ball slammed into my left side, swiping me off my feet and driving me into the ground. I knew it was Jack when he tucked me into his chest the same way he had when we'd gone over the cliff. He smelled warm and welcoming, like an open fire, and as the tumbling beast thundered nearer, I clutched him as hard as he clutched me, buried my face against his shoulder, and held on.

Like before, when the wyvern had flipped the car, there wasn't any discernible noise or sensation, just a terrible assault of thunder and pain and dust. The ground shuddered like it was coming apart, and then it was over. I panted, wrapped in Jack's arms and not caring.

He lifted his head and looked to my left, his jaw flexing. Dust and grit rained from his hair onto my face. I coughed, and he looked down, his eyes widening as though he were surprised to find me alive beneath him.

I coughed and croaked. "Is it dead?"

"It's down…"

The wyvern let out a gods-awful whine that spurred Jack into motion again. He pulled me off the ground and into a run. I looked back to see the creature thrashing about, clawing its own eye out.

"There… goes… my… knife," I said, between breaths.

Jack snorted, the sound combining with the memory of Jack twice tucking me in close, not to kill but to keep safe.

18

DAY

Jack stood between the tracks, staring into the enormous tunnel mouth.

There was no light at the end of it, just complete darkness.

If I went in there, I wasn't coming out.

"We'll go around," I said.

"There is no going around, unless you want to take a week's detour in minus twenty temperatures."

The tunnel burrowed through the mountains. I didn't really want to climb the snow-capped peaks either, but that wall of black would eat me, just like everything else out here.

Jack held out his hand.

Was he expecting me to take it?

He looked up. His bangs fell over his eyes while the rest of the messy locks fell about his cheeks. His shirt had lost a few buttons and his once perfectly pressed black pants had grayed, edges frayed.

"Take my hand. I'll walk you through it," he said, like having a vampire escort you into a dark hole in the ground was perfectly reasonable.

"It's fine..." I rolled my shoulders and started forward, plunging into the dark. Immediately, the chilled air sank beneath my skin and sucked out all my warmth. I'd gotten deep inside the dark soup before stumbling over a railroad tie. At least, I hoped it was just a railroad tie. It was so dark I could have been walking over dead bodies without knowing it.

Jack's fingers claimed mine. His were surprisingly warm.

"How long after this?" I'd spoken quietly, but my voice still barreled ahead in an endless echo. We wouldn't be sneaking past anything living in here.

"Three days. We're making good time."

I lifted my free hand and could barely see it in front of my face. Jack walked confidently beside me, his vampire eyes adapted for complete darkness. They'd lived in it once, before deciding our world better suited them.

I stumbled again and swore. I didn't hear Jack laugh, but I could hear his smug smile in his silence.

"You don't have long to save your demon friend's soul," he said, dropping that bombshell at my feet.

"Why do you care?" It came out harsh, even for me.

"I don't, not about him."

"Right, so why bring it up?" He was trying to distract me from the fact I was drowning in darkness. I'd take it.

"Do you know how to help him?" he asked.

"No," I admitted. "I was getting close, but I thought I had more time... and then Etienne happened, and here we are." I wouldn't be able to save Rafe. He'd be stuck as soulless. It hadn't been my fault. If anyone was to blame, it was Lilith, but she wouldn't fix him. To think he'd be a cold, heartless bastard for the rest of his very long life when I knew how he'd been very different before... it hurt inside, like many things hurt inside lately.

"I can help you," Jack said.

I walked on, his warm hand in mine. In the dark, there was nothing else to see or feel or even hear, just my thudding heart and our footfalls. "Why?"

"Must I have a reason?"

It mattered, because I'd owe him, if he helped me. "Always." I waited, but with no answer forthcoming, I sighed. "How then?"

"You must summon both the phantom and the demon into the same summoning circle. The demon summoning is easy enough, but once inside, the incubus will have to perform a similar summoning to pull the phantom to him. Only Raphael can reclaim his soul, if the incubus is strong enough."

That didn't sound so bad. Rafe was a brawler. I'd once seen him knock a vampire twice his weight on his ass with two punches. He'd used his tail to poke him in the eye first, but even so, Rafe had floored him in less than a second. But Rafe had been angling for a fight back then. Now, soulless, he'd told me there was nothing wrong with him. Would he fight for a soul he believed he didn't want? "The books said it had to happen within a few days of him losing his soul. It's already been that long."

"The summoning must happen before the phantom feeds again. As there's little for them to feed on around the station, his soul should be safe for a while."

That didn't change the fact that, to get home, we still needed to get through this tunnel, whatever lay beyond, and the phantom-infested barrens.

"Why help me, Jack?"

"I assume you care for him."

"No, yes, but I mean, why are you saying this?" His hand still wrapped mine in warmth, and it felt… right, in all the wrong ways. I knew I should push him away. I could get through this tunnel without him, although it would take longer. I shouldn't want to feel his touch, should I? Just knowing he was here chased away my fear of being alone in a big wide world I had no experience in.

"Lilith is a powerful ally," he finally answered. He wanted to help Rafe so he could get Lilith on his side.

"Yeah, except maybe she doesn't want him restored…"

"Why wouldn't she—ah—" he cut himself off.

"Ah?" I frowned. "What does 'ah' mean?"

A metallic twang rang ahead, like a distant bell chiming, growing louder and louder.

"Ah," Jack said.

"Ah again?"

"I was concerned this might happen."

"What—" The chime pinged through the tracks and traveled on behind us. "Ah," I said. A train. Of course it was.

And I couldn't see either exit.

"It's fine." He drew me to one side. "Press close against this wall." He lifted my hand, pressed it against cold brick, then held it there.

It wasn't fine. These trains were huge and loud and hot and would fill this tunnel, boiling the air with steam. Jack would think it was fine. He didn't need to breathe.

"We should have gone over the top," I muttered.

The light came first, a growing pinprick in the distance. The tracks twanged and hummed, signaling imminent danger. Brighter, the light glowed. I couldn't hear the engine yet, but soon it would be screaming.

Light filled the tunnel with shades of gray, bleaching Jack's frown. He stared up the tracks. Fine, my ass. His face was pinched with worry. He saw me looking and frowned harder. The train's whistle screamed. I yanked my hand from under his.

Distant thunder rumbled the air. It wouldn't be a quaint puffing train. They never were. More high-value cargo, maybe, and this time, I'd be a single step from its huge wheels.

I pressed my back against the wall and spread my hands to hold myself in place. I'd have preferred to face the rakshasi again.

"Lynher..." He had to say it loud with the engine rumbling closer.

"Will you stop calling me that." I looked away from the light and up at Jack. The light turned him ghostly, but his eyes shone. Even now, with his lips set in a grim line, his expression locked, he had *something*, and I felt that same powerful pull from him, like he could absorb all the light and noise and make it disappear out of sheer will. But as the engine thundered and the tracks jumped, there would be no vanishing this iron beast. We just had to get through it.

His hand found mine again, and I let it.

A hot wave of wind pushed ahead of the train. My hair lashed around my face. I couldn't look. Not anymore. The noise was too much. I squeezed my eyes closed, my heart thumping against my ribs. The whistle screamed again.

When the train launched past, it tried to rip me from the wall and throw me under its wheels. The wind pulled at my body, its fingers digging in, hoping to dislodge me. I couldn't breathe, and when I did, steam sizzled my tongue. Jack's arm, pinned across my chest, held me to the wall. On and on the wheels raced by, then the carriages clattered, their hinges clanging and moaning, and then it was over. The wind rushed out, dragging with it the steam and dust.

I gasped.

It was over.

A tingling shiver ran down my spine.

Gods, what a rush.

Jack's arm opened, letting me step forward. I slumped over and panted hard, bracing my hands against my thighs. "Damn…"

The train was fast dragging the light away, and when Jack didn't say anything, I looked up. His smudged gray outline slid down the wall and slumped on its ass.

"Jack?"

He wasn't moving. I reached for his shoulder, managed to find it, and stroked upward to his neck. His skin burned hot beneath my fingertips.

"Jack? What's wrong?" I traveled my fingers higher to his jaw and cupped his face. Was he out cold? Was he hurt? I couldn't see enough to know. Why wasn't he answering? "Wake up."

I roamed my other hand up his hard chest, feeling for a sign of life. I couldn't feel a heartbeat or hear him breathing, but I was doing enough of that for the both of us. "Dammit, Jack, you prick… You can't leave me here."

He gasped.

His hand locked on my wrist, holding my hand off his chest. "*Lynher…*" he growled.

In the dark, his eyes threw their silvery glow, and between one moment and the next, the ruthless, blood-hungry thing he was inside peered out from behind his gaze. Then he blinked, and it was gone, along with their strange shine.

"What happened? Are you hurt?"

"Nothing… No, I'm… " He audibly swallowed. "She knows."

"She?"

He looked down, saw how he had my wrist trapped, and let go so suddenly I rocked backward.

"We need to hurry." He was up and moving and gone, leaving me to scrabble around in the dark, following the tunnel wall so I didn't turn myself around and head out the wrong way. He found my hand again, but the touch wasn't nearly as soft or warm as before. He pulled me along, barely letting me get my feet under me. "Hurry or I'll carry you out of here."

"I'll shove my stake in your heart before I let you carry me anywhere."

When we made it out the tunnel, dusk had the sky bleeding red. Jack freed my hand and marched on between the tracks, his limp awkward again. "Keep up!"

I was hungry, tired, and thirsty, but I wouldn't be the one slowing us down. The station was a few days away. We'd make it, even though the *she* Jack had mentioned had realized her overseer wasn't where he was supposed to be. It had to be the queen. Who else could render him so useless? Who else could make him afraid? And who else would he be running from, if not the only monster worse than him?

19

NIGHT

Something was wrong with Jack. More wrong than normal. He'd stumbled a few times in the last hour. Every dusk on this journey, he'd gone off to feed, but not tonight. Tonight we weren't stopping, and it showed in Jack's weariness, but he wasn't the only exhausted one.

Blisters burned my feet, I staggered too often, and my belly had turned to knots trying to eat itself. I needed rest, fresh water, and another rabbit wouldn't go amiss, but Jack hadn't replied when I'd asked him to stop, and now it was night, and we were both weak, resulting in a whole lot of stupid.

Jack stumbled and fell to his knees, muttering a curse. I circled in front of him, planted my hands on my hips, and stared him into looking up. "We rest."

"Can't." He gritted his teeth and pulled on his leg, trying to make it work again. My wretched human heart did a little sympathetic flip, and rolling my eyes, I offered my hand.

"She'll find us," he said, grasping my hand and allowing me to pull him back onto his feet. He tried to straighten his wrinkled and stained shirt cuffs, like he thought he could put all of his pieces together and recreate that impeccably dressed gentleman act. That ship had sailed. I knew I looked like shit, but he looked like death. His cheeks had hollowed and his hazel eyes had grown hard and metallic. If he smiled, I'd probably see fangs.

"If *anything* finds us, we're as good as dead," I said. "There was an old building back there." I nodded back the way we'd trudged. "We should rest up inside for the night."

He was still fixated on his cuffs, trying to make the fabric lie correctly against his wrist, probably so I wouldn't see the tight lines around his eyes. He was in pain. Had he been human, he'd have been panting and sweating, but now he was suffering; all that human nonsense was just baggage he'd discarded along the way. The more vampiric he looked, the more he was hurting.

Maybe I should leave him for "her."

The station couldn't have been much farther. I peered into the dark, *sensing* home was close. If I stuck to the tracks and stayed quiet, I'd make it.

"Miss Aris?" Jack said. "You are the hostess, are you not?" He'd found his overseer tone again, and even as pale as the ghost he pretended to be, he lifted his chin and found some typical VG haughtiness. "Gerome taught you to care for everyone, even those you despise. So help me."

How many humans had reached out to him, begging for help? How many had he slapped down? How many orphaned children had he sent to the farms? And he had the nerve to plead for *my* help. A human. It must have cost him a great deal of pride to ask.

I should leave him to die. Something out here probably ate vampires. Or maybe his queen would find him in the dirt. It was all he deserved.

Kensey wouldn't leave him. Even knowing everything Jack had done, Kensey never turned anyone away. "Anyone can be saved," he'd told me once. Gods, my brother was too damn good for this world.

"Go then," he grunted, tugging at his leg and hobbling forward. "But stay on the tracks. The iron will keep you safe from most things."

I sighed at his back, swore under my breath, and grabbed his arm. "*Gods and spices*, we're going back to the shed. Don't argue or I will leave you. I should leave you..."

He leaned close, trying to maintain some dignity as we stumbled back along the path. I'd been up close and personal with Jack too many times, but this was the first time I'd felt him tremble. Part of me enjoyed seeing him weak, but a smaller part, the softer part, found the change alarming. If something like Ghost was afraid of the queen, the rest of us had no chance against her. If she was really coming, how could I stop that?

We hobbled back to the shed, half hidden in the undergrowth. It was easily missed and made for good cover at night. I rested Jack against the wall on one side and crouched against the opposite, watching him rub his leg.

"You should leave," he said sometime later. "Why haven't you?" He'd pulled his coat closed but shivered anyway. It wasn't the cold making him shiver; he didn't feel it. It wasn't the pain from his leg either. Something *inside* was making him sick, and it had started after he'd blacked out in the tunnel.

"Your queen is doing this to you from a thousand miles away. She's in your head, right?"

He nodded tightly and rested his head against the wall. His eyes fluttered closed. "It's a little more complicated than that, but simply put, yes, she's in my head."

"Can't you... stop it somehow? Block her out?"

He either smiled or winced. In the shadows, I couldn't tell which. "No."

He was resisting her. I hadn't known such a thing was possible. Did resisting his queen make him different? Gerome had told me the vampires were all the same at their core. They knew nothing beyond their service to the queen. Drones were the most obvious example of the control she exerted, and although more *human* in appearance, Jack had the same genetic design.

"Why run?" I whispered.

His expression twitched. "Have you never wanted to see outside your prison?"

"I'm not in a prison."

Now he definitely smiled. Bastard. "You should leave me. Why haven't you?"

"Because you want me to." Maybe staying with him was stupid, but vampires didn't send their prey off with no hope of chasing them down. And the times he'd saved me…? Maybe those times had been to get back to the station, but not this time. He was sick, and he'd told me to leave, even though we both knew he could kill me, drink my body dry, and make himself right as rain by morning. The only possible explanation was that Jack cared that I kept on breathing.

"Why do you think the station will keep you safe?" I asked.

He opened his eyes and lowered his gaze. "It is my *only* sanctuary, Lynher Aris. My first and last hope." He paused, his glare fixed on mine, mining it for something I couldn't fathom. "I don't expect you to understand. You understand so little. That is Gerome's legacy."

"How well did you know Gerome?"

"Well enough." He grimaced. "You are like him. Every night you lie and manipulate with that silver tongue of yours. Gerome was a master of the dance."

He spoke of someone I didn't recognize. The Gerome I knew was kind and true and good, like Kensey.

"I don't trust you," Jack added. "I watched you at the station, before all this, from the moment we met on that platform and you strode through a crowd of vampires like you had all the power in the worlds. You wrap the Dark Ones around your little finger. They believe you work for them, but you have them all working for you, and none of them see it. You're human, and you hide behind that weakness, turning it into a strength. You, Miss Aris, are unsettling. I've only met one other like you, and she's currently in my head, demanding my return."

I swallowed, not knowing what to say. For one, the way he'd described what I did made it sound brilliant. And I was damn proud of that. Gerome had taught me well. But he was a Dark One too, and to hear him spill my secrets so easily reminded me that he knew too much. Ghost was dangerous. And he would die as soon as he got back. He had to, for the sake of the station.

He shivered and hugged himself harder, gritting his teeth.

"What's it like?" I asked quietly.

"Like my mind is glass, and she's shattering it, piece by piece." He gave his head a tight shake. "I am irrevocably tied to her. It is the way of all vampires."

"Why fight her?"

"Because the alternative," he hissed, "is worse."

I shouldn't care.

And I didn't.

Straightening my legs next to his, I folded my arms and watched him mentally battle the unseen. His suffering should have been cathartic. He surely deserved it. And yet…

"How many people have you killed?" I asked.

His eyes remained closed as he replied, "You keep asking as though you expect the answer to change. The answer never changes. The numbers are countless, and I will kill again, because it is what I am."

"And you've never saved anyone? Not a single soul?"

Lashes fluttering, he fixed his gaze on me. "Not until you."

"We aren't saved yet, are we. And let's not pretend you're saving me for any reason other than to get you into the station."

His lips lifted at their corners. "I don't need you to get into the station, Lynher."

So arrogant. Even weak, he believed the worlds revolved around him. "It won't give you sanctuary without me."

Opening his folded arms, he pulled up a sleeve to reveal his wrist. In the dark, his tattoos looked like thorned ropes binding him, and now that I knew about his queen, I wondered if she had put those marks there, like shackles. Apparently, I was supposed to see something in those swirls, so I looked closer. Tilting my head and leaning forward, a different smudge caught my eye, this one hidden beneath the more solid lines of ink. It was faded, barely there at all, but I couldn't unsee it.

"That's not possible." I grabbed his shivering arm, yanked his sleeve higher, and pulled his wrist closer. An embellished x. Just like mine. There was no mistaking it.

"You should know by now, Lynher Aris, anything is possible at the Night Station," he said, slyly.

He was marked.

He truly didn't need me to secure sanctuary. He already had it.

My library office *had* opened for him because he was part of the station too.

The mass-murdering vampire known only as Ghost was under *my* protection?

"How?" I hissed.

He was closer and looking at me with his half smile, the one I wanted to rip from his lips. That smug smile, the delight in his eyes, he was suffering but loving this moment.

The station hadn't always saved good people, but it knew what Kensey and I tried to do, how we tried to save people from the likes of Jack, and it had always supported Gerome and our work. Why risk it all by inviting Jack inside?

I dropped his arm and scuttled back, hugging my legs to keep myself as far from his reach as possible. "I don't believe it."

"I didn't think you would," he whispered, resting back and pulling his coat closed again. "You have your little white lines, Lynher, and gods forbid anything or anyone dare cross them." His voice trailed off, his mind drifting into sleep, or whatever the vampire equivalent was.

I stared at him, trying to unravel the mystery of Jack, of Ghost, of the overseer with no name who I was supposed to keep safe. I'd never questioned the station before. Now I questioned everything.

DAY

A sheen of perspiration shimmered over Jack's pale skin, and his eyes had lost their shine. But staying in the shed was not an option. He again told me to leave, even as I scooped him up and lay his arm around my shoulders. Leaving him wasn't an option either. He knew too much. If his queen found him, or one of the VG did, the entire station would be compromised. Mark be damned, I was fixing this and him.

So we limped along the tracks. The day was clear, sunlight pouring down. Jack sagged more with every step.

The station was close.

We could do this.

Kensey wouldn't quit. I'd never quit in my life. I wouldn't start now.

The tracks snaked through the land, and we followed, dipping down into the brush to shelter from the sun. My throat was parched and the blisters on my feet had blisters. None of that would get any better anytime soon. The only way to save us was to keep moving forward, one step at a time.

When Jack fell for the fourth time, we crumpled among an oak's twisted roots, and this time, Jack wasn't getting back up. He'd fallen awkwardly on his side, his head resting on an ancient root, eyes open but unseeing. I hated him for his weakness, hated him for everything he'd done to my people, hated him for what he was and for *this*. And I hated that I was supposed to help him.

"Your queen is a bitch for doing this. Why couldn't she torture you once we'd gotten back, huh?" I swept his hair back from his cheek to look at his face and see if he'd heard. His lips ticked. "This is stupid. Why do this to you? What good are you to her if you're a wreck?"

"Survival of the fittest," he rasped.

She'd rather he die than return weak.

I hated her too. Everyone hated her, but she'd never featured in my life until now. Gerome had told me that she was like a vast breeding machine, constantly birthing new vampires, like a hideous fat ant in her throbbing nest of vampires. Her breeders tended to her every need while her body made more of them. The very idea of her made me want to retch up the nothing in my gut.

I fell against the oak beside Jack and looked up. Leaves fluttered, dappling the sunlight. Normally, I'd have enjoyed the daylight. Before these last few days, I could have counted on one hand the times I'd felt sunlight on my face.

"How long?" I asked, pulling my knees close to my chest.

"Another night, perhaps," he said. His lips were cracked and white. Vampires didn't die like normal people. They dried up, turning pale first. Then their skin shrunk around their bones, and eventually, they just stopped before turning to dust. It was a wretched way to go, and one I'd always thought fitting, but as I watched it happen in slow-motion to Jack, I found it inconvenient. If he'd just hurry up and die, I could at least leave him.

I still had my stake.

Taking the weapon from its place against my back, I twirled the point against my finger. It wasn't as sharp as before. Rakshasi blood stained the point, but it would kill a vampire if struck home, straight through the heart. I just had to punch it in real hard. Right now, Jack didn't look as though he could fight back.

He pretended to breathe, so he was strong enough for some bullshit. If I staked him correctly, it would be quick. A mercy, really.

I tightened my fingers around the stake, getting a good hold. The angle was awkward, with him on his side and me upright, coming in from his left. Really, for maximum impact, I should strike from the front and hope I didn't hit a rib.

"We should move on—" He got his hands under him and tried to push up

I had my opening.

A mercy.

Necessary.

For the station and all the lives I protected within it.

I was reaching for his shoulder before I could talk myself out of it. My fingers sank in. I gripped and thrust the stake forward.

Light and heat flared between us. My mark sang, seeking to protect me like it had with the rakshasi, but then a sudden, vicious stab of pain snapped up my arm, snatching control of my body and sending me reeling away.

Fiery agony lashed and hissed.

Gods, what!

It hadn't been my mark protecting me; it had been his protecting *him*.

Shock buzzed through me. My ears rang. Then Jack slammed into me, knocking me onto my back. He straddled my thighs, one hand pinned at my waist, the other holding my wrist back, keeping the stake at bay. I saw his eyes then, saw the infinite sea of power behind them, and something else inside, something hungry and dark and full of want and need, like he could swallow the entire world and not be satisfied.

He struck.

Pain flashed and died, killed by the venom infecting my veins. His cracked lips sealed over the bite. His jaw moved, coaxing *my* blood over his tongue and down his throat. It didn't hurt. My vision bloomed, all the colors of the day blurring into blues and oranges, and it all felt so perfectly fucking wonderful. I wasn't hungry anymore. And the sores on my feet had vanished. I could lie right here, in Jack's arms, and never leave. Inside, I screamed in silence. But his venom had snuffed out my voice too.

He stole my life gulp by gulp.

It was always going to end this way, so why fight it? I had a hold of his shoulder with my free hand and tightened my grip, wanting more of this peaceful bliss, wanting more of him pressed against me. He'd held me in his arms, folded me close to keep me safe, but this was different. This was better. His murderous embrace felt like coming home.

20

NIGHT

Lynher…? Gods… why…?"

An urgent, angry voice dragged me from the warm, quiet place, and as the familiar stranger muttered and swore, blaming me, a tingling spilled life back into muscle and bone. Then the aches returned, and my stomach growled, or maybe that was Jack who'd growled.

He shoved the stake in my face. "I'm taking this!"

Tucking the stake into his coat pocket, he started pacing and running his hands through his messy hair. Considering all the leaves turned over at his feet, he'd been pacing a while. He looked better. I, on the other hand, felt like I'd been turned inside out—again.

I groped at the numb patch on my neck, sweeping away cool, congealing blood. "You… bit me."

He growled a frustrated sound, striding back and forth, his leg better, thanks to *my blood*. "You *leech*."

I sounded like I'd leaned too hard on the whiskey. But the warm, fuzzy feeling in my head was all Jack's doing. I should have been angrier. It was there, a ball of hissing, spitting rage, but the venom had dammed it behind the afterglow. His venom was *inside* me. Once it wore off, I would kill him this time. Properly.

"We need to move," he snapped, grimacing down at me like this was my fault.

Screw him and this. I rolled onto my side, waited for the forest to stop spinning, and got my knees under me enough to kneel. Standing was next. Just… after the trees stopped swaying.

"You bit me." I was on my feet, and then Jack was in front of me, a tall and exceedingly handsome barrier I needed to push through. With his tilted lips, all warm and pink, and his hazel eyes, so human and bright and trying to burrow inside and make me *feel* for him. He looked *good*, like maybe he could wrap me in his arms again and hold me tight like nobody had in *so long.* Gods, no. "Get out of my head, vampire!"

His lip curled. "The venom will wear off."

"Fuck. You." I tried to shove him, but he neatly stepped aside, almost sending me reeling again. I stumbled into a walk instead and stared forward, hopefully heading in the right direction.

"You tried to kill me," he said, circling in front to block my path with all his frustratingly delicious maleness.

I pulled up short and huffed through my nose. "No, I didn't…" Had I? Oh right, I had.

"I *told you* I'd retaliate. You can't attack a vampire and expect it not to react. Did Gerome teach you nothing? You're lucky I'm… I had enough control to stop, else you'd be dead and I'd be well-fucking-fed." His gaze dropped to my neck, and he swallowed, probably remembering what it had felt like having me crushed beneath him, his fangs in my throat.

Gods, he was hot when he was angry, and now that he'd lost all that half-dead grayness, his snarl made me want to sink my fingers into his hair and rip a kiss from his lips—that was the venom talking.

"You *deserve* it," I slurred and reached to grab the stake from him. He swatted my hand away, then, changing his mind, snatched at my fingers and pulled me along.

"We have to move."

I yanked free again, spluttering, "Grab me again and you'll discover my knee in your nuts. Maybe then you'll wish your bitch queen had gelded you."

I was mostly certain all those words had arrived in the correct order.

"We don't have time for this!" he snapped back, all fired up on my blood. "I will throw you over my shoulder if I must."

"You will do *no such thing*." I pointed, my finger all I had to threaten him with. "I am done with you. Done! I'm going home to my people, and if there's any justice in this world, your queen will find you and do whatever it is you're so afraid of, because it's all you deserve." I turned around and stomped ahead, hopefully in the general direction of our destination. It didn't matter. I couldn't spend another second in the same space as him.

"Listen to me."

Nope. Wasn't doing that.

"Caine marked you."

I stopped, cleared my throat, felt my heart thudding too fast, still trying to filter out the venom, and turned back. "What?"

He rubbed the back of his neck, his fingers massaging out an ache instead of manhandling me. "Caine knows where you are."

"Caine?" The horrible one. The one who had eyed me up like his personal piñata. The one who had bitten first and almost killed me.

"Your blood... The taste..." He ran his thumb along his bottom lip. The tip of his tongue traced the same path. "You're claimed, which means you can't outrun him or walk away. He'll find you."

That was definitely very bad and I should have been afraid, but seeing as I was all drugged up, emotions would have to come later. "Then why hasn't he found us already?"

"Because you're walking right back to him... at the station."

"Can't you just"—I waved a hand—"do your thing and order him to stand down?"

He laughed like I was a damn fool. "My position as overseer has been *revoked*."

Oh gods, why did everything have to be so hard? *"Caine doesn't know that."*

"By now, he does. They all do."

"How?" Was there a VG super-fast telegram I didn't know about? Did they still have electronic communications?

"It's… complicated."

"Then lie," I said, squaring up to him. "You're so good at pretending to be something you're not that he'll never know."

His nostrils flared, and the pretty smiles and kind-eyed act fell away, revealing the cold, hard overseer he truly was. "Do you even hear yourself?" he hissed. "You live a lie. With every breath, you believe you're a *human savior*, and all you're doing is delaying the inevitable. You and your brother—you don't make a difference. You save a few hundred a year. The farms kill that a day. You're a silly woman in an elaborate dress, playing with predators. You think I'm pretending? Take a look at yourself, Lynher Aris. You have no idea what's going on around you, but you could… if you'd open your eyes."

I wanted to hit back, to swear at him, call him a leech again, but his words—so close to my own—had pulled the fight right out of me. Because he was right. It was pointless. I wasn't even saving them for them; I was saving them for Kensey, because he needed a cause. He needed hope, but I knew it was all lies. I lived in the dark. There was no winning this war. There was no resistance in far-off continents. There was just one station, one beacon in a whole world of darkness, and outside its walls, I was as much a tool as Jack was.

Jack sighed through his nose and lifted his face to the sky, muttering words I didn't catch. "Lynher… just… come with me." He held out a hand. The same hand that had pinned me down while he'd *fed on me.*

The venom must have been wearing off, because tears swam in my vision, and I hated them too. "*You. Bit. Me.*"

He swore and dropped his hand. "I didn't kill you."

"So I'm supposed to be grateful!"

He grabbed for me, like I was a doll he could throw around. I recoiled and stepped around him, marching ahead. "This way?"

"Yes." The sound of his steps followed behind.

The tracks soon reappeared through the brush as the sun set, spilling bloodred rays across the sky. I walked on, his venom leaving me colder with every step. Why had the station chosen him? And when? It wasn't right. It wasn't fair. It mocked everything Kensey tried to do. Gerome would have known; he'd have had all the answers by now.

Night stole all the heat from the air, but I was still too angry to care. Jack kept my pace, staying in the corner of my peripheral vision. Was his queen still hunting him, or had my blood made that go away too? I didn't care. Once we were back at the station, I'd deal with him, like I'd deal with Etienne and anyone else who considered me weak. Screw them all. This little fish was poisonous.

The tracks funneled farther into the dark. I walked and walked and walked, the railroad ties passing beneath my boots in time with my heartbeat, until a band of brilliant twinkling lights blazed in the distance. The Night Station. I sobbed in relief.

Jack's arm blocked my path, jolting me to a halt. "Look..."

A silhouette darkened the tracks. A shadow, really, but not a phantom. This figure was solid.

Caine. I could *feel* him, his charm, like a thousand spiders scurrying across my skin, trying to find a way *inside*.

A burbling growl rumbled through Jack. He handed over the stake—"Please refrain from using it on me"—and walked ahead. The starless night painted him and Caine in shades of black. They didn't look so different in the dark.

Hopefully, they'd kill each other.

While they worked on that, I'd be back at the station. I dropped down the side of the tracks and cut through the brush, catching glimpses of the pair of vampires through bare branches. Physically, they appeared evenly matched, neither one heavier nor bigger. I almost wished I could stay and watch them throw down, but with sanctuary so close, I wasn't risking a delay.

"Almost home," I whispered to the station, sensing its protection extending toward me, eager to embrace me. I'd get inside, clean the blood and dirt off, and wear whatever the station had in the closet, rebuilding my armor, and then I'd seek out Etienne. Had it been day, I'd have gone straight to Kensey, but the risk was too great. Night was my territory and my strength. I was so ready to climb back into the role of hostess and forget this nightmare had ever happened.

"It took you long enough to bring her back," Caine chuckled, his voice carrying in the quiet.

What?

Caine had known Jack had me?

Didn't matter.

Jack limped to a stop in front of Caine. He'd emphasized the limp, pretending to appear weaker than he was, reminding me how nothing about Just Jack was real.

I wove around patches of brush, each footfall carefully placed. Caine probably knew where I was, but I was relying on Jack to keep him and anything else out here occupied. The station was so close, I could almost taste its cinnamon and citrus air.

"Are the preparations complete?" Jack asked.

What preparations? Didn't matter…

"Etienne is… difficult," Caine replied.

"The fae always are."

A twig snapped under my heel. I froze, holding my breath. Fae? What did they mean? And why were they talking about Etienne? Unless…

Could Jack have orchestrated the kidnapping? Had he made Etienne lock me inside the carriage with him? No, none of that made sense. Having me gone only to return me again was a pointless exercise. Unless they had wanted me out of the way for… something.

I squinted into the shining station lights.

So close…

Once back inside the station, I'd be strong again.

The vampires had fallen quiet.

The sound of my thudding heart filled my ears.

A glance over my shoulder revealed the vampires were no longer where I'd expected them to be. They weren't on the tracks—or *anywhere*.

My heart picked up its thudding.

They weren't fighting because Jack was working *with* Caine. They wanted me gone to get to Etienne, to prepare for something…

The queen?

Oh no… no, no, no…

Gods and spices.

That fanged bastard. Telling me to leave him…. Keeping me safe… He didn't need me to get inside the station; he'd needed me out of it, leaving it unprotected. Bringing me back home was a part of that.

I still had the stake. I clenched it tighter. It wasn't much, but I'd killed a rakshasi with it.

The station lights twinkled.

Bushes rustled behind on my right.

Run, my instincts demanded. Ice trickled down my spine.

Running never worked out well.

The vampires didn't want me dead, or they'd have killed me by now.

I drew in a breath, lifted my head, stepped from the brush, then kept right on walking like it was broad daylight and nothing in the dark could touch me.

Jack wanted me alive. He'd told me as much. He wouldn't hurt me now, or let anything else do so.

"Come out, come out, wherever you are…" I whispered. Plenty of other creatures lurked in the dark around the station. Every night, they watched through the bright station windows, eyes full of envy. They knew me. For decades, they'd coveted sanctuary and my and Gerome's role in it. And here I was, in their space… ripe for the picking.

Bushes rustled on both sides of the tracks. I didn't think phantoms rustled anything, so whatever it was, it had a physical form. That narrowed it down to a few hundred possible human-eating nasties. Good. Let them come.

I wouldn't run.

The lights were closer, throbbing and flickering. I fancied I could hear twinkling laughter from inside. There were a hundred different species of Dark Ones inside those walls too, all with teeth and minds just as sharp.

I had to keep walking.

My heart pounded like a beacon to vampires.

Distantly, something howled. The sound rolled on and on across the empty land.

My blood raced, urging me to run and close that last fleeting distance.

But all the hungry things watching me from the dark were waiting for exactly that.

I was Lynher Aris. Nothing would stop me from walking back through those station doors. "You can't have me," I told the dark.

The unmistakable sound of a phantom screamed to my left, coming in fast.

"Come at me, then," I seethed, keeping my head up and my eyes locked on the station.

I could make out the beautiful figures on the platform. Women in frills and lace. Men in patterned silk and polished shoes. The breeze whispered me closer, sprinkling a taste of magic in the air.

The phantom flew in, a wave of black liquid hissing over the tracks, but it didn't reach me. Jack appeared, his forearms crossed, his station mark blazing.

"Back!" he yelled.

The phantom whirled around itself, spiraling like oil down a drain.

I walked on, *around* Jack.

More phantoms spilled into the light.

"Lynher! Get down!"

No, I wasn't doing a damn thing Jack said. He wanted me to live, then he could make it happen. I was going home. Fuck everything else. Fuck him and Caine's so-called claim on me, and the queen, and the phantoms, wyverns, drones, rakshasis, demons, fae. Fuck all of them.

They. Needed. Me.

The mark on my arm sizzled to life, the station reaching out, as safe as a mother's hand, a mother I'd never known.

Come home, it said. *Come back to me, my child.* How had I ever doubted it?

A vampire roared behind me, and then huffed a breath, as though it had been hit. Caine or Jack, it didn't matter. Just a few more steps.

Silvery sparks exploded on the platform, a small celebration of Rafe's arrival. His wings flicked, scattering sparks around him, startling the crowd and alerting them to the scene beyond the white line.

Do. Not. Run.

Rafe pulled his wings closed and cocked his horned head, his stupidly pretty face cut into a frown. He didn't approach, didn't appear in front of me and wrap his arms around me to take me off somewhere. He could have, but maybe he'd learned his lesson, because he stayed behind the white line.

Phantoms howled above. Light flashed behind me, washing over them, driving them back, and with every step, the mark on my arm grew hotter.

One liquid shadow broke from the others and plummeted toward the tracks, flooding the last few meters between me and the station platform. It looked like the others, just threads of night around an invisible core, but there was something different about this one. It stayed between me and the platform, between me and Rafe, and it seemed to *see* me.

I stared back, light throbbing off my mark. Maybe it was the same phantom that had taken Rafe's soul? "You and I have unfinished business, but now is not the time..."

It shot skyward, but I'd likely see it again.

Rafe knelt and reached out his hand, a jaunty grin lifting the corner of his lips.

I closed my hand in his and let him pull me onto the platform.

"Welcome home, Lynher Aris." He stepped away, and as I took that final step over the white line, breathing a sigh of relief, he bowed low, the gesture sweeping and overly dramatic, so typically Rafe.

It was more than good to see him, even if he was broken.

I was home.

My lip wobbled.

I clenched my teeth, straightened my shoulders, lifted my chin, and headed through the open doors.

21

NIGHT

Rafe followed me inside a random residential room, and I let him, too exhausted to argue. I'd only made it a few steps inside when the entire room blurred, color spilling into color. My empty gut flopped, and my head spun. I reached for a wall, and then it was done. The suite the station had provided was full of all the things it knew I loved. Cushions and books, plush couches and day beds. A spread of fresh food overflowed the dining table. Candles lit. Glittering cutlery. Even a bottle of wine and a black rose. If I didn't know any better, I might have thought the station felt… guilty.

"It's good to be home," I told the space.

Kicking off my boots, I sighed with relief, not caring that I trailed mud and leaves behind me. My mind itched from Rafe's presence, but he was the least of my concerns. A glance behind me and I caught him eyeing the food like he wanted to open his wings, fall over it, and claim the entire spread as his.

"Rafe… where's Etienne?" I asked.

"Etienne?" His top lip arched.

"Yes. Etienne."

"The shy Frenchman?"

"Where is he?"

His frown was back. "You disappear for a week and then you reappear on the tracks, lit up like a star, rags hanging off your bones, with vampires fighting in your shadow, and the first thing you ask is where's the Frenchman?"

"I'll explain. I just need to find him. And then..." *find Kensey.* I had to know my brother was okay, and I couldn't wait until dawn. I patted my pockets. "Pencil..."

Of course I didn't have a pencil. My clothes weren't Lynher Aris's clothes.

Rafe rested a hip against the table. "A what?"

"A pencil, do you have one?"

"Darling, why would I have a pencil?"

Gods and spices, why would he indeed? I needed to think, to fix my thoughts and focus. The closets. Heading into the bedroom, I reached for the closet door and froze. The woman looking back at me in the floor-to-ceiling mirror had eyes sunken into their sockets, her hair was a rat's nest, her hips jutted, and her skin was the color of dishwater. I'd seen healthier corpses.

Rafe's reflection loomed in the doorway. A moment of fear flicked through his mismatched eyes. Fear for me? Was that possible without his soul?

Later. I'd deal with him and everything else later. I had bigger issues.

I yanked open the closet door and grabbed the first dress hanging on the rail. Pockets. They were everywhere, hidden in the seams, the underskirt, the boned waist. Inside one of them, I found a pencil and a small piece of paper. Quickly, I scribbled a note to Kensey.

I'm okay.

Are you?

Folding it in half, I turned to find Rafe close, his wings open and loose, his shoulders sloping. He stiffened the moment I found his gaze.

"Take this..." I could trust him, couldn't I? It didn't matter. I had to know. "Place it under the antique pitcher in the eastern hallway. Do you know where that is?"

Nodding once, he plucked the note from my fingers and left.

I heard the main door click closed and shuddered out a sigh.

Weakness rushed in, and before I could stumble to the bed, I dropped to my knees, fell forward, and sobbed. Once one gulping gasp was out, the rest followed, and I couldn't stop. I cried out all the hurt inside, but more came, spilling over, and it was all I could do to breathe and exist.

Jack was out there. Caine too. Maybe the queen was coming here? I had to deal with Etienne and show the station residents all was well. I had to check everything *was* well, that the station hadn't been compromised, but above all, I needed to know Kensey was okay. Because if anyone had hurt my brother, I'd burn them alive and send them to whatever place they called hell.

I wanted to crawl into bed and hide, but it was night, and nothing was over, not yet.

Showering was a new kind of hell. I couldn't get warm, no matter how high I cranked the heat up. Naked and shivering, I pulled on the dress, the same one I'd rummaged through. Each buckle sealed shut and ribbon tied off rebuilt my image. There would be no fixing my hair, so I took a pair of fabric scissors to the locks and hacked them off, creating a messy bob.

I emerged from the bedroom halfway back to my old self and found Rafe leaning against the table, his wings illusioned away. He still had his horns, though.

"Has anything happened?" I asked, grateful no hint of my breakdown lingered in my voice.

"Anything?" He double-blinked, surprised by my new look.

"Is anything wrong. Has anything... bad happened since I've been gone?"

He picked up an apple and turned it over in his hand. "Besides the normal? I don't believe so. But it's not my job to monitor your station. I was off doing demon things for much of your absence. In fact, I hardly noticed you'd gone."

I headed for the door. So, if everything continued as normal, whatever Jack was planning might not be in place yet. I'd find Jack, but first, I had to find Etienne. He'd started all this. He'd have answers.

"Eat." Rafe bit into his apple, the crunch loud.

"I will." I reached for the door handle.

"Humans need food," he said around his mouthful. "I read it in a book."

"You can read?" I tried the handle and found the door stuck closed.

"Ha. Ha."

Pulling on the door didn't help. Rafe had just come back through it, so it could open. I tried again, rattling the handle and putting weight into the pull. "Oh, come on…"

I glared at Rafe, and he raised his hands in surrender. "It worked fine earlier."

The skeleton key. I patted my dress down, searching each nook and pocket, finding them all empty. "Oh, this isn't fair. I have to get out there." I wandered in circles, talking to the walls. "I have to find Etienne. You can't lock me in. Jack and Caine are working to hurt us and you. That has to be more important than anything else."

A chair skidded out from under the dining table, its legs scratching across on the parquet floor.

Rafe's chewing stopped. He arched an eyebrow at the chair and me. "I'd say the station agrees with me."

Gathering my skirts, I sat at the table, grabbed a chunk of bread, and picked at it, stuffing bite-sized pieces into my mouth. "Happy now?" I fumed.

Rafe snorted, earning a scowl.

"Fine." Reaching for the water and cheese, I loaded my plate. I did have to eat and drink before I fell down and couldn't get up again. And going after the VG while weak was a terrible idea. I knew that… but too much was happening while time ticked on.

I ate methodically, taking little pieces, knowing too much would likely come back up again. Rafe simmered, a thousand questions in his blue and green eyes, but he ate enough for ten incubi. They were nothing if not gluttonous for all pleasure.

Lost in dark thoughts, I almost missed Rafe freeze up. Then he plucked a knife off the table and threw it with lethal accuracy at the wall.

"What the—"

His wings popped into existence.

"Rats!" he hissed, picking up another knife.

"Stop!" I launched from the chair.

A mouse darted along the skirting board. The first knife Rafe had thrown with terrible accuracy had lopped off the tip of its tail.

"What's the matter with you?" I cupped the mouse and brought it close to my face. Its whiskers twitched, and its mouse hands rubbed its pink nose. "It's just a mouse."

Rafe had spread himself against the far wall, wings out and crackling. "Bring it closer and it dies."

Raphael, Lilith's favorite incubi elite, was afraid of… mice? I set the mouse down on the table and returned to my chair, hiding a laugh by clearing my throat. The mouse sat on its haunches, stroked its nose, and then without fanfare, its body dissolved into a pile of white sugar, which was, in fact, what it had been made of. In the sugar lay a tiny folded note.

"What sorcery is this!" Rafe lowered his knife and peeled himself off the wall, venturing closer to eye the paper as though expecting it to scurry up his leg.

I filed the knowledge that he was afraid of rodents in my "useful for later" mental pile and picked up the note, grinning. The note had to be from Kensey. Nobody else knew how to send sugar mice between night and day, which meant he was okay. He'd probably be angry and demand to know everything, but it didn't matter. He was okay, and that was…

The scratch-like handwriting was not Kensey's.

I read the note and let it fall from my fingers.

Rafe pinched the note's corner between his finger and thumb and frowned. "'Your brother is in our care. Do not search for him.' You have a brother?"

Kensey… Someone had Kensey.

I couldn't believe it. Lies. It was all lies.

Was it Etienne? He'd know about the mice. Kensey could easily have told him. He had Kensey. I would rip his damn heart out of his chest and have Rafe eat it.

"Rafe…?"

"Darling?" he purred, sidling closer.

"I need your help."

"Of course." He tossed the note aside. "I am forever your faithful servant." He bowed again, and when he looked up, his grin was full of demon teeth, his tongue forked. "For a price."

The rage Jack's venom had bottled up inside me seeped through and heated my veins. "We're going to destroy every last vampire in this station, and we won't stop there. Anyone who has dared wrong me, who thought me weak, who trapped me in that damn carriage… I'll make them wish for death."

He straightened, planted a hand on his hip, and eagerly wet his lips. His two-tone eyes shone. "For that, you had better believe I'm having you all to myself for a week."

Ugh, incubi. "An hour," I countered.

"An hour?" He laughed. "An hour is nothing. Three days." He leaned forward and stroked his warm finger along my jaw, spilling wholly inappropriate shivers down my spine. "And nights." He was so close I could taste his sweetness on my tongue. His magic wrapped in close, trying to convince me Rafe was the air I needed to breathe. "They have your brother, whom you're apparently fond of, whoever he is. What are three days and nights with me in exchange for rescuing sibling love?" His words touched my lips.

This close, with his intentions clear, he was a vision of sin and all the forbidden things Gerome had told me never to touch. "What do you know of love?"

He blinked slowly, his black pupils devouring the color of his eyes. "I know it tastes delicious."

"A day and night. I can't give you mo—"

His mouth sealed over mine, forked tongue thrusting in. I might have pushed him off if I didn't already know this was how incubi sealed bigger deals, and besides, I already owed him this. His touch lured a small, vulnerable part of me out of hiding and stirred it fully awake. He tasted of wine and revelry, of bad things that, if indulged, would kill, but you'd die with a smile on your face, and I wanted more of it. All of it. All of him.

I lifted my hand and thought about wrapping my arm around his neck and pulling him down, but if I did that, I'd give him too much, and these strange, off-kilter feelings weren't real anyway. I was tired, strung out, raw, and afraid. He was the closest thing I had to a friend. Weakened, I kissed him back, slowly, carefully, keeping the real need behind toughened barriers so he didn't rip me open and take everything. But gods, it felt good. He kissed like he were making a promise, like this was the beginning of something dark and dangerous he'd deliver on. Kensey was in trouble, the station was balanced on a knife's edge, and I didn't want to be alone in this.

He pulled away first, his eyes bright, back to their multicolored state. They didn't seem so soulless anymore, and in my weakness, I pressed a hand to his cheek, looking him in the eye. I *would* fix him as soon as I'd dealt with everything else.

I stroked a thumb around his smile, over its design, making his lashes flutter. It would have been a dark moment had he died on the tracks. I had no regrets from then or from the deal we'd made. When we saved Kensey, my brother didn't have to know how. I did my best work in the dark.

I told Rafe everything I dared of my plan. Most of it would get back to Lilith. If she ever asked him outright, he wouldn't lie to her, but he had a knack for slithering around the truth when it suited him.

He listened, reclined sideways in a chair, one leg thrown over its arm, as relaxed as if we were discussing what new raucous the Corvus twins had been causing. Perhaps it was exhaustion or the kiss, or maybe part of him had taken root inside since our deal, because I didn't recall him looking so distracting before. I'd known he was built for stamina. Most incubi and succubae were naturally attractive, and if they weren't, they fixed it with illusion. But Rafe looked the same. A waistcoat with nothing beneath, leaving his arms bare. Black leather pants, which defied gravity and clung to his waist. Boots up to the knee, sporting a small heel.

"… listening?" He rolled his eyes when I blinked. "As dashing as I am, sweetness, you need to pay attention to—"

"I was…"

"—my words, not where you want to wrap your tongue when we're done."

"That wasn't what I… That's not…" I straightened at the table and shook my head. My mind had wandered for a while there…

Rafe grinned.

"You did something to me, didn't you?" I said, waving a hand to encompass all his incubus-ness.

His grin became a wicked slash. "You made a deal with an incubus. What did you expect?"

"But we've…" I swallowed, not sure what I was trying to say. "We've gotten close—"

"Kissed before?"

Gods, he was loving this. "*Yes.*"

"A chaste peck. When you were young, full of experimental ideas, and I was… nicer." He shrugged and examined his sharp nails. "Things have changed."

He was well put together, and lying on his side, one leg bent, the other stretched out, the pants so snug they tucked into all the right crevices, allowing me a fantastic view of his—

I pulled my stare away and buried my head in my hands. "This is a problem."

"Only if you let it become one."

He was up and moving closer, and I could feel that too, like he was hard-wired into all my neglected feminine parts. I was regretting our deal.

"Now then, Lynher Aris, hostess extraordinaire—"

"Rafe…" I looked, and there he was, standing right in front of me, all six-feet-something of male demon designed to seduce, minus the wings. A good thing he'd hidden them or I'd be climbing him like a ladder. Dammit. I stood so I didn't have to stare at his navel, his waistcoat not quite meeting his waist, leaving a glimpse of golden skin. My fingertips itched to skim there, and afterward, my tongue would follow. Now we were almost eye to eye. Close enough to kiss. I should have stayed sitting. Clearing my throat, I tried again. "I need white paint."

He raised an eyebrow.

"Lots of it." Patting my dress, I found a pencil and a small piece of paper and scribbled a note before folding it up and handing it out. "And rugs. All the rugs. They're all over the station. You'll need to visit the empty rooms to collect them."

Rafe opened the paper, read the words and frowned.

"And I need this all to happen in the day," I added. "Can you do that?"

Dropping his chin, he nodded and lifted the folded note. "And this?"

"That is… an invitation. You'll know what to do with it when the time is right."

He tucked the note inside a discreet back pocket.

Rafe gave me a charming smile and offered his hand. "A visit to the Grand Hall seems like a fantastic way to show the guests you're alive and well." His smile ticked, and his gaze fell, roaming over the dress and its deliberately low neckline. He shivered all over and rolled his shoulders, shaking the desire off. "The anticipation is divine."

His tail snaked around my ankle, but at my narrowing eyes, he unraveled it and chuckled, sweeping a hand toward the door. "Please, go ahead, my sweetness, so I can admire your ass as you walk away."

He was impossible. "Slut," I groused with a smile.

"You know it."

I lingered at the door, not because it was locked—I'd already tried it and it had fallen open—but because I was back in my life again, walking the halls, seeing to the needs of my guests, playing among monsters. Only, it wasn't the same as before. I'd seen some of the outside. I'd seen the mud-thick farms and the people locked in the dark, awaiting their fate. I'd watched a little girl run for freedom, only to die in the mud.

Jack's words haunted me: "*Take a look at yourself.*"

Some things would change around here.

But first, I had a vampire infestation to eradicate.

Rafe's hand gently landed on my shoulder. He'd probably meant it as a comfort, but the touch startled me back into the present.

"It will be all right," he whispered into my hair. "I'm with you."

When he said things like that, I wished I could believe him. I gently eased his hand off. "I'm stronger alone."

I opened the door and walked back into my life.

Nothing had changed. Gaslit chandeliers made the light sway and dance and catch in the eyes of all the predators in the Hall. The huge clock ticked away the minutes. Dark Ones mingled and laughed and danced, and twirled and lied and did all the things they did to each other's faces and behind their backs. And it all felt so… needless. I pinned my smile on, like always. I didn't have my knives and would have felt naked without them before, but now, their loss was insignificant.

Familiar guests dipped their heads as I passed. A few of my staff took my hand and squeezed as they passed by wordlessly, handing out drinks.

The Dark Ones must surely have thought me dead. Humans didn't do comebacks. But here I was. A strange kind of power made my bones feel heavy—*stronger*—like they had outside, when I'd walked to the platform. I was home. This was my castle. Nothing could touch me or mine here.

I saw Rafe among the fray, champagne flute in his hand as he discreetly watched me watch them all. A jinn—her skin a glass-like green and her gown made of metal loops threaded with silk—moved in close, her innate heat enough to carve a path through the others. She met my eye, dipped her chin, smiled, and moved on. Many did the same, or wished me well, or thanked me, but for what I wasn't sure. I took it all gracefully, remarked on their beauty and stealth, whatever their favorite trait was, and so we danced. Me their little fish.

A few VG were scattered about, but not enough to suggest anything untoward was happening, and both Jack and Caine were conspicuous in their absence.

I spotted the elven couple, recalling Jack's comment to Caine about the fae. They were both looking my way. By the time I'd made my way around the room to where they'd been standing, they'd vanished among the crowd.

Enough with playing nice.

Where the fuck was Etienne?

I needed explanations. I needed to know Kensey was okay.

The clock chimed four times. Dawn would be upon us soon. Perhaps Etienne was with my brother, hiding in daylight. The note had come from there. If he was, I needed to get to him.

The reception bustled, as it always did. The Corvus sisters complained noisily at the desk, chirping their displeasure about some irritation.

"Excuse me, I'm sorry to interrupt, but have either of you seen Etienne?"

They blinked at the same time. "Oh yes," the one on the left said. I could never tell them apart. "The east wing hallway. By the blue door."

"Thank you." I turned away.

"Miss Lynher?" She tipped her head and blinked again, then made a tiny motion with her forefinger and thumb. "He takes the lost things, did you know?"

"I'm sorry… what?"

They shook their heads in unison, rippling their curtain-like black hair. "She doesn't know," one said. "Never mind…" said the other. Something caught their attention in an adjacent room, and away they went, leaving me frowning after them.

With their strange words chipping at my focus, I headed deeper down the hallway and stalled as Etienne stepped from a room ahead. My heart stuttered because he looked like the same man who had come to me, his eyes full of hope that I might let him stay in Night. The same friend I'd thought was trustworthy and safe. But he'd shut me in that carriage with a killer. That reality did not match who I knew this man to be, but why?

"Etienne."

He flinched but quickly grinned. *"Oh, Mademoiselle,* you are safe!" He flung his arms around me in a display of emotion I could only absorb. When he pulled back, tears swam in his eyes. "When you didn't report at the end of your shift, and then Kensey's note said you weren't there for breakfast, we thought—"

"Kensey!" I grabbed his arms and held him still, staring into his eyes. "Is Kensey all right?"

"Y-yes... He's fine. Well... I mean, he's not fine. When you didn't come back—" His doe eyes widened. "I've been trying to hold it all together. I hoped... I hoped you'd come back—"

"Come back? *Etienne, you trapped me in a carriage with Ghost.* I wasn't ever coming back from that."

"What...? I d-did what? No... No, that wasn't... I didn't. I could never..." He fell into French and babbled a string of words I had no hope of understanding, then stepped back, his hand shooting to his mouth to silence himself.

He didn't look like someone who would maliciously try to kill me. "All right, Etienne. Let's talk." I slipped the skeleton key from my pocket, grateful to have found it there again, and slotted it into the lock in the door he'd emerged from.

"Oh no, don't!" He pulled on my arm, but I was already over the threshold, walking into a gloomy suite. Just one candle on a central table lit the entire room, but what I could see shimmered and shone. Pots, candelabra, glasses, vases, an umbrella, a hat. The more I looked, the more of the strange collection I saw gathered on chairs and tables. So many odd items, all out of place. A watch, a boot without its partner, one of the creepy dolls Kensey and I had hidden years ago.

"Etienne... what is all this?"

He fell back against the closed door like he could hold back the truth. "I just—It's... I can't help it. Sometimes... I see things and I... I take them. Just little things. They aren't missed. I know it's wrong. Buttons. Buttons are my favorite."

"What?"

"Buttons. I don't know why. They have magic, did you know? Some are keys to memories. Not my memories. Others… I see things. Sometimes, I…" He hung his head. "I know how it sounds. I tried to stop, but when I stop, it's like… it's like I go insane if I can't…" He trailed off.

"You stole all these things *from our guests*?"

"I…" He wrung his hands.

The Corvus sisters' words about lost things. Compulsive stealing… buttons with magic. Something wasn't right here. Something wasn't right with Etienne. "Etienne, show me the station's mark."

He swallowed but held out his arm, and there the mark was. Caine had mentioned Etienne was being *difficult*.

He chewed on his bottom lip, awaiting my assessment.

"Were you on the platform with Ghost and me? Did you seal us inside?" I asked.

His lips pinched. "*Oui*. I think I did. I didn't want to. But… I had to."

"Why?"

"Because they told me to," he whispered, eyes haunted.

"Who told you?"

His shoulders fell. "The fae. They said they just wanted you… displaced for a few days. That you'd be safer *away* because of what's coming. I'm sorry! I thought I was doing a good thing." Groaning, he buried his face in his hands. "I'm sorry… so sorry."

Jack's words about the fae. Etienne's time with Kensey. Etienne's "*thefts*" and his "*being difficult.*" There was more here than manipulation, so much more. I looked closely at my assistant, seeing him from a different perspective. I'd initially assumed him to be naïve and inept, but that wasn't it at all.

The fae had gotten to him and made him remove me, but they could only have done that with leverage.

I touched Etienne's face, making him look up. Tears wet his cheeks and made his eyes shine, and there, behind the anxious exterior and his attempt to always do good, behind it all, something darker flashed and was gone.

Gods, did Kensey know Etienne wasn't even Etienne? Was that why he was so adamant that Etienne had to work with me, at Night, because he knew he was a Dark One too? *Oh, Kensey Aris, you are in so much trouble.* "Etienne, it'll be all right. I just need you to be honest with me. Do that and we can work this out together. All right?"

A few years ago, I'd been handed a fae babe to keep it safe. A babe with dark hair and dark eyes and golden skin. I saw those same features in Etienne now. Grown, but still there. He wasn't even French. That too was a lie and part of the human wrapping. Whatever Etienne was, it was nothing human.

Kensey knew. He had to. A human babe did not grow to adulthood in a couple of years. He knew, and he'd sent him to work for me without telling me!

"Dammit, Kensey."

"The fae, they knew me…" Etienne whispered. "When I went to their room after the succubus was killed, *they knew me.* They knew my name, and they knew… They said I didn't belong here. They said I was their son, and I… I so wanted it to be true. I've never had a family. I don't remember any parents," he rambled. "And …" With a wrenching breath, he whispered, "I did not want to be human anymore."

I sighed. "None of us do, Etienne."

"But they knew things, Miss Aris. *Private things.*"

"Things like your compulsive theft?"

He nodded. Thievery was common enough among changelings. With their true natures repressed, they manifested tics and quirks. He was lucky he was sane.

"Aoife and Connaught told you to trap me with Ghost?"

"They said, on that night, I'd find you beside a carriage, and I was to… *see that you stayed inside,* just for a little while, for your own good. They promised I'd get to go home with them. But the train left, and the door was locked, and then you were gone. I went to them. I told them it was wrong, and they… laughed." He hiccupped a sob. "I'm sorry. I'm so sorry. I don't know what I was thinking. It was wrong. Don't… please don't make me leave."

I could see he was sorry, but that didn't change the fact that he'd made a deal with the fae. Such things were as binding as night and day. "You agreed to go with them?"

"I didn't know what that meant. It's like they got inside my head and made me do things."

"Did you eat anything when they revealed who they are to you? Did you touch anything unusual?"

"I… touched her, Aoife. She opened her arms and I went to her. It felt so right. Like home, *tu savoir*?"

I remembered the same feeling in Jack's arms as he'd almost consumed my life. "Anything else?"

"She kissed me… on the forehead, and it was the most wonderful feeling, like I finally belonged."

I could imagine how it had gone during the day. Kensey knew what Etienne was. He couldn't have failed to notice Etienne's differences, especially as they were close. But after telling the young Etienne how bad the Dark Ones were, Kensey couldn't tell him he was one of them. So Kensey had left out the important parts, and Etienne had walked right into a trap because of it.

"Etienne, we are your family now. The elves… they gave you up. It was give you to Kensey and me for safekeeping or to the VG. Granted, you were… smaller then. I'm not entirely sure how you got to be a man in a few years, but I figure Kensey will know." After I chewed him out for not telling me my new assistant and his boyfriend was a damn changeling. "I believe you… but I can't trust you. Around them, you'll… be different. More like them. You won't even know it until it's too late."

His face fell.

"We will deal with this later. Your honesty is appreciated…" Naturally, he didn't lie. He was an elf. He couldn't lie. He just… got creative.

"I want to make this right," he said, coming forward and taking my hands. "Please?"

"I have to find Kensey. There was a sugar-mouse note. I thought… Did you write it?"

"No. I haven't seen any notes."

Then someone else had sent it, which meant Day was compromised, and we were all in trouble.

22

DAY

Kensey wasn't in the station, but my brother had left before. It didn't necessarily mean he'd been *taken*, even if the note had implied as much. The day staff had seen him at the end of his last shift. Wherever he was, he couldn't have gotten far.

"Do you think someone has taken him?" Etienne asked. He stood behind me in the music room, keeping his distance. He'd stayed close as I'd searched every corner, every hidey-hole, every secret place I knew.

The note hadn't written itself. I still wasn't wholly convinced Etienne *hadn't* written it.

"C'mon…"

We could do no more in the day. I rarely returned to Night during daylight hours, but if someone had taken Kensey, time was not on my side. The spiral staircase returned us to the station's Night realm. Thick timber shutters sealed the windows closed, blocking all light. Some light still leaked through, slicing the dark like razor-sharp spears. It was normally enough to keep the vampires from roaming the halls. Most guests would be safe in their rooms, sleeping or doing whatever the Dark Ones did during the day. Only a few staff remained. They acknowledged me as I hurried by.

Rafe flashed into the hallway ahead, prompting a squeak from Etienne.

"It is done," the incubus said, his gaze reading me and my changeling shadow. I couldn't tell him about Etienne's origins with Etienne present, but by the way his gaze snagged on Etienne, I wondered if he knew. I'd hoped he'd have told me, but then, it seemed that lately, everyone had secrets.

I nodded and stiffly walked by him.

"Hello, lover..." Rafe purred behind me, his attention lingering on Etienne for a sexual snack.

"He's off-limits," I said, walking on. "Believe me, you do not want to mess with that bloodline."

We turned a corner, and there was Jack, standing between bars of sunlight shining through the shutters, his hands atop his cane. I froze, Etienne stumbled into my shoulder, and Rafe let out a rumbling growl. He looked the picture of male elegance in his lace-lined dark suit, like we hadn't spent a week scrabbling around in the dirt, trying to survive each other. His hair was swept back, his face stern. I hadn't expected to see him in the day—or looking so like... Jack.

"You look well, Miss Aris." Closing his eyes, he bowed his head.

Rafe was a blur, his wings thrown open in a blast of crackling heat.

"Don't!"

He swung for Jack.

Light swallowed us, flooding the hallway and washing out my vision. A few seconds of furious blinking revealed Rafe pinned to the wall, Jack's hand around his throat. With Jack's sleeve pulled back, the station's burning mark shone brightly on his wrist.

"Don't make me hurt you, demon." Jack's fangs gleamed.

"Try it, vampire." Rafe smiled, and it was nothing like the smiles I'd seen before, like he'd gladly sink his rows of sharp teeth into Jack's throat and wouldn't stop there. "We'll see who's left standing."

Jack was marked by the station. Rafe was not. Rafe couldn't win this, not inside these halls.

"Stop!" I snapped. "Jack, put him down."

The overseer swung a glare at me that would have dropped me to my knees had I not spent a week of hell with him. It struck that vulnerable prey-like part of me, and as his charm tried to slide across my thoughts and travel deep, I held his shimmering eyes, daring him to dive deeper. "Put. Him. Down."

Whether it was my tone or his regaining control over himself, he dropped Rafe and backed off, avoiding the shafts of light to straighten his cuffs and cover the sizzling mark on his wrist.

"I wish to speak with you," he said. "Alone."

A burbling growl sounded from Rafe again.

Jack had the answers to everything. "Do you know where Kensey is?"

Lifting his head, he nodded toward the nearest door.

"Take Etienne," I told Rafe and slipped my key into the room's lock. "I'll be fine."

Rafe's predatory glare hadn't faded, and as I opened the door, letting Jack enter first, Rafe narrowed his eyes on me. He was easy to dismiss as just an incubus, but no simple incubus served Lilith. Rafe was as dangerous as the demon he served, which I often forgot—until moments like these, when malice made his eyes burn and the veins in his wings glow with unknown power.

He hated being shut out, but I stepped into the room and closed the door on him.

The strange décor threw me. Sleek glass and steel tables, and a window where there shouldn't be one. It overlooked a twinkling city that no longer existed because Jack and his kind had torn the old world down.

"What are you doing to my station?" I folded my arms and kept the door at my back. His only escape and mine.

The room's startling change had thrown him too. He lost himself in admiring the new features and touched the ultra-smooth table, running his hand along the sleek chair-backs. Maybe it had hidden meaning to him. The station often provided its guests with the things they wanted most, but Jack wasn't really a guest and never had been.

"The situation is delicate," he finally said, turning away from the modern splendor to face me.

"I'm listening."

"What you're doing here… it can't be sustained."

"It was fine before you came along."

"No, it wasn't. Did you think the missing carriages went unnoticed? Did you think a sanctuary for all races on the edges of both worlds would slip by the queen?"

I swallowed to moisten my suddenly dry throat. "Where's my brother?"

"I don't know where Kensey is."

I wanted to slap my brother's name off his lips. "Liar."

"Look…" He stepped forward, bringing him closer, but stopped as I tensed. "Lynher, you hate me, and I understand why. But there's more happening here than you can possibly imagine. You're a small part of a bigger plan, and I'm… I'm trying to keep you alive."

"*You're* trying to keep *me* alive?" I snorted a laugh. "Funny, it didn't feel like that when you had your fangs in my throat."

"Granted, that… that wasn't my finest moment. I was weak, and I am what I am. It wouldn't have happened had you left me, like I'd suggested."

Oh, and didn't he look convincing as the sheepish, guilt-ridden vampire, with his big human eyes and that silly lock of hair that had fallen across his forehead. I couldn't believe anything my eyes told me or the words coming off his silver tongue. "You spoke to Caine like you'd planned all this from the beginning. And Etienne… he's…"

"A changeling. Yes, I know. And yes, I know what's happening here."

"And you didn't think to tell me? We spent all those days and nights together, and you didn't once say that Etienne was compromised."

He looked up. "Etienne's origins were the least of my concerns. Keeping you alive was—"

"Why, exactly? You've never explained that part. Why do you need me alive, *Just Jack?*"

He swallowed hard and tossed his gaze about the room, hoping to find his answers in living walls. "This station is an anomaly. There are no others like it anywhere in this realm or a dozen others. Gerome said…" He wet his lips. "It has great power at its heart, a power my queen seeks. She's coming here. She was coming before I arrived—"

So it was true. His monstrous queen was coming to my station. I couldn't fight that. I could barely fight him. All of this had begun with him, and it would end with him too.

"You are not fit to bear that mark on your wrist!" I hissed. "You are not worthy of sanctuary. I have no idea why the station marked you, but you will never be one of us!"

"Lynher, listen…" He reached out, and I slapped his hand away. "I'm trying to stop her, to buy some time to figure it all out. I'm not working against you. The station is—was everything to me. Once. Long ago."

The hate was so strong it blurred my vision and made my clenched fists ache. If the station meant so much to him, why was he hurting us? Why was he hurting me? "I want my brother back. Where is he?"

He reached again.

"Touch me one more time and I will break your fingers. I don't care if the station retaliates."

He sighed and gave up on trying to invade my personal space. "My best guess, the fae have him. They used Etienne, yes? They took from him the knowledge to use against you."

"Why? I've never hurt them."

"Because the fae will always be on the winning side, and they know what's coming."

"The VG is preparing the station for her arrival. Caine had the elven couple manipulate Etienne to get you out of the picture. He likely threatened them too. He knew he couldn't kill you inside these walls… but none of that matters. Every guest logged in the guest book when she arrives will be turned over to her. And every resident too. Lilith. Whatever is in Room 3B. These walls will become bars and it will all belong to her."

"That's… impossible."

He looked sorry, not angry or mean, just… sad, like it was already over. "I'd planned to have more time here to find a way to stop her, but my unexpected arrival at the farm, it drew my queen's eye back to me. I was due to report back to her and tell her everything about my stay, everything about… you. But my…" He licked his lips. "Our escape from the farm enraged her. She knows I'm here. She doesn't know I'm marked, but… it won't matter. She's coming, Lynher. She's coming and everyone inside these walls must kneel or die."

"Is she coming here for us or for *you*?" I snarled. "Her overseer who got away? That's what your marks are… She put them on you, didn't she? She covered you in ink to claim you, like Caine claimed me, only far, far worse. She wants you." I prodded him hard in the chest, and he backed up a step. "This is all about *you*."

His eyes widened, and he let fear filter through all that arrogance and poise. Terror. My theory was close enough to tear away his mask and reveal the scared nothing vampire inside. He wanted my help, but I wasn't Kensey. I'd seen what Jack and his kind did to people. He didn't deserve sanctuary, and I didn't care if he was marked. I was the Night Station now.

"Get my brother back and maybe I'll help you, Just Jack." I brushed by him and opened the door.

"Lynher, wait. *I have no sway over the fae—*"

I closed the door behind me, shutting off his pleading, fearful tone.

The number of VG listed in the guest book had doubled since my weeklong *break*. More vampires was always a bad omen. Was the queen's arrival imminent? Jack had seemed to think so, but I couldn't trust a word he said. The only fact I was certain of, was that she wanted her overseer back. He'd admitted as much, and now he was hiding in my hallways. She was coming for Jack, I was sure of it. If I removed him, it might postpone or stop her arrival altogether. Every second he was under my roof risked the lives of my guests and my family. And nobody survived hurting my family.

Room C46 caught my eye on the register: Connaught and Aoife, the elves who had promised Etienne a life with them in exchange for imprisoning me with an overseer. His mother's kiss had charmed him. Changelings were human until their twenty-first year, making

Etienne as susceptible to the fae as the rest of us. He'd have told her anything, done anything, after that kiss, just to feel her love.

He'd told them about Kensey and probably about the notes my brother and I passed back and forth. They'd have used a note to lure Kensey into Night, suspecting my brother would go anywhere and do anything for me. The elves had played on my love. So, it was time I played on theirs.

After checking in with my staff, I resigned myself to my library. Finally alone, I tucked myself behind my desk and closed my eyes for a moment. When this was over, I'd sleep for a week. Kensey would make pancakes. Trains would come and go like the tide, and things would go back to the way they were meant to be. I just had to stop an overseer and maybe the queen of vampires…

"I could do with you here, Gerome," I whispered and imagined him leaning against the desk, his soft smile a comfort in these dark times. He was dead because of vampires and so were hundreds of thousands of people. Countless farms kept people like cattle, and when they were done with them, they drained them, shoved them into windowless rooms, and burned them to ash. I couldn't wait for the resistance to reach our shores. The time to fight was now.

The wall clock chimed six times, bringing me back to the present.

Night was here.

My shift had begun.

And this shift would bring an end to it all, one way or another.

Etienne was at the main desk, scanning the guest book. As I approached, he looked up and pulled a smile onto his lips. It seemed genuine, but so did the one I threw back at him.

"Etienne, tell the guests that there's to be a Midnight Ball," I told him. "Everyone is to attend."

He grabbed a notebook and pencil and mumbled as he wrote. Peering over his shoulder, I noted how his handwriting differed from the sugar-mouse note. He caught me looking and doubt stuttered his smile. He knew I'd never trust him again. Through no fault of his own, the Dark Ones had ripped his life away. I just hoped their promised one matched up to his expectations.

"Inform the staff it is to be extravagant and glamorous. I'll get the station on board, but I need *everyone* in attendance."

"Everyone?" he asked.

"Everyone."

"What of… what about… *Resident Three B*?" he whispered.

"Not them." Whatever existed in 3B had never left the room anyway and would have no interest in such frivolous things. "But everyone else must be there. Even Lilith. To miss it would be to miss the station's grandest of celebrations." I added a flourish and wore my role well, attracting the eye of those lingering nearby. Rumors would fast spread. Few would want to miss the station's first and likely only ball.

He scribbled furiously. "What are we celebrating, ma'am?"

"My return from the dead."

He frowned, knowing me too well. He'd heard the threat hidden in my words. "I'll see it done." When I turned to leave, he called me back. "Has there been any news of our… mutual friend?"

"I'm working on it."

The halls soon filled with Dark Ones, each tipping their hats, no doubt while sharpening their claws behind my back. I wondered if any of them had been eyeing my throne during my absence. A good thing only those station-marked could host. Jack didn't count. The day a vampire became a host was the day I burned the station down.

Preparations had begun to dress the Grand Hall, and thankfully, the station was playing along. Brightly colored gossamer drapes hung in waves from the ceiling. Colored shades made the chandeliers twinkle, raining color across the floor and the many gathered below. The VG gathered too, pockets of black and red among a sea of color. The guests had found all manner of beautiful clothes in their closets. They all shone like precious gems, and from the gallery landing above, I watched them spin and twirl to the rise and fall of the music.

The elves arrived near twelve, the pair in matching purple and cream, hair done up in elaborate curls and pins. They looked good enough to eat and drew more than a few gazes, including mine. So beautiful. It was always the beautiful ones who had hollow hearts. Gerome had told me that. Would he approve of my actions tonight? I'd never know, but I liked to think so. No doubt he'd have had another way of saving everyone, but I wasn't Gerome.

I spotted Rafe on the outskirts of the growing crowd, cradling a lit pillar candle in his hands. He knelt, placed the candle near his feet, straightened, and looked over his shoulder, up at me. The old Rafe would have winked and grinned. This one smiled, but it wasn't entirely harmless. If it wasn't for our deal, I wouldn't trust him with any of this.

Lilith sashayed up the stairs and came to rest against the rail beside me, wearing the body of a stunning redheaded woman. Her silk dress, what little there was of it, was startling in its plainness. "What are you up to, my little Lynher?" she purred.

"You look good in green."

"It's emerald, dear. Green, indeed." She flicked her long fingers. "You make me sound like a maid."

Rafe's attention slipped to Lilith and lingered. A quiet moment passed between them, then he was through the crowd largely unnoticed, which was a first for him. I hadn't known he could do subtle.

"I see you have not restored his soul." She gripped the banister. Was it my imagination how her knuckles whitened?

"If you're so eager to see him restored, why not do it yourself?"

"I do not care either way. There are plenty more incubi I can call upon to serve me, but you care, and I like to watch you watching him. I admire the dance you perform around him and he around you, as though you both assume I cannot see your intentions."

I almost laughed. "I have no intentions toward Rafe."

"You will." She stroked my cheek and ran the tip of her tongue along her top lip. "You have no idea, darling. Without his soul, Raphael is unrestrained, making him… as boundless as fire. He will *consume* you from the inside out and perhaps this station with it."

I batted her hand away. "This is a night for celebration. I'm kindly asking you not to ruin it."

She laughed and curled her fingers into her palm. Her gaze lingered as she backed away, and then she descended the sweeping staircase, meeting Rafe at the bottom step. He said a few words, none of which I could hear over the music, and then he leaned closer. He cupped her cheek, and for a moment, I thought they'd kiss, but his cheek brushed hers and his lips moved, spilling secrets into her ear. When he was done, Lilith looked up, straight into my gaze. Her snakelike eyes gleamed with something I dared not interpret, and then she left the room.

He'd told her enough. Maybe everything. I'd expected it but hoped he'd resist. Soulless, he was a threat, but one I understood. I descended the stairs, and the moment I stepped off the bottom step, he swooped in, snaking an arm around my waist. Another night I'd have thrown him off, but tonight I needed him close, for more reasons than I cared to admit.

"Jealous, my darling?" he asked, walking me among the dancers before clasping me close. "Calm your human heart. You must resist my charms or all here will know I have bespelled their hostess."

I fought back a laugh. "My human heart is fine, thank you, and I am not bespelled."

His hand slid down to my lower back, where his fingers spread, delivering a wave of warmth that wasn't entirely natural but wholly welcome. The fingers of his other hand entwined with mine, and then we were moving to the music as one, falling into its rhythm. His hips moved, his body a song of sensation that lulled the strung-out portions of my mind. His touch soothed, and the heat of him seduced, but I knew it was all incubi tricks and could pull away when I chose.

The clock caught my eye. I had time for a little moment to call my own in the madness to come. There was no crime in dancing with a Dark One.

"Our forbidden love is doomed, you know, Lynher girl." His lips brushed my forehead, his tone soft and intimate.

"Is it?" I asked. I'd folded my arm around his back and felt his muscles move through his waistcoat fabric. His warmth soaked deeper, like the sunlight I'd felt on my face while making my way back home. Maybe it was our deal or part of me that couldn't help herself, but in all the times I'd had Rafe in my arms, whether to hit him or to hold, he'd never felt safer.

"I am promised to another… a witch," he sighed dramatically.

"Don't let Lilith hear you call her that."

"Shh." He leaned back and pressed a finger to my lips, eyes sparkling with mirth. "She keeps me chained, and if—when I misbehave, she whips me." He yanked me close, overacting his part. "Five wicked lashes for every indiscretion."

"Only because you like it."

He chuckled, and I rested my head against his shoulder. I could pretend too, couldn't I?

"Only true love's kiss can free me from the wicked queen." His voice rumbled through our bodies.

"I thought she was a witch?"

"Whatever."

"Well then, you'd better find your true love if you're to be free…" I trailed off as he stilled, our dance over.

"May I cut in?" Jack asked, his presence ripping away all comfort.

I pulled out of Rafe's arms, straightened in front of the overseer, and nodded tightly. Rafe melted into the crowd, throwing a withering glance behind him. People twirled and sparkled and laughed, and I knew I should take Jack's offered hand. He'd arrived at the perfect time, yet taking his hand would begin the final dance, the turn of the final cog in this grand game, and I remembered so well how he'd kept me safe in a world determined to destroy all the good left within it. He wasn't good. Far from it. I couldn't think of him as anything but a queen's pawn.

The grand clock above us clunked and whirred, beginning its midnight chimes. All the while, Jack's gaze fell into mine, neither of us moving.

"Lynher?" He blinked, hand still outstretched.

Chime.

Eleven to go.

The midnight train's shrill whistle cut through the night. More guests arriving, the beat of station life ticking over like a heart. All around, Dark Ones grinned and hungered and believed themselves on top of the worlds, dancing on the bones of the dead.

I took Jack's hand in my left and reached behind me with my right.

Chime.

He'd pulled me with him over a cliff into raging waters, keeping me close then and later when the wyvern had attacked. Maybe Jack was different, but what did it matter? He'd killed countless, and he'd kill again. All vampires were a scourge on the world. This moment might be the only one I had to fight back.

Chime.

Behind my back, my fingers closed around the stake. People danced and nudged us, the world still turning while we stood frozen.

Even now, his eyes were honest but sad. Did he know this was an ending? Could he sense the tension and the station holding its breath?

"I know where Kensey is," he said, hoping for a lifeline?

My heart raced. "Where?"

Chime.

"With the elves. They drugged him with goblin fruit. He'll be all right."

I still had his hand in my left, his fingers gentle and warm. He'd always worn his unremarkable act like I wore my dresses. We both had roles to play in this world. Our lives were not our own.

The train thundered into the station, rattling the huge windows and filling the outside air with rolling steam.

"They told you this?" I asked. I had to be sure.

Chime.

"I… have a key." He reached into his pocket with his free hand and removed a skeleton key. A key exactly like mine.

That was impossible.

I had the only key.

He smiled sheepishly, like this was all a silly joke, and wasn't it amusing how the station had picked a mass murderer and marked him to keep him *safe*. And now he had a host's key.

There was only mine and… *Gerome's*.

An overseer was a station host.

No, not possible. That key didn't belong to him. It couldn't. The station would never betray me. He had to have stolen it.

I snatched my hand from Jack's and stared at his impossible key. A sickening sense of dread and grief pulled at what I thought I'd understood.

Gerome's key had been cracked on one side.

Chime.

"Turn it over."

Jack held out his key and flipped it over in his palm.

A jagged crack marked its spine.

I tried to breathe, to fill my lungs, but the air lodged in my throat. Laughter and light danced around us, swirling and spinning, too bright, too sharp.

Looking into his sorry eyes meant looking into the eyes of Gerome's killer.

"It was you…"

Chime.

He wanted the station's power for his queen. It made sense now. The games, the distractions, his infamy. The fae had trapped *him* inside the carriage, not me, and spun a lie to protect themselves. Because they knew what he was. The Ghost. The most feared overseer. And here he was, his machinations at work. He had Gerome's key. He'd driven a railway spike through Gerome's heart. He had control.

"Your brother will be fine," he said, his lies making a mockery of his so-human appearance.

He was a monster born of the suffering of others. He didn't care about me or my brother. All he cared about was his queen and how she could control the station. As long as I breathed, that was never happening.

"Gerome was like a father to me and you killed him!"

"Lynher—"

"Whatever happens, the worlds will be better without you in them." I grabbed his hand and yanked him forward, right into the stake I plunged between his ribs. Lilith's words came back to me, about how intent mattered to the station's protection. I did not *intend* to kill Jack with this stake, or even really hurt him. This was all just a harmless distraction.

Yet nothing had ever felt so right, so perfect. Someone screamed, and then the rest of the crowd joined in. A crescendo of shouts and cries rose all around, and the guests fled. The station didn't protect him because my intention wasn't to harm, just to distract.

Chime.

Jack clutched my arm. His key fell from his hand and rang against the floor.

I stared into the eyes of a monster. "I hope you rot in hell."

His face fell, contorting with rage or fear or some other fake emotion he could wear at will. "What have you done?"

The vampireguard rushed in like when Lilith had killed his stand-in. So many of them, each one the queen's drone, each one filled with hatred and a hunger for innocent people. From every door they poured forth, boots thundering like an invading army.

Come… I silently urged. *Come to your overseer's rescue.*

I threw my head up and caught sight of Rafe on the landing, his wings clamped, his hands gripping the rail.

"Now!" I yelled.

Chime.

He took from his pocket my folded note, and with a flick of his fingers, he folded the note into a small paper bird and launched it over our heads. Jack saw, and even while in pain he frowned at the fluttering paper bird, his attention on that and not on Rafe pulling free a rope looped around a hook on the wall. The wall drapes fell open. Their trailing edges cascaded over the ring of candles Rafe had placed around the room. Flames licked and leaped up the fabric, rising higher, sealing the countless vampireguard, Jack, and me inside a ring of fire.

Jack's snarl was more from surprise than malice. He stepped back, groped for the stake in his chest, and yanked it free, but it was too late. Light from the white symbols I'd asked Rafe to paint on the floor joined the firelight. They'd been hidden beneath rugs. Now activated, the summoning power shone, but I wasn't bringing a demon here… I was sending something like one away.

"Lynher… don't." Jack wore his fear openly on his face. His look begged me to free him.

But I wouldn't.

Chime.

Rafe's paper bird flew above Jack's head. Jack looked up, and the bird poofed into ash that rained down on him. His name had been written on that simple piece of paper, the name I'd insisted on calling him, giving it power. *Just Jack.*

The trap had been sprung. A stake in the chest wouldn't kill him, but death was too good a fate for a monster like him anyway. No, there was a special place reserved for him and all the wretched vampireguard infesting my station. A place between worlds. A place as evil as their human farms. A place vampires called hell, where demons roamed.

Chime.

One more to go.

"Stop this at once!" He settled the full weight of his glare on me. "Your ignorance will see us all killed and your precious station lost. Imprisoning me won't stop *her*. She's coming tonight. You're sealing your fate!"

The black-and-red vampires swarmed in, surrounding us. They could attack. My mark wouldn't protect me, not inside the summoning circle, a space between worlds.

Chime. The clock had rung its final bell. The reverse summoning was sealed.

"It's too late." I smiled. "For all the people you've killed"—I stepped back—"for those still locked in the dark"—I again moved back, the vampires hissing as they parted behind me—"I hope you suffer like them, *Just Jack.*" One more step and the circle would let me out. Only me, the summoner, because my name hadn't been on that piece of paper.

Jack's eyes widened. So kind, those eyes. He'd almost fooled me, but Gerome had taught me well, and now my teacher, my friend, my father's death was avenged.

"This is for you, my friend," I whispered, taking the final step.

An arm swooped in from behind, locked around my throat, and hauled me back against a hard chest.

"Caine, stop!" Jack threw out a hand, the one holding the stake. "*Don't*!"

He took a step closer, but Caine's hold on my neck tightened, choking off my air. I gasped and dug my nails into his arm, trying to pry him off.

"She'll kill us all." Caine's voice rumbled down my spine. He smelled of decay and dust.

It didn't matter. The circle would close eventually, even with me in it. They were all going to hell, and if I had to go with them, so be it. The station would be safe. Kensey was alive. I knew that much. He'd be okay.

Jack came closer. "Let her go," he said, his glare fixed over my right shoulder, where Caine bowed his head, leaning in close.

Caine breathed deeply, his lips close to my neck. "This pretty little thing was always going to be mine."

The vampires seethed and simmered, bubbling in agitation, realizing their fate. None could escape the fire.

"All of you!" Jack raised his voice. "Don't touch her. Let Miss Aris go."

Caine's rage shivered through me. "You *are* a traitor, just like our queen told us."

Jack's shoulders dropped. He tilted his head, his hand still reaching, the stake in his grip. "No." And he smiled his cruel, hard smile. *"As your overseer and the Queen's Chosen, I command you— hand Miss Lynher Aris over to me. She's* mine."

The power in his words rippled through the crowd, calming them. Caine panted close to my ear, his body strumming as he fought Jack's control.

"Our queen's voice is mine, her will my own." Jack's vampire eyes shone. *"And I command you to* ***let her go****."*

Caine threw me forward, and suddenly, I was in Jack's arms again, just like when we'd gone over the cliff. He folded me in close. I waited for him to bow his head and tear out my throat in front of his subjects, because he was everything I'd been told, everything to be feared. I looked up, met his eyes, and let him see how ready I was to die for my cause. But he didn't look enraged, or lost to bloodlust, or even monstrous. He looked like the man who'd gotten turned around in my station and found his way to my library.

His hard smile broke apart. He pulled me close and said, "I did get that dance after all." And then he moved, turning me around while stepping forward, and with a strange expression of sadness on his face, he shoved me through the flames.

23

NIGHT

Heat wrapped around me then spat me out. I staggered backward, almost falling. Rafe's sparks rained, his presence simmering to my right, but I couldn't look away from beyond the rippling wall of fire. Inside, Jack had the stake raised. Caine turned toward him, and dozens of VG sprang into motion, lunging to attack Jack. Caine reached out, fangs bared to kill—

The summoning circle collapsed.

The fire gasped out.

The white marks sizzled to nothing, forever scorching the floor.

Soot and embers fell from above like dirty snow.

But the vampires, Caine, and Jack were gone.

"Lilith's tits, it worked," Rafe breathed.

They were *all* gone.

At the end… Jack had… *saved* me?

"You're looking burned around the edges, darling…" Rafe mused. "Are you all right?"

"I'm fine," I mumbled. I stepped over the burned summoning marks and entered the circle. Nothing remained. No hint that the vampires had ever been here.

My boot scraped something hard. I looked down and choked on a gasp. Gerome's key. The sight of it summoned a great swell of emotion that lodged in my throat. Scooping it up, I cradled it in my palm, closed my fingers around it, and finally said goodbye.

Jack and his entourage were gone, their infestation over.

The train's whistle screeched its alarm.

No. Not over.

Jack's final words about the queen…

Darkness boiled outside and beat against the windows, trying to choke off the station's lights. The train whistle blew again and cut off.

The entrance's arched double doors rattled on their hinges. The windows rumbled too. The dark was trying to get in.

The mark on my arm burned to life, funneling both power and pain through my skin, and mine wasn't the only one. The marks of any staff who had drifted back into the Hall sizzled to life. Dark Ones had spilled back in too, drawn to the force outside, searching for a weakness.

"What is that?" Rafe asked, his face tipped upward. Enormous shadows played across his entire body, wings and all. They played across everyone, sweeping and searching. And I could feel her then, the thing that had been inside Jack's head, the same terrible world-hungry presence I'd glimpsed in his eyes. The darkness inside him hadn't been his at all; it had been his queen's.

And she was here, just like he'd said.

I grabbed Rafe's hand, ignoring his querying look of surprise.

The air thinned and stretched, lacing pain through my ears and skull. Some of the staff cried out. Some fell to their knees. The Dark Ones looked on, each one so small, as inconsequential as everyone else.

All the station's shutters slammed shut in a procession of booms that rocked the air, the ground, and thumped through my body. The world tipped, as though I were falling but standing still. Unbalanced and strangely detached, I fell to my knees but didn't feel myself strike the Hall floor. Something was wrong. I pulled on the air, trying to draw it into my lungs, but it was too thin, too far away.

Ahead of me, Rafe turned around, trying to see whatever he needed to fight, but he could not fight this. None of us could.

The shutters ceased their slamming, the air popped, my mark blazed so brightly it bleached all color from the world, and then, with a final gasp, all the hurt and noise and pressure vanished.

Murmurs quickly chased away the fresh, new quiet.

Rafe grabbed me and hauled me to my feet. "Do your thing," he mumbled, shoving me forward. I smiled at the approaching Dark Ones, like I always did, feeling broken and strangely unhinged inside.

"What is this?" a female jinn asked, gesturing at the closed shutters. Embers fizzled beneath her green-tinted skin, sparking like fireworks. "Are we prisoners?" she asked, her Middle Eastern accent strong.

"No, it's just… a precaution." I had no idea what it was. "The vampire queen was moments away from breaching these walls, and so the station protected us. We just… need to give it a moment."

"What happened to the overseer? Was this your doing?"

More Dark Ones circled in. Others tried the shutters and the doors, but the station was locked down. In all the stories I'd read, this had never happened.

"It's fine." I lifted my hands. "The threat has passed. Return to your rooms. When the station is ready, it will allow us transit again. Please… relax. Enjoy our hospitality."

The jinn's expression spoke of her distrust before she turned her back on me.

"Allow me to take you away from all this…" Rafe's whispers were mighty tempting, but I was still the hostess and my brother was still missing.

"No."

He opened his mouth to argue.

I stopped him with a raised hand. "I don't need you for this."

His pretty eyes narrowed, and his wings ruffled as they often did when we disagreed.

"You've done enough."

What happened next, I had to do alone. Not with another demon whom I already owed a debt. This wasn't his fight, and without his soul, his motivations were dubious at best. I couldn't have him anywhere near my weakness—Kensey.

He laughed me off with a shrug and turned away. "Fine, sweet thing, but don't be too long… Our time alone begins at dawn."

I sighed, glancing at the closed shutters. "Rafe, we didn't agree to that."

"We didn't *not* agree to it either."

Really? I was exhausted and still reeling from everything that had happened, and he was pulling the damn deal card now!

"Only if I get my brother back and he's fine. I'm not doing *our thing* without knowing he's okay."

Rafe spun around and bowed dramatically. "I'm soulless, not heartless." He vanished before rising, leaving me in a room full of wary predators.

Outside the fae's room, I braced a hand against the wall and bowed my head. I was shivering from the adrenaline comedown and couldn't shake it. For all my games and outward show of strength, I was crumbling inside.

I just had to do this one last thing while the station did whatever it was doing…

On the walk from my library, where I'd collected an essential item that would help in what came next, the guests who weren't hiding in their rooms had steered clear of me. I'd need to reassure them they were safe, and find Etienne, and clean up the burned debris in the Hall, and welcome the new arrivals, and a thousand other things, and uphold my deal with Raphael. The station cogs kept turning, even if the shutters were closed to whatever was outside. I had to trust it. There was no room in my body and heart for anything else.

I slipped my hand into a pocket and squeezed Gerome's broken key. Tears blurred my vision.

"Not now," I whispered, dabbing the wetness from the corners of my eyes. I couldn't fall apart just yet. I had to keep it together for Kensey, for whatever I found beyond this door.

Straightening, I knocked.

Etienne opened the door, looking pale. He stepped aside, and there they were, the beautiful pair of elves, Aoife seated in a Queen Anne chair and her husband, Connaught, standing behind her. They looked like a glorious portrait. There was no sign of my brother in the main room, but these suites had adjoining bedrooms. He could be in one of those.

Elves were at the top of their food chain, mostly because they liked to eat the fae below them. Connaught and Aoife were no exception. As ethereal as they appeared in their flowing pale blue silk-and-lace gowns, with their featherlight blond hair and pointed ears, they could turn into vicious killers at the click of their beautifully lithe fingers.

"Miss Lynher," Aoife greeted, her tongue scandalously pink behind her pale teeth and lips. "Is it done?"

"Aoife, Connaught." I dipped my chin respectfully. "Is what done, exactly?"

"The vampire situation has been dealt with?"

"The overseer and his entourage are gone, yes. As for whatever was outside… that remains to be seen."

"Good. That is good." She looked over her shoulder at her husband, who stared back at me. I hadn't yet seen him blink. "You must be wondering about our part in this?"

I sighed, failing to hide my exhaustion. "You gave Etienne to us to keep him safe, correct?"

"Indeed, we did. He was born here, in this realm, and as such, the vampires believed it their right to take him. Naturally, we could not allow this, so we arranged to hide our son among you here, at the station. He will return home with us once he reaches maturity."

Etienne shifted uneasily. He seemed pretty mature already, certainly old enough to make his own choices, but the fae did things differently, and as human as Etienne appeared, he was fae beneath the lies.

So many lies spun like webs all around me.

I'd never found them so tiring before.

"You had Etienne trap me in a carriage with Ghost. Why?" I asked, ignoring the rasp in my voice.

Again, Aoife looked at her husband, perhaps expecting him to explain, but he just stared through me, trying to solve the puzzle of how someone like me had so much power beneath this roof. They all coveted it. I hadn't realized how much until Jack had brought it to a head.

And he'd saved me… in the end.

"In the hope you'd do what you've done. The overseer was a weakness. You saw to it that he was suitably distracted, thus undermining their queen. We knew you'd succeed."

They knew I'd fucking succeed? "How convenient an answer." Fae couldn't lie, and they did everything in their power to get around that weakness. "Is my brother here?"

Connaught broke out of his statuesque stance and lifted his head. "Your brother is our insurance that you'll keep Etienne safe until he matures. He will stay in our care while Etienne is in yours."

I still had strength enough to feel anger. "So, you do have him?"

"Yes."

My cheek twitched. "Is he here?"

Connaught glided across the floor and disappeared into a side room. He returned with Kensey, bound at the wrists and gagged. My brother's eyes flew wide on seeing me, and then narrowed. He was furious, and he wasn't the only one.

"Etienne." I pitched my tone like I normally would when asking him to perform his station duties, and like the good member of staff he was, he came forward.

A knife dropped from my sleeve and into my palm. I grabbed Etienne by his collar and pulled him around, hugging him close. The blade fit snugly under his chin. It was a simple blade, borrowed from one of the kitchen staff on my way here. It wouldn't hurt a fae, but Etienne was as mortal as me.

Aoife's hand shot to her mouth, smothering a graceful gasp.

Connaught yanked on Kensey, reeling him back in. My brother's muffled protests bubbled, and considering where his gaze was, he was more concerned for Etienne than his own damn life. He and I would have words after this.

"I've had a really bad few days," I said. "Without going into details, I discovered a fae spy within my staff, and I don't appreciate being lied to when it comes to my family. And make no mistake, Etienne *is* my family. He's actually a damn good assistant, and to learn that he's been compromised made my bad few days even worse. Frankly, I'm right on the edge of doing something reckless, so if you'd like to test that theory, please continue to hold my brother hostage, and we'll see how far I'm willing to go to get him back."

The station's mark helpfully flared as a reminder of who they were fucking with. I'd thank it later.

Connaught sneered, appearing more striking in his fury. Fucking elves. They were some of the most dangerous guests under my roof, but they also loved their family like I loved mine. They were afraid. Afraid of the unknown entity that was me, afraid of the station, and afraid of vampires. I understood all that.

"Release Kensey."

"Only if you agree that Etienne will give up his place beneath your roof and return with us as soon as he's reached maturity," Connaught replied.

"I can't agree to that. You handed Etienne over to me, a human, and we do things differently. Until he turns fae, Etienne is his own person who makes his own choices. You don't own him here like you would in your world. You chose to give him up. He is free—besides my holding a knife to his throat, but you haven't given me much choice in that. Now, let my brother go."

"You marked him. You claimed our son. We do not trust you, Lynher Aris. How can we trust someone who banished an entire retinue of vampireguard and their overseer to the demon realm? Your brother is the only thing you care about, and to keep you in line, we must keep him."

"I don't mark people. The station does that. You handed him over, and the station embraced him… I'm as much a servant of the station as anyone."

"This station is not as benign as it appears!" the male elf snapped.

This was getting us nowhere.

Kensey was mumbling behind his gag and trying to writhe free of Connaught's grip. My brother was stronger than he looked, and if he got a hit in, the situation would turn messy. I still hoped to walk out of here with both Kensey and Etienne, but if it came to it, I would kill Etienne to save my brother. But there was another equation in this—the way Kensey was looking at Etienne. Kensey would trade himself for Etienne's freedom, because my brother was one of the good ones, and the fool loved Etienne. I hoped that gag stayed in before he opened his mouth and put his foot in it.

"This is unnecessary. I have no reason to want to hurt Etienne or keep him from you. If you're afraid he likes it better among humans, that's your problem to solve, not mine. Let my brother go. I'm not asking again."

Etienne hadn't fought, likely because he believed I wouldn't hurt him. He could keep on thinking that right up until I cut his throat, if required.

Aoife flicked her wrist. "Let him go, love. She is but one human, albeit in a position of power she doesn't understand."

Her keen eyes told me she absolutely knew I'd kill Etienne to save Kensey. She was the reasonable one.

Connaught relaxed his grip on Kensey and untied his wrist bindings. Kensey pulled his gag free and threw it at Aoife's feet as he strolled by.

"Lynher, you can let Etienne go now," my brother said, his voice ragged from his ordeal.

I could.

But there was still the little fact of how they'd lied to us and used their son to manipulate me, and if one Dark One believed I was a soft touch, they'd all get ideas.

I flicked the blade, opening a thin bloody line in Etienne's neck. It wasn't deep, it wouldn't kill him, but it might scar. Etienne sucked in a breath through his teeth.

"Lynher!" Kensey barked.

"What is this!" Connaught raced forward.

Lifting my hands, I backed off. The knife had gone—I'd tucked it safely away but could easily whip it out again. "Don't fuck with my family."

Connaught looked at me as though he'd love to rip my spine out and wear it as a scarf. Aoife just looked cold, like she'd come close to seeing her son bleed out in front of her. They had made him mortal. This was their doing, all of it. My family were not tools to be used.

"We're done here," I told them.

Etienne slipped a hand into Kensey's, and they hurried from the room. I'd almost made it out behind them when Connaught added, "Don't make enemies of the fae, Miss Aris. You will not survive the repercussions."

Smiling, I caught the door handle, bowed as I pulled the door closed, and said, "Don't make an enemy of me, or you'll find the station doors permanently closed to you. Good night, Connaught and Aoife. Sleep well."

24

DAY

I allowed Kensey and Etienne to return to Day without me. Kensey wouldn't have gone, but Etienne had urged him on, saying I needed time to fix the fallout from the reverse summoning. And I did. I went through the motions, trying to smooth over the drama left behind from the scene in the Grand Hall. The shutters were still locked tightly, allowing no entry or exit. There were questions, most of which I couldn't answer. Were the VG coming back? How safe were the guests from the vampires and from me…

With dawn creeping through my bones, I unlocked the Day door and descended the spiral staircase, seeking sanctuary. Kensey would soon come looking for me, and I wasn't ready to go over everything that had happened. I'd fall apart in front of him, and then nothing would get done.

My bedroom shutters were closed too, holding back something. I wandered to the dresser, with its large ornate mirror, and almost didn't recognize the woman looking back at me. She seemed confident, proud, strong even, but I saw how her smile was broken and worn out. We'd survived, Kensey and me. We were okay. Why, then, didn't it feel like a victory?

A knock sounded at my door. It could only be Kensey or Etienne. Neither would go away until I spoke with them.

Sure enough, Kensey smiled when I opened the door. I so wanted to fall into his arms, but dawn had come, and I had one last promise to uphold.

He opened his mouth to ask his questions, but I spoke over him. "I need Etienne to cover my shift for a day and a night. Can you ask him to do that? And can you watch him…?"

My brother closed his mouth and frowned. "Are you all right?"

I'd never willingly missed a night shift.

"I will be." I rubbed my forehead where the tiredness had collected into an ache.

"Are we safe?" he asked, not for himself, but for every single human that helped run this strange corner of the world.

"We are, for a while, I think. Until the shutters open, at least."

He moved as though to enter my room, or maybe to draw me into his arms, but if I let him hold me, all my defenses would crumble, so I held him back. His face fell in confusion.

"We'll talk. I promise," I told him. "I need some time, that's all."

I knew Rafe was behind me the second my brother's gaze flicked over my shoulder, but it was more than that. I'd made a deal with an incubus. His presence warmed my blood and made my exhausted body hum in anticipation.

"I see." Kensey's frown darkened.

"It's not…" What was the point in explaining? He'd already assumed the worst. "Kensey, will you help cover for me?"

"All right," he agreed, "if that's what you want." He meant Rafe, and no, this wasn't what I wanted, but it was a whole lot more complicated than where his mind had gone.

I closed the door on my brother's disapproving scowl and felt that same emotional wave clog up my throat. I just had to spend a day and a night with Rafe—then it would all be over. I could go back to my life, to the way everything had been before, and forget any of this had happened. The carriage, Jack, the farm, and those poor people trapped in the dark rooms…

"I'm sorry…" I told Rafe.

"Sorry?" He didn't bother hiding the surprise from his voice. "Whatever for?"

Facing him was one of the hardest things I'd ever had to do. He wore an open cotton jacket, barely more than a decoration over his bare chest, and the pants were cotton too, thin and loose. No shoes. He rarely wore them. He hadn't changed his appearance in all the years I'd known him, until the phantom had taken his soul. Now he stood there, his wings arched elegantly behind him, his smile and eyes hollow, just decoration on an empty husk.

"I can't fix everything. I can't fix you."

He was in front of me, his thumb wiping my cheek. "Your face is leaking." He lifted his thumb to his lips and licked away the tear he'd collected.

"You know what tears are, Rafe." He'd seen me cry a thousand times as a child, but like everything between us now, this was different, because he was different. Maybe I was too.

"But I never expect to see them again on you." His fingers brushed up my cheek and into my hair. He pulled me in, and I didn't fight him. I was weak and alone and lost, and I'd agreed to this, and it felt right. So right. "There's nothing to fix," he said, voice rumbling as his arms sealed around me. "I don't need a soul."

More tears fell. I squeezed my eyes closed and crushed his silly jacket in my grip. Only someone without a soul would think they didn't need one.

"Everything is easier now," he said. "Clearer."

I'd broken him. I couldn't fix everything, and now he was forever changed. The phantom would have feasted on other souls by now, and even if it hadn't, it would be long gone. He was the closest thing I had to a friend, and I'd ruined him.

"Let's get on with this, then…" I swiped at the useless tears, tore free from his arms, and headed for the bed. "I agreed, so…" I pulled my dress sleeves off my shoulders.

Rafe's fingers looped in the fabric and hitched the sleeves back up. His skimming touch sent shivers down my back. My breath caught, and my thoughts careened off course to where his fingers might go next. I could do this. It was necessary and hardly a chore. I'd thought about it often enough, especially of late. He made it impossible *not* to think about lying with him, and that dark part of me, the one that had gotten me through the last few days, *wanted* this. It always had.

But why was he pulling the dress back on?

"What—"

He turned me to face him, his warm hands on my shoulders. There was anger in his eyes, but I couldn't imagine why. Wasn't this what he wanted? Without a soul, he surely didn't care how he got it. His hands stroked down my arms, and then he took my hand and led me to the bed. I went, as compliant as a lamb being led to the slaughter.

He set me on the edge of the bed and knelt to unlace my boots. Curious, I watched him with his head tilted down, his hair fallen around his short horns, and then found my gaze wandering up the arches of his closed wings. I'd never seen him fly and wasn't entirely sure flying was their main purpose. Demons were… different in more ways than I understood. I'd read books and spoken to Gerome, but I had not told him about Rafe. Like Kensey, he wouldn't have understood either.

Rafe pulled one boot off and then the other, and taking one foot in one hand, he ran his other up my calf, lifting his gaze at the same time. His touch felt divine, as though he could brush away every ache. Maybe he could. We had a day and a night. I was about to find out what he could do with those clever hands.

My heart thumped too hard in my chest, like maybe I wanted this to happen. Maybe I wanted to kiss his soft, inviting lips.

"Lie back," he ordered.

I swallowed and did as he asked, struggling to take my eyes off him.

He ran his hands up my thighs and around my hips, dipping them into my waist, and then placed a knee on either side of me and crawled up until we were eye to eye. His tail wrapped around my ankle, holding firm.

His wings lay open, cocooning us inside this small moment in time. His breathing matched mine, his lips so close I just had to lift my head to seal the kiss that was surely coming. I wanted this, wanted him. I had wondered about it for years, since I'd grown into my body and started looking at males *differently*. I'd bedded a few of the staff in my early teens, mostly as a distraction. But Rafe was untouchable, the forbidden, and therein lay the sweet irony. To touch him, to run my hands over lean muscle and smooth skin, to tip his head up, to taste the line of his jaw, to tease my tongue in and draw the real him out. None of it was real. All of it was his demonic seduction, but that didn't mean I couldn't enjoy him. This was the perfect excuse to take that forbidden last step.

"You must never let them see you, the real you," I heard Gerome tell me from long ago. *"And never love them, Lynher."* He'd seemed so sad then. *"The Dark Ones will never love you in return."*

Rafe and I had made a deal. This meant nothing.

His eyes searched mine, and the moment stretched, both of us caught between action and inaction. I'd imagined him grinning. I'd thought he'd be a tease and impossibly arrogant now that he'd gotten his wish. But there was none of that on his face or in his body, just a tight hint of anger or maybe frustration. As I watched, the color in his eyes darkened, eaten by his expanding pupils, and the truth of him simmered to the surface. Lilith's errand runner, now so much more.

"Rest," he said, breathing in as he pushed away.

I propped myself up on my elbows and watched him stalk to the dresser. He spread his hands on its surface and bowed his head. His wings shuddered and pulled closed, sealing their oily colors inside. His tail lashed, a sure sign he was angry. I didn't understand. I'd been ready for him, more than ready.

"What is this? You make a deal and then you don't want me?"

"It's not that," he hissed and looked up at our reflections. His mismatched eyes were black, wholly consumed. "A day and a night. That was our agreement."

"Yes, but—"

"Don't argue, Lynher. Not on this." Then he was gone, sparks raining in his wake.

Day and night came and went, and I slept through it, grateful for the space Rafe had given me, if troubled by his strange behavior. I'd assumed he'd return to collect on our deal, but when dawn came around again and he still hadn't come, he'd forfeited his chance, leaving me suspicious and curiously bereft. Had he bargained for the day and night to make sure I rested? Why would he do such a thing when he'd had the opportunity to have me in all ways, like he'd always wanted. His actions didn't fit him. The Rafe I'd grown up with would never have missed an opportunity to bed anything, but this new Rafe was more complicated.

I ate breakfast with Kensey, eyeing the closed shutters, wondering if they'd ever open again. He didn't mention Rafe, and I didn't mention how Etienne was fae. Maybe we'd get to that, but not yet. I told him everything that had happened with Jack, even the moment he'd saved me from Caine, at what must have been a huge cost to himself. Kensey didn't trust it but agreed my actions in trapping the overseer had been the right thing to do.

"Jack said some things…" I swirled a silver spoon in my tepid coffee and wrapped my fingers around the mug. I'd struggled to get warm since returning from the *outside*. "…about Gerome."

Kensey's chewing slowed. "What *things*?"

"Gerome was good, right?"

"He raised us, didn't he? And I know for sure you were a pain in the ass—" I threw a napkin at my brother. He caught it and laughed. "That overseer was trying to twist you around to his thinking. He wanted you and this station for the queen." Kensey poked his tongue into his cheek. "Did you believe him?"

"No, of course not."

"We'll figure it out. We always do." He downed his syrupy coffee. "While you were *away* and I was going out of my mind, news came in. The vampires have pulled out of England," he said around mouthfuls of pancake and syrup. "And there's movement on the West Coast. They're withdrawing their advance and pulling out of some European territory."

"Any idea why?" I picked at my bacon, feeling full and well rested for the first time in forever.

"None. But if they're giving up land, it must be good. They *never* give up land. Maybe they've overreached? Whatever the reason, it has to be good news for us."

"Maybe." Vampires on the move was never good news, and the feeling of that thing outside the station, trying to boil its way inside... That thing—their queen—was no normal vampire.

I said my goodbyes to Kensey and headed into Night while it slept, stepping back into my role. It felt better to be back in my boots and dress now that I'd had time to recover my wits. Etienne was waiting for me. I reeled off instructions for the evening and felt the comfort of the role fall back onto my shoulders.

Everything would be all right.

I unlocked my library door, and Etienne followed me inside, reciting his list of tasks for the day.

A cane rested against my desk, its silver top reflecting the light from the doorway.

For a terrible, heart-stopping moment, I knew Jack had returned and looked for him in the shadows. But he couldn't be here. It wasn't possible.

I clicked my fingers, and the lamps spluttered to life, chasing away the dark.

He wasn't here. I even checked under the desk, feeling partly foolish but mostly aware that someone had been here.

"Isn't that Ja—"

I picked up the damn thing before Etienne could say the name and brought it down over my knee, snapping it clean in two, then tossed the two pieces onto my desk. "Now it's firewood."

Etienne eyed the two pieces like they were snakes. "I'll er... I'll dispose of it, shall I?"

"Incinerate it, and when the shutters open, I'm tossing the ashes onto the tracks."

When had Jack had it last? In the ballroom? I couldn't recall, but I didn't think so. Perhaps someone had found it and placed it here. But how had they gotten inside my room?

Something else caught my eye in the floor-standing mirror across the room. It reflected Etienne and me, as it should, but there was something wrong with its picture, something off-kilter.

As I approached, the clear outline of a handprint appeared in its center. Using my sleeve, I tried to wipe it away, but the mark stayed. I tried again, rubbing harder. The handprint didn't budge.

"What is it?" Etienne asked.

Leaning so close my breath misted the mirror's surface, I frowned at the handprint. "It's on the other side of the glass."

"That's… not possible. Is it?"

"Etienne…" I straightened. "Cover every mirror in the entire station. Every room, every floor. Collect all the hand mirrors, pocket mirrors, all of them. Get it done. I can trust you with this?"

"Yes, naturally, but…" He pulled his glare from the mirror. "What does it mean, ma'am?"

I tentatively pressed my hand against the imprint. Ice nipped at my palm, trying to freeze my skin to its surface. It burned cold. "Someone is trying to come through."

The shutters behind the mirror threw themselves open, startling me into reaching for my knife. Milky moonlight poured in and over the mirror and Etienne, spreading its icy touch throughout my library. There was no blackness boiling out there, no terrible queen about to smash the glass and claim us all, just starlight and…

That couldn't be right.

I drifted closer to the window. Etienne approached too and drew in a breath. Beyond the glass, countless moon-licked rooftops climbed toward the sky. Great domes jutted from those angular peaks, some topped with bent and rusted crosses, their arches and elaborate carvings all cracked and crumbling. Stone gargoyles stood sentinel on the corners of marble facades. The buildings were barren and ruined, half tumbled into empty streets, but they were not the same buildings I'd looked upon my entire life.

This wasn't my view, and from the architecture, it wasn't even my continent.

"So beautiful..." Etienne whispered, moonlight turning his face ghostly pale. "Where are we?"

"I have no idea."

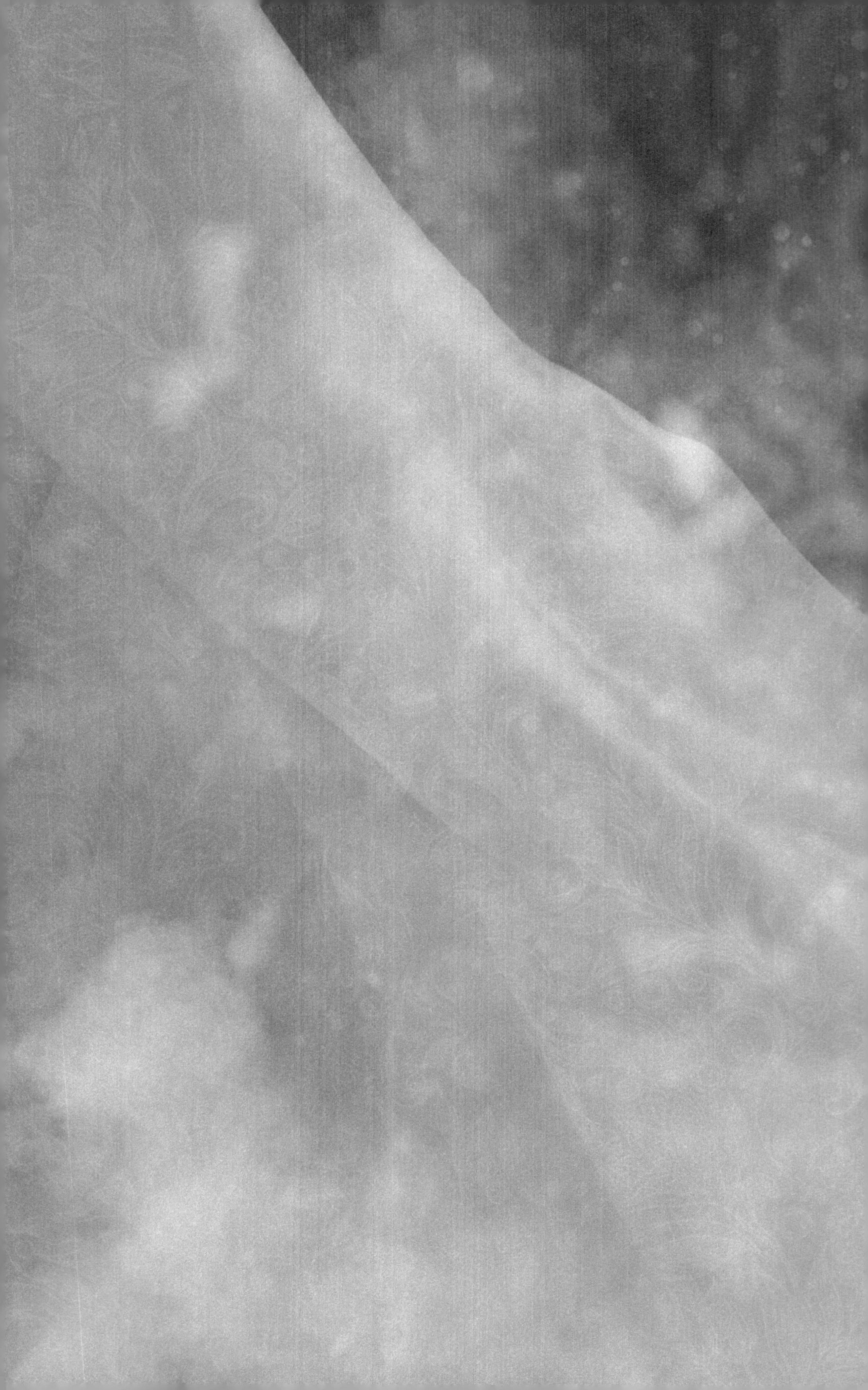

To be continued in Night Scourge, Daybreaker #2
coming from Pippa DaCosta in 2020

cryhollow.tumblr
cryhollow.twitter
Lynher

cryhollow.tumblr
cryhollow.twitter
Jack

cryhollow.tumblr
cryhollow.twitter
Rafe

cryhollow.tumblr
cryhollow.twitter

Kensey

www.ingramcontent.com/pod-product-compliance
Lightning Source LLC
Chambersburg PA
CBHW030426310726
48979CB00009B/1628/J

* 9 7 8 1 9 1 6 0 0 9 2 4 0 *